HOLY DEATH

INSPECTOR WEST

PETER MULRANEY

ISBN 13: 978-0-6481046-8-1
Cover image: Noah Silliman on Unsplash

This edition published 2018.

✸ Created with Vellum

To the people standing in the thin blue line between us and trouble.

CHAPTER 1

FR MAURICE SKINNER opened the door at the back of the old church. A stream of pale yellow light escaped into the night and bathed the solitary vehicle standing in the car park behind the building. Darkness reclaimed St Frank's minibus when he closed the door behind him.

Fr Skinner had no need for a light to guide him on his way. The pale moonlight penetrating through the low cloud was more than sufficient to illuminate his path. Besides, Fr Skinner knew all there was to know about walking in darkness.

Dressed in priestly black, the old priest stepped into the night and merged with the darkness. He walked across the expanse of the yard separating his residence from the old church on autopilot. His head was still locked in the discussion he had been having with Robert Sturm, the supervisor of the men's shelter located in the old church.

He was still ruminating on his impending enforced retirement when he reached the side door of his house. He was not happy that Bishop Kerry had turned down his plea to stay on as the chaplain of St Frank's. He'd devoted the last ten years of his life to the men who used the shelter, and couldn't see why he had to stop just because of some stupid rule.

Even though he was turning seventy-five, the Church's compulsory retirement age, he'd argued that at least he was available to do the job. The bishop had insisted that there was no way he could allow him to stay on, as their insurance didn't cover priests beyond seventy-five.

He was furious, but what could he do? The bishop held all the power. After his meeting with the bishop, he'd sulked all the way home and spent the evening complaining to Robert.

As far as he could tell, the bishop had no-one else to look after the needs of the poor souls that called St Frank's home. It wasn't as if the seminary was bursting with new recruits to the priesthood. God, if things don't improve Robert will be right, he thought, and we really will be importing more priests from Africa and India.

On the threshold of his residence, Fr Skinner rummaged in his pockets for his keys. Standing in the dark, he silently rebuked himself for not having replaced the spent bulb in the security light that usually illuminated his approach to the door. He'd meant to replace it earlier in the day but had forgotten all about it, thanks to his meeting with the bishop. Too late now, he thought, as he felt for the keyhole.

After a couple of fumbled attempts, he managed to slip the key into the lock and turn the handle. As he opened the door, he felt a firm push in the middle of his back, and stumbled into the dark interior of the house.

He crashed onto the floor, hitting his head on the leg of the hat-rack standing in the hallway. He heard the door close behind him, and blinked as the light came on. A pair of firm hands grabbed him by the collar and roughly dragged him up into a kneeling position. With his head locked between two strong hands smelling of cigarettes, he couldn't turn to see his assailant.

A cold fear rose up from deep within his gut. He thought he was going to wet himself.

'What do you want?'

The silence was broken by a voice that Fr Skinner did not recognise.

'I hope you've said your prayers, Father.'

CHAPTER 2

DETECTIVE INSPECTOR CARL WEST sat at his desk with his hands wrapped around a cup of hot coffee. His head hurt. He wished he'd exercised a little more restraint during the previous night's celebration of Harry Fuller's promotion to detective sergeant, and hoped he'd only have to manage a quiet day of paperwork in the office. Detective Constable Lisa Templar was due to join them tomorrow to replenish the ranks of his diminished team and, despite his headache, he was determined to have things ready for her.

He took a sip of his coffee and started work. He'd only managed to log on to his computer when the telephone on his desk rang. He listened as Operations gave him the details, and then went out into the squad room where, like Carl, DS Harry Fuller was nursing both a cup of coffee and a hangover.

'You look like death warmed up, Harry.'

'You don't look much better, Boss. Hope we're having a quiet one.'

Carl shook his head and immediately regretted it.

'Our luck's just expired. That was Operations. That fire at Gladesview House last night is looking like arson, and they've discovered a body in the ashes. Mike Jonas is already there. Grab your coat, we need to go take a look. I'll drive. You don't look like you're up to it.'

'Thanks, Boss.'

The front entrance of Gladesview House was sealed with crime scene tape, the handiwork of the uniformed patrol that had responded to the fire alarm along with the fire brigade. After negotiating their way through the cordon, Carl parked their silver Ford in the car park located just inside the gate, and they walked over to what was left of the old mansion.

Gladesview House, which had housed an aged-care facility for retired Catholic priests, was little more than a blackened ruin. The roof had collapsed on the eastern side of the building and one of the exterior walls had fallen into the garden. The house and gardens, which had given their name to the suburb surrounding them, had been gifted to the Church from the estate of an elderly Catholic dowager in the early nineteen-fifties, twenty years before Carl had been born.

Carl spotted Dr Mike Jonas, the police pathologist, standing with a fireman wearing a fire investigator's jacket next to a window of the ruined building.

Carl walked over to join Dr Jonas and the fireman, while Harry went to speak with the uniformed officer in charge of the crime scene.

'Hi, Mike. Wasn't expecting to see you today.'

'Morning, Carl. This is Tim Ryan.'

'Detective Inspector Carl West.' Carl extended his hand. 'What have we got?'

'One incinerated body, and a broken window that Tim reckons doesn't look right,' said Mike.

'How do you see it, Tim?'

'Looks like the fire started in this part of the building, Inspector. We had one of the sniffer dogs here earlier, and she pointed to a spot in the corridor outside this room. And, there's a burnt petrol can on the floor there as well.'

'That's usually pretty convincing evidence,' said Carl.

The fire investigator smiled and pointed at the broken window in front of them. 'See that glass over there on the floor. It's too far in from the window. I'd expect to see broken glass just below the sill, either inside or outside, unless there'd been a gas explosion. Then it would be all outside. See there, the rest of this window isn't even cracked. Looks like your arsonist may have broken in through this window, Inspector.'

Or that's what he wanted us to think, thought Carl, as he looked in through the broken window at the charred remains in the far corner. 'Didn't anyone notice this guy was missing during the evacuation?'

'It was chaos when the brigade got here, Inspector. The fire ripped through the place pretty fast, which is why the roof in this part of the house collapsed. In a building this old the roof timbers would be as dry as kindling. I gather it wasn't until they got to the hospital that the night nurse realised Bishop Knight was missing.'

'Is everybody else accounted for?' asked Carl.

'They're all in University. Most are suffering from smoke inhalation, but the couple we pulled out of this part of the building before the roof collapsed are pretty seriously burnt. I'm no doctor, Inspector, but I suspect you could have more than one death on your hands,' said the fire investigator.

'Where's this night nurse?' asked Carl.

'In the hospital with the others. She's pretty badly burnt herself. The fire chief reckons she deserves a medal. Apparently, the crew had to restrain her in the end for her own safety.'

Carl turned to Mike Jonas.

'Guess it will be a while before you can tell me anything about Bishop Knight's demise.'

'I'll let you know if the cause of death is other than smoke inhalation after the post-mortem. Not much I can do here given the state of the body. I'll have the crime scene boys do what they can once the site is secure,' said Mike. 'I doubt we'll get much but you never know. By the way, how's Harry?'

'He'll survive.'

Dr Jonas smiled. Carl knew Mike was one of the lucky ones that didn't suffer any ill effects from imbibing more alcohol than he should. Maybe it was simply because in his line of work he had consumed a lot more than most.

Carl went in search of Harry, and found him leaning up against a patrol car talking to Senior Constable Charlie Head.

'Morning, Inspector,' said Charlie. 'I guess I can hand over jurisdiction if you're here.'

'Eventually, Charlie, but I'm leaving you in charge of the crime scene until we get the forensics. Have you had a chance to interview the neighbours?'

'We've done the rounds, not that it's done us any good. No-one saw or heard anything until the fire brigade arrived with their sirens blaring. They're lucky the place had a monitored fire alarm, otherwise it would have burnt down without anyone noticing. Besides, the call came through at two in the morning, according to the patrol we relieved a couple of hours ago.'

'Given the location, I guess the neighbours were all safely tucked up in bed at that hour. I know I was.'

'What did you find out from the fire inspector, Boss?' asked Harry.

'He thinks the place was torched, and that the arsonist broke in through the window of the room where the body is, which I understand we think is Bishop Knight.'

'Do you remember him, Inspector?' said Charlie.

'Can't say I do, Charlie. What can you tell us about him.'

As a member of the St Vincent de Paul Society, with a nun for a sister, and a wife that worked as a social worker for the diocese, SC Charlie Head was Carl's usual source of information on all things Catholic.

'Bishop Knight,' said Charlie, removing his cap and scratching his bald head, 'was the bishop forced to retire when that child abuse scandal broke about ten years ago. They reckoned he was protecting some of those pedophile priests.'

'Can't say that I remember,' said Carl.

'It was in all the papers,' said Charlie.

Carl looked at Harry, who shrugged his shoulders and then pulled out his iPad mini and made a note to research Bishop Knight.

'Guess we'll be doing some reading,' said Carl. 'Thanks, Charlie.'

'What did Dr Jonas say about the body?' asked Harry.

'Too early to tell. He'll have to do a post-mortem to determine if there is anything more to the bishop's demise other than smoke inhalation. Either way, we're dealing with a homicide and a crime scene that has been flooded with water and trampled over by firemen in big boots. I'm not confident we'll get many clues as to who was playing with the matches.'

They watched as a white Ford Transit van negotiated its way through the crime scene cordon and parked next to the patrol car. Forensics had arrived.

'Good morning, Inspector. Where's Dr Jonas?' asked the sergeant from Forensics, as the crime scene investigators climbed out of their van.

'He's around the back of the house, Sergeant. I'll leave you with Charlie. Give me a call when you're through and let me know if you agree with the fire investigator.'

'Okay, Inspector.'

'There's not much we can do here for the moment, Charlie, and it sounds like we might have to wait a while before we can talk with the survivors. Come and see me when you get back to the office.'

They had almost reached the car when Carl's smartphone rang. He threw the car keys to Harry while he listened to the caller.

'Not a good day for the Catholic Church, Harry. Looks like they've lost another priest. Take us to St Frank's Shelter in Mortlock Street.'

FROM THE STREET, St Frank's looked like a church that had seen better days. The iron roof was spotted with rust and the large front door badly needed a fresh coat of paint. Even the stained glass windows, bathed in late morning sunlight, had no sparkle. The driveway to the car park at the rear of the building looked more like a track through a field of grass than a roadway. The car park itself, which at some point in time had been a paved surface, needed some serious attention from a lawn mower as well. The residence located across the car park from the old church building appeared to be in a similar state of dilapidation.

A patrol car, a silver Ford sedan, and a white van were parked adjacent to the house. A faded blue minibus, with St Frank's painted on its doors, was parked outside the rear door of the old church building.

Carl's favourite uniformed officer, PC Jane Priest, was waiting for them at the line of crime scene tape. He'd had a short, lust fired affair with her the year Peter James had been shot; before DS Nina Strong had joined his team and permanently changed his perspective on relationships.

'Morning, Inspector, and congratulations, Sergeant,' said PC Priest, as Carl and Harry approached her.

'Thanks,' said Harry.

'Well, it's good to see we still have one living priest,' said Carl. 'How are you, Jane? Haven't seen you for a while.'

'First day back from leave. Spent three weeks hiking in New Zealand with a couple of friends.'

'What's it like over there? I hear it's a great place for hiking.'

'We walked all over the South Island. The scenery is fantastic. It's even better in real life than what you'd expect from seeing Lord of the Rings.'

'That sounds like a ringing endorsement. I'd love to see it, if I can persuade Nina to take me there,' said Carl. 'She likes to go to foreign places.'

'I'll give her the hard sell when I catch up with her,' said PC Priest. 'I'm supposed to be having coffee with her tomorrow.'

Carl was continually amazed at how the women in his life seemed to get on together. He didn't know too many men who were still friends after having had affairs with the same woman.

'Who's here?' asked Carl, switching back to work mode.

'Dr Worthington, from the pathologist's office, and Sgt Lang's team from Forensics. The body is just inside that door there.' PC Priest pointed to the door in the side of the house facing the car park.

'Who found the body?' asked Carl.

'Robert Sturm. He's the manager of St Frank's Shelter. He's given us a statement.'

'Where is he?'

'Over there.' She pointed to the back of the church.

'Harry, let's go and see what Dr Worthington has for us, and then we can have a chat with Sturm.'

PC Priest spoke into the radio clipped to her vest to let her partner know they were approaching the house, and lifted the tape for them. Carl and Harry walked along the blue plastic sheeting leading to the door. As they approached, the door opened and Emma Worthington, a tall woman in her fifties, with twenty-five years' experience in crime scene investigating as a pathologist, came out to meet them. One thing Carl liked about Emma was her thoroughness. Not much got past her attention to detail.

'Ah, Carl, wasn't expecting to see you here. Heard you'd gone to Gladesview,' said Emma.

'We'll have to wait for Mike to do his thing on that one. Body looked char-grilled to me. No recognisable features, so he's got some work to do before we'll know for sure who it is, and if he died in the fire or before.'

'What makes you think there might be a possibility of before?' asked Emma.

'The fire investigator reckons someone may have used the window of the room where they found the body to enter the building,' said Carl. 'What have we got here?'

'A very dead Fr Maurice Skinner. Broken neck. Pretty forceful snap, I'd say. Nothing accidental about it, by the look of it.'

'How long's he been dead?'

'That's always an educated guess, Carl, as you know, but I'd say less than twelve hours, and no science involved in working that out either.' Emma smiled. 'The guy that found the body told us he'd been talking with Fr Skinner up to around ten last night. He discovered the body around nine thirty this morning. Simple mathematics.'

'The Forensics' boys having any luck?' asked Carl.

Dr Worthington walked over to the door. 'Dean, do you want to come out and say hello to DI West and the newly minted Sgt Fuller?' She smiled in Harry's direction. 'I hear you boys were not on your best behaviour last night.'

'Last time I go drinking with your boss,' said Harry.

12

Emma smiled. Harry wasn't the only one Mike Jonas had drunk under the table.

Sgt Dean Lang appeared in the doorway, camera in hand. 'Morning, Inspector. Harry.'

'I know it's early days, Dean, but what's your scene looking like?' said Carl.

'I don't think this place has been cleaned since Adam was a boy, Inspector. We've got enough stuff in this carpet to set up a museum. What might be of interest to you though is that set of muddy footprints on those paving stones.' He pointed to the stones that abutted the side of the house. 'See how it looks like someone was standing there, and then walked along the wall towards the door? There's some of that mud on the carpet, just inside the door.'

Carl looked at the track of muddy footprints and wondered just how much care, if any, the killer had taken to conceal his identity.

'So, are you telling me it will be some time before we have anything that might identify our killer, apart from muddy shoes?'

'I reckon we'll have enough material to identify anybody who has entered this place in the last ten years. Might make it a bit of a challenge finding anything belonging to your killer, Inspector, but when you do find him, I can tell you he'll have big feet, going by the size of those footprints.'

Carl took another look at the trail of mud, and agreed with the sergeant's assessment.

Harry made a note on his iPad.

'Where's the body?' asked Carl.

Sgt Lang stepped out of the doorway. The body of Fr Skinner lay face down on the carpet just beyond the edge of the open door. 'Looks like he was killed right here, either answering the door or as he was going in when he arrived home last night' said

Sgt Lang. 'And, that security light up there,' he pointed above his head, 'which has a heat activated switch, is not operational, so it's possible the killer was waiting here in the shadows when he got home from his chat with his mate across the paddock.'

'Thanks, Dean.' Carl turned to Dr Worthington 'If those footprints belong to our killer, we might get lucky,' said Carl. 'Doesn't look like he's gone to much trouble to hide his tracks. Who knows what else he's left behind for Dean to find.'

'I'll examine the bruising around the neck when I do the post-mortem but I wouldn't hold my breath. It's not like he squeezed, so there may not be any impressions we can use,' said Dr Worthington.

'Okay, Emma. We'll leave you to it and go and see what Mr Sturm has to say for himself.'

Carl and Harry walked across the car park and knocked on the door at the back of the old church.

The door was opened by an overweight, middle-aged man with cropped grey hair, wearing a green knitted sweater over a white shirt, black trousers and very big, shiny black shoes.

'Robert Sturm?' asked Carl, holding out his badge.

'Yes.'

'Detective Inspector Carl West, and this is Detective Sergeant Harry Fuller. Do you mind if we come in?'

'No, no. I've been expecting you. Come in. Come in. Can I get you a coffee or a tea?'

'I could use a coffee,' said Harry.

'Inspector?'

'Coffee, thanks.'

Carl looked around the kitchen they were ushered into. The

interior of the kitchen didn't match the exterior of the building. It was all stainless steel appliances and sleek marble bench tops. The money spent on renovations had obviously been spent on fitting out the interior of the building.

When Robert had made coffee and offered them a slice of carrot cake, they sat at the white top table to talk, in a room filled with the aroma of freshly made coffee and cake. Harry placed his iPad mini on the table next to the plate holding his piece of cake.

'What exactly goes on here, Mr Sturm?' asked Carl.

'St Frank's is a halfway house, of sorts,' said Robert. 'It was set up by Maurice when he retired as prison chaplain, ten years ago this month.'

'Why did you say of sorts?' asked Harry, before sampling the cake.

'Well, we don't take just anyone. Maurice wanted to help older men who had served long prison terms. As you'd no doubt appreciate, some of them find it extremely difficult getting back into society and almost impossible to obtain any meaningful employment. A lot of them end up reoffending for the sole purpose of going back inside, where everything is familiar.'

Carl nodded. He'd heard that story several times over the years.

'How many residents do you have at any one time?' asked Carl, taking a bite of the carrot cake and wondering who had made it. It tasted even better than the home-made carrot cake he bought at Lena's, his favourite lunch-time eating place in the city.

'We're licensed for twelve, which is a little ironic when you think about them being housed in an old Catholic church,' said Robert.

Carl hoped Harry would have some idea what that was supposed to mean.

'This is nice cake,' said Carl. 'Who's the cook?'

'I'll take that as a compliment, Inspector. It's one of my mother's recipes. As you can see,' he patted his paunch, 'I'm a man who enjoys his food.'

Carl smiled. Robert Sturm reminded him of the rotund Friar Tuck from the Robin Hood TV series he had watched as a boy.

'So, Mr Sturm, what's your role here?' asked Carl.

'St Frank's is a joint venture of the Church and the State, Inspector. The Church provides the buildings and the personnel to run the place, and the State provides the residents. The State also provided the money to convert the old church into a hostel with independent living units, and this residence.' He waved his right hand around the room they were in. 'I'm the live-in supervisor, and Maurice was the administrator and chaplain to the men.'

'Where does the money to cover operating expenses come from?' asked Harry.

'The residents pay a nominal rent for their units and meet most of their own living expenses. Maurice and I get stipends. Maurice got his from the diocese, like any other priest, and I'm a Christian Brother. We meet our other expenses through fund-raising and donations.'

'Are you fund-raising to repair the roof?' asked Harry.

'We were until last week, but then a local builder offered to replace the roof as part of a government sponsored training activity for his apprentices, and Correctional Services has agreed to send a community work order group around to paint the outside of the building, once the new roof is on,' said Robert, with a smile. 'All we have to do is find the paint. It'll be nice living in a building that looks like somebody loves it, for a change.'

Carl was starting to warm to Robert Sturm.

'How long do most of your residents stay?' asked Carl.

'Most stay around six months. Sometimes it takes a bit longer to find them suitable accommodation.'

'Do any of them find employment?'

'Most of them end up on the age pension, Inspector. We try to get the younger ones back into the workforce but it's not easy. Generally, they start off in our gardening team to get used to a work routine, and then we help them negotiate their way through the employment services. We've managed to get quite a few back into the work force over the ten years we've been here.'

'Where does this gardening team work?' asked Harry.

'Mostly on Church properties, Sergeant, under the supervision of a qualified gardener. You've probably seen some of them working on the gardens around the cathedral, and they look after gardens in several parishes. And, we have the contract for maintaining the gardens at Gladesview House, the priests' retirement home. The boys really like working there.'

'We've just come from there, actually,' said Carl.

Robert's hands went to his face. 'Dreadful business. Absolutely dreadful. I don't understand why anybody would want to burn down an old folks' home. Bit of a strange coincidence though, don't you think, Inspector?'

Carl's blank look prompted Robert to continue. 'I just heard on the radio that they think Bishop Knight died in the fire. Maurice and Bishop Knight were great mates. They were at the seminary together. In fact, they were ordained on the same day, and now it looks like they've gone off to heaven together.'

'Well, I guess that brings us to why we're here, Mr Sturm. I know you've already made a statement, but can you walk us through from when you last saw Fr Skinner and when you found his body this morning?' said Carl.

Robert looked at his hands. Carl noted that Robert Sturm had large hands.

'He was sitting where you're sitting, Inspector, right up to around ten o'clock last night. He came over most nights for a cup of tea and a chin wag before he went to bed. Anyway, last night he was pretty worked up. He'd been to see the bishop during the day to ask, beg actually, to be allowed to stay on after his birthday. The bishop refused. Ordered him to pack up and move into Gladesview, according to Maurice.'

'Why wasn't he allowed to stay here?' asked Harry.

'Seventy-five is the compulsory retirement age for priests, Sergeant. Maurice reckoned he had another good ten years in him. The bishop saw it otherwise.'

'How was he when he left you?' asked Carl.

'He'd calmed down a bit but he was still fuming. He knew there was nothing he could do but that didn't mean he had to be happy about it. It wasn't so much that he had to retire. He was fretting over who would replace him. It's not like the bishop has anyone else to send here in his place.'

'What did you do after he left?' asked Carl.

'I went in to watch the late news in the common room with a couple of the residents.'

'Did you hear anything after he'd left?'

'Inspector, when these old guys watch TV they have the sound up pretty loud. Anything could have happened over at Maurice's place without me hearing it.'

'So, what happened this morning?'

'I went over to see if Maurice was okay when I got back from driving the boys to work. That was just after nine o'clock. His car was gone, so I thought he must have gone out. I was about to come back here when I noticed the door off the patio was open. I thought he must have forgotten to close it properly behind him. Anyway, when I went to close the door I found him lying on the floor. When I touched him he was cold, so I knew right away he was dead. At first I thought he must have had a heart attack or something. Then I realised his neck didn't look right. That's when I called you guys.'

Robert looked at Carl. 'You know, Inspector, I've known Maurice for twenty years. He devoted his life to helping people who made mistakes and ended up in prison. I don't think he deserved to die like that. I hope you catch the bastard that did this.'

Carl waited a couple of moments before asking, 'Do you have any idea who might have wanted to kill him?'

Robert Sturm moved his head slowly from side to side. 'Not the slightest. To be honest, I've only ever heard people thanking him for what he'd done for them. As far as I know, Inspector, the only person Maurice regarded as an enemy was the bishop, and I can't imagine Bishop Kerry being a killer.'

Carl took out one of his cards. 'Thanks, Mr Sturm. If you think of anything, you can always get me on this number. By the way, did you give a description of Fr Skinner's car in your statement?'

'Yes, Inspector. I guess the killer didn't want to walk home. Can't think of any other reason why anyone would've taken Maurice's old bomb.'

'Would he have had to drive past here?' asked Harry.

'No, the front of Maurice's place opens into Austin Street. He could have gone out that way.'

'What time do your residents usually get back for the day?' asked Carl. 'We'll need to talk to them.'

'I'll be collecting the gardening team at three thirty. We should be back here by four. The others are usually back before five these days. They don't like to stay out after dark,' said Robert.

Carl shook hands with Robert Sturm and thanked him for his help.

As Carl and Harry walked back across the car park to the priest's residence, the coroner's van arrived to collect the body. They waited for the body to be loaded before suiting up in their protective clothing to search the house.

The carpet in the entrance hall may have needed some attention but the rest of the house was relatively clean. The room Fr Skinner had used as an office was neat and tidy. There were no papers on the ancient desk but there was a new looking iMac computer. The combination of ancient furniture and high tech equipment made Carl think of his own office.

Harry touched the mouse with his latex enclosed hand. The screen came to life.

'I wonder what his password is?' said Carl.

Harry opened the top drawer of the desk and picked up a faded blue card with two words written on it. Father and Forgiveness.

Harry typed Forgiveness into the password field for the user listed as Father, and the screen opened to a desktop crammed with icons, on a background that he recognised as a photograph of the gardens at Gladesview House.

While Carl looked through the rooms of the house, Harry systematically worked his way through the files on the priest's computer. It was obvious from the number of photographs stored on the hard drive that Fr Skinner had been a keen photographer, with a penchant for landscapes and old buildings. After he had opened files in several folders, Harry concluded that the priest had used the computer for both his personal interests and for performing the administrative duties associated with running St Frank's and organising fund-raising events.

'Harry, come and take a look at this.'

Harry followed the sounds of Carl looking through a room to a bedroom at the front of the house. A large double bed took up most of the floor space and there was a mirrored wardrobe attached to the wall opposite the entrance of an en-suite bathroom. The bed was made, but the covers were dusty to the touch.

'Take a look in there, Harry.' Carl pointed to the wardrobe.

Harry slid one of the mirrored doors along its track. The wardrobe was full of women's clothing. The floor was littered with shoes and handbags covered in a thin layer of dust.

'The en-suite's got women's stuff in it as well,' said Carl.

'It doesn't look like anyone's used this room for a while,' said Harry.

'The room next door has a single bed that looks like it's been slept in recently,' said Carl, 'and a wardrobe with what appears to be the priest's clothes. I'd wager he's been sleeping in there in recent days.'

'I thought Catholic priests were supposed to be celibate or have they changed the rules?' said Harry.

'Not as far as I know,' said Carl. 'Something to ask Charlie when we see him.'

'Maybe he had a live-in housekeeper,' said Harry.

'Looks like she hasn't been home for a while,' said Carl. 'What did you find on that computer?'

'Files about St Frank's, details of fund-raising events, heaps of photos, a few letters.'

'What are the photos of? Not little boys, I hope. God, I hope we aren't going there.'

'I haven't looked at all of them yet but he seems to have had an interest in landscapes and old buildings. Some of his photos are pretty good, they look like they were taken by a professional. The few photos of people I looked at appear to be of old men, so I guess he kept a record of who passed through St Frank's.'

'That could be handy. Get Dean to take a copy of the hard drive so we don't have to lug that iMac into the office.'

Harry left to speak to Sgt Lang.

Carl took another look inside the wardrobe. The style of the dresses didn't look anything like the outfits Nina wore. They reminded him of the clothes his grandmother had worn.

He wondered just what they were going to unearth, as they peered into the life of the priest in their efforts to find his killer.

CHAPTER 4

IT WAS NEARLY one o'clock by the time Carl and Harry returned to the office. Carl's head had cleared and he was looking forward to lunch, despite the generous piece of carrot cake he had consumed at St Frank's.

'I'm going to Lena's to buy something for lunch. Want anything?' said Harry, as he parked the car.

'One of those prosciutto baguettes and a flat white would be good.' Carl handed him a twenty and headed towards the building, while Harry walked around into the street and down to Lena's.

As Carl was settling into his office, Dr Jonas dropped in on his way to conduct the post-mortem of the body believed to be the mortal remains of Emeritus Bishop Michael Knight.

'I hear you've picked up another body, another priest in fact. What happened?'

'Emma's assessment at the scene was that someone had snapped the priest's neck,' said Carl.

'So that one's definitely murder, then,' said Dr Jonas.

Arriving back from Lena's with their lunch, Harry walked in and joined them.

'We spoke to the manager of the shelter at St Frank's, a guy

23

called Sturm. He told us the priest, Fr Skinner, was a close friend of this Bishop Knight. If your body is the bishop, bit of a coincidence them dying on the same night, considering one of them was murdered. I wonder if there is more to it.'

'Time will tell, Carl. The bishop's dental records are on their way to the lab, so I should have a positive identification for you once they arrive. I'll let you know if I find anything else of interest, like a broken neck.'

Dr Jonas headed off down the corridor to the elevators.

'Your lunch, Boss.' Harry handed Carl the bag holding his baguette and placed the cup holding his coffee on the desk. 'Do you really think there might be some connection?'

'Who knows, Harry? But it does seem a bit strange that two old priests, who just happen to be friends, end up dead on the same night.'

They took ten minutes out to eat lunch and discuss the changes set to engulf Harry when he got home that night.

'I hope you know what you're doing, Harry. I wouldn't want her old man on my case, mate. I've seen what he's like in court.'

'He's nothing like that in real life. Besides, it was partly his idea that we move in together. He reckons it's cheaper to have a trial run than what it is to get divorced.'

'Yeah, he's definitely right on that score. I don't recall it being much fun either.'

'Do you know much about this Lisa Templar that's starting with us tomorrow?'

'I had a look at her file yesterday. Could be interesting to work with. I gather she was a teacher before joining the force.'

'Well, maybe our report writing will improve,' said Harry.

'I don't think we need to worry too much about our report writing, apparently she taught Maths. Let's just hope she's as good a detective as the chief seems to think she is.'

'How long has she been with the force?'

'Not all that long, actually, she's one of those mature age recruits. A couple of years, I think.'

Carl faced his computer and opened the file HR had sent him. 'Yeah, two years last month. So, she's not totally green, and she's been out of school long enough to lose the teacher attitude.'

'I hope you're right about that last bit.'

Carl finished the last of his baguette and scrunched up the paper bag, before tossing it in the general direction of the bin. The ball of paper hit the wall, and joined the others on the floor in the vicinity of the grey metal can.

'Guess we'd better find out what we can about this Fr Skinner. Someone obviously wanted him dead, so he must have pissed somebody off. See what you can find out about him from Corrections, while I sort out who we need to speak to in the bishop's office.'

While Harry was being passed around the switchboard at Corrections, Sgt Dean Lang walked up to his desk and handed him a copy of the hard drive from the priest's computer.

'That should keep you out of mischief for a while, Harry. Couple of hundred gigabytes there for you to play with.'

'Thanks, Dean.'

He waved off Sgt Lang with his free hand as a voice came onto the line that was not the switchboard operator.

'John Wilmas, Sergeant. I understand you want to talk with someone about Maurice Skinner. What exactly do you want to know?'

'Hi, John. Where do you fit into the Corrections' picture?'

'I'm the chaplains liaison officer.'

'Great. Did you know Fr Maurice Skinner?'

'Yes. I knew him. Just heard about his death on the radio. Is that why you're calling?'

'Afraid so, John. Wondering if you'd heard anything that might shed a light on why anyone would want to kill him.'

'He was popular with the inmates, so I can't imagine anyone I know wanting to kill him, Sergeant. Maurice was the longest serving chaplain we'd ever had, and we've got a queue of guys lining up to go to St Frank's when they get out.'

'That sounds pretty impressive. What was he like?'

'He'd been here for years before I arrived, and he certainly made my life easier. I was sad to see him go when he retired. We need more guys like him working with inmates. To be honest, I've never heard anyone say a bad word about him, let alone threaten to kill him. Maurice being murdered doesn't make sense to me, and I'd pity the poor bastard that did it, if you manage to catch him. Don't think he'll last very long inside.'

'Thanks, John. You have my condolences.'

Carl appeared at Harry's desk as he put down the receiver. 'Get your coat. We've got an appointment with a Monsignor Rivers over at the cathedral.'

The Catholic cathedral stood in a garden setting on the southern side of the square in the centre of the city, a short walk from Police Headquarters. The Church Offices were housed in a building on the eastern side of the city block entirely taken up by the cathedral grounds. A young woman met them in reception and directed Carl and Harry to the monsignor's office on the upper floor.

The building had been constructed in the second half of the nineteenth century and, despite renovations dating to the latter part of the last century, there was no elevator. Carl and Harry climbed up a dimly lit stairwell, with threadbare carpet covering each step, to a long narrow corridor and found the monsignor waiting for them outside his office.

Monsignor Rivers introduced himself and invited them into his office.

'I've pulled Fr Skinner's file from the archives for you, Inspector.'

The monsignor placed a faded yellow folder on his desk. 'I'm afraid none of the old records are digital, so we'll have to sift through this.'

'Have you had a chance to read it, Monsignor?' asked Carl.

'No, not yet.'

'Do you mind if we have a look?' asked Carl.

'Not at all. It's always interesting reading these old files.' Monsignor Rivers turned the folder so that Carl could see the papers as he leafed through them.

'We've got his application to enter the seminary, a transcript of his academic record, details of his ordination.'

'We've been told he was ordained on the same day as Bishop Knight,' said Harry. 'Is that true?'

'I'd have to check, Sergeant. As you can see,' he said, pointing to the date, 'Fr Skinner was ordained fifty years ago, before I was born.'

'You might want to locate Bishop Knight's records, Monsignor, in case it turns out we're dealing with his murder as well,' said Carl. 'I assume his file would be more extensive than this.'

'Yes, there's an archive devoted to the term of each bishop.' The monsignor made a note and turned back to the folder holding the records of Maurice Skinner.

'Looks like his first appointment was as assistant parish priest to Lawton, in the south-east, where he served for two years before being appointed as parish priest at North Summit, up in the hills, for a little under three years. Then it appears he was assigned as prison chaplain, a post he held for the next thirty-five years, until he turned sixty-five. He's been running St Frank's, which he persuaded the bishop to set up, ever since.'

'Is it usual for a priest to spend nearly all of his life as a prison chaplain?' asked Carl.

'Depends on a person's charism, Inspector. It seems Fr Skinner was especially gifted in that area. I know from my own dealings with him that he was particularly devoted to the interests of men who had made mistakes in life. He wanted to help people start again.'

'Where did he live all that time while he was the prison chaplain?' asked Carl.

'He's lived in the house attached to St Frank's for the last forty years, as far as I know. The church building there hasn't been used as a church for a long time. It was known as St Francis of Assisi's when it was a parish church, which is why Fr Skinner chose to call his centre St Frank's, but it's had a multitude of uses over the years since it was decommissioned as a church.'

'How does a parish get decommissioned?' asked Harry. 'Where do the parishioners go?'

'In this case, Sergeant, they went to the suburbs. No doubt you noticed that St Frank's is surrounded by office buildings. It's been that way for a long time.'

'Are there any records of complaints of any nature against Fr Skinner in his file, Monsignor?' asked Carl.

Monsignor Rivers leafed through the pages. 'There's not much here apart from details of his living arrangements, records of his stipend and car loans, letters of commendation from Correctional Services and details of his recent stay in hospital. He had a heart attack a couple of years ago, which is one reason why the bishop wanted him to retire.'

'Did he have a housekeeper?' asked Carl.

'Yes, the details are in here. See,' the monsignor pushed the page over to Carl. 'Mrs Monica Newbury. She was Fr Skinner's sister. She became his housekeeper after her husband died about twenty years ago. She passed away last year. Lung cancer, I believe.'

'If there were any complaints lodged with the bishop against Fr Skinner, would they necessarily be in his file, Monsignor?' asked Carl.

'That would depend on the bishop and the nature of the complaint,' said Monsignor Rivers, dropping his hands into his lap and leaning back in his chair.

'Don't get me wrong, Monsignor, but if, say, there'd been a sexual abuse complaint against Fr Skinner, would you expect to find a record in this file?' asked Carl.

'If the complaint had been made under the current protocols, of course.'

'And, if it had been made before the current protocols were put in place?'

'I think we'd have to search through the records of whoever was the bishop at the time, Inspector, and I couldn't guarantee that we'd find a written record either. Things were done differently in those days and, if my experience is anything to go by, the further back we go the less likely it'll be that we'll be able to find any records.'

'Who would you say Fr Skinner's friends were, Monsignor? Did he associate with other priests?' asked Carl.

'He was a very private man, Inspector. He didn't mix much with other priests. He rarely attended any functions after he retired as prison chaplain. In fact, most of his cohort are dead. The remaining few, like Bishop Knight, were residents of Gladesview House. I take it you've met Robert Sturm?'

'Yes, we interviewed him this morning.'

'I'd say Robert would have been his closest friend these days, apart from Bishop Knight, who I understand he visited every

Friday, and I believe he kept in contact with a lot of the men he'd helped over the years.'

'That doesn't sound like much of a candidate list of killers to me,' said Harry.

'It's hard to understand why anyone would want to kill him. I've only ever heard good things about him and the work he was doing. Was there anything taken from his house?'

'Not that we can tell. The only attractive item in the whole place was a new looking iMac computer, and it's still there. So I think we can rule out robbery as the motive, unless the theft of an ancient VW Golf counts,' said Carl, standing. 'I'll let you know if we'll need to look at Bishop Knight's files, Monsignor. By the way, who was the bishop when Fr Skinner was ordained?'

Monsignor Rivers looked at the record of Maurice Skinner's ordination. 'Bishop Patrick Walsh. He's been dead for twenty-five years. Killed in a car accident in the mid-north, if my memory serves me correctly. That's when Bishop Knight took office.'

'Give my condolences to Bishop Kerry,' said Carl.

Carl exchanged cards with the monsignor, and then he and Harry retraced their steps to the cathedral gardens. They were about to head back to the office when Harry spotted an ancient, light blue VW Golf parked in the street behind the cathedral, which he pointed out to Carl.

'Call Jane and get her to check the details of Fr Skinner's car.'

Carl walked over to where the Golf was parked while Harry made the call. There were several parking tickets attached to the windscreen wipers, and a bunch of keys hanging from the keyhole in the ignition.

'Looks like it's been here all day, going by the number of tickets,' said Carl.

'It's his car, Boss,' said Harry.

'Get on to Operations. Ask them to send a patrol and to get Forensics over here. Tell them we'll wait until someone arrives.'

CHAPTER 5

CARL WAS SETTING up his case files when DS Nina Strong came into his office at the end of her shift. She leant across the desk and kissed him.

'Heard you had some excitement today. Are you ready to come home or should I catch a cab?'

'Grab a seat, sweetheart. I'll be with you in a minute.'

While Carl finished setting up his case files, Nina took the opportunity to scroll through the emails on her iPhone.

'Okay, sweetheart, let's get out of here. We'll be back soon enough. I have a briefing in the Incident Room first thing in the morning,' said Carl.

'Not bringing that file home with you?'

'There's not enough in it yet.'

Carl came around from behind his desk and kissed her lightly on the lips. 'Come on Mrs West, let me take you home.'

They left Carl's office and walked to the elevators.

'I hear you have two murder investigations on the go,' said Nina.

'Well, I've got two bodies, but Mike thinks one of them died of smoke inhalation. Emma is fairly certain the other was helped on his way. Broken neck.'

'Do they think the fire was arson or an accident?' Nina asked, as they stepped into the elevator.

'The fire investigator reckons it's arson, so technically you're right. I have two murder investigations. Funny thing is the victims knew each other.'

'So you might only have one.'

'Bit early to jump to that conclusion, don't you think?'

Nina shrugged her shoulders. 'What does Harry think?'

'Harry's too distracted to think straight at the moment, and I'm not talking about all the excitement of making sergeant.'

Nina laughed. 'I hope he knows what he's doing.'

'He'll be alright, once he gets over the novelty of it. I'm sure Jessika will sort him out. Probably just as well, we've got Lisa Templar starting with us tomorrow.'

'Hmm. I'd better keep an eye on you two for her sake.'

'She should be okay. It's not like she's a fresh young thing we can lead astray. She's around my age, for starters. She's one of those graduates with life experience the chief thinks we need more of.'

'That will be a change for you. I hear you seduced the last female member of your team, Inspector.'

'Yeah, well some things can't be helped. You should have seen the way she threw herself at me.' Carl smiled at her across the roof of the car, as she opened the door and slipped inside to sit beside him.

'Aren't you happy I couldn't resist your charm?'

'Happiest inspector in the force.'

'Do you think you would have married me if the chief hadn't found out about us?'

'What sort of question is that?'

'Well, you had all those other affairs before I came along. Girls talk you know. Jane's told me some interesting stories about you.'

'Yeah, well you're the one that got me, and I'm happy about that. Speaking of Jane, I saw her today. Said she'd been hiking in New Zealand.'

'I'm catching up with her tomorrow. Guess I'll hear all about it.'

Carl swiped his pass to open the exit and drove out onto the street.

Life had changed for Carl since he'd met Nina. No more casual affairs. No more spending the night alone, wondering what was wrong with him.

He'd nearly lost her when she went to visit her parents after DCI Rankin had carpeted him for having an affair with his sergeant. Some idiot had driven his truck up the back of her car when she'd stopped at a stop sign. The impact had pushed her car across the intersection into a tree, killing her parents and the family dog, and putting Nina into hospital for weeks.

They'd both had unsuccessful marriages before they'd met, and had been wary of making the commitment to a long-term relationship, until they'd nearly lost the chance to make a go of it.

Carl's first wife, Virginia, had divorced him before he'd made sergeant. She'd hated the shift work nature of police work, and had told him she wanted to be with someone who'd spend more time with her than his job. Virginia had wanted children, but she'd refused to bring a child into the world to be ignored by an absent father who was always on call. She'd had three children with her accountant husband since she'd left Carl.

Nina's first marriage had ended when she'd come home early from an aborted stakeout, only to find her lawyer husband in bed with one of his legal secretaries. It had taken her a long time to rebuild her trust in men, but somehow Carl had gained her trust.

Nina wanted children. Carl wasn't confident he had what it took to be a good father, never having known his own father, who had been killed in Vietnam six months before Carl was born. He always felt at a loss around kids, even though his cousin's kids adored him.

After Nina had recovered from her injuries, they'd decided to make the commitment, and got married. Now they were working in different Major Crime teams under DCI Rankin.

'Any progress on that case you're working on?' said Carl.

'We picked up a small-time dealer this morning that told us his supplies were delivered by a courier driver, from the same firm that Jordan worked for.'

'Anything come from that?' said Carl.

'We've interviewed four drivers but nothing's come out of it. I think they're all too scared to talk. They don't want to end up with a bullet in the head like Jordan. Can't blame them, I suppose, but it sure makes finding his killer difficult.'

'Still no idea who the source is?'

'DI Reid thinks it's some guy called Ron Zeitz. We've got him under surveillance.'

'He must have something concrete to get that approved.'

'We've had an anonymous tip-off that this Zeitz guy is a big-time player. We need to connect some dots before we can move on him. You know what the chief is like.'

Carl nodded. He'd had his share of similar arguments with DCI Rankin, so he appreciated DI Reid's predicament.

'Did you make that appointment with Dr Merry?'

'Would you believe I can't get in to see her for another three weeks?'

'Is that going to be a problem?'

'Not really. It only means we'll have to wait a little longer to find out if there is anything we have to worry about before getting pregnant.'

'I suppose a few more weeks of practice won't hurt.'

'Like you need to work on your technique. Give me a break!'

'There's nothing wrong with fine tuning, is there?'

Nina laughed. 'My mother was right. All you guys want to do is play games.'

'Hey, at least I only play home games.'

After ten minutes of driving time they were outside their apartment. Nina collected the mail, while Carl parked the car in the garage before joining her inside.

They changed out of their work clothes. Carl opened a bottle of shiraz.

'Guess you'll be getting used to mineral water in the not too distant future,' said Carl, handing Nina a glass of the wine.

'Don't get any ideas about me doing this pregnancy on my own, sweetheart. I'm expecting more than moral support.'

Carl looked at the glass of wine in his hand.

'May I remind you, Mr West, that what's good for the goose is good for the gander, and if I'm the goose having our child, you're the gander.'

'I'll drink to that.'

They spent a few minutes sipping wine, before moving into the kitchen, where Carl supervised Nina's preparation of lamb curry and rice, one of the dishes she had almost mastered.

They had consumed most of the red wine by the time the lamb curry was ready to enjoy, and long before Carl got to play another home game.

———

Harry arrived at his apartment and found Jessika, dressed in tight fitting shorts and a body hugging tee-shirt, cleaning the bathroom. He felt himself getting excited just by looking at her. He stopped in the doorway of the bathroom.

'Hello, sweetheart.'

Jessika jumped at the sound of his voice.

'When did you get here?'

Recovering from her surprise, Jessika stepped over to him and wrapped her arms around him. 'Dad let me off early. I've been here since just after lunch.'

Harry ran his hands over her smooth bum and pulled her close. They kissed as if they hadn't seen each other for weeks, instead of only the night before.

Jessika eased out of the embrace and patted the lump in his trousers. 'Down, Tiger, I'll play with you later.'

Harry tousled her cropped red hair, and walked out of the bathroom into the living area of the one bedroom apartment that had been his home for the last two years. Now that his attention was focused on the room, and not Jessika's backside, he noticed that a few things had changed since he'd left for work that morning.

'What do you think?' Jessika asked, from the bathroom doorway.

Harry surveyed what his mother had lovingly described as his bachelor's pad, when she'd helped him clean on the weekend. She'd warned him that Jessika would want to brighten the place up a bit with a few feminine touches. That warning, however, hadn't prepared him for the transformation he was now looking at. She'd turned the place into one of those apartments he'd only seen in the pages of the household magazine that came with the weekend paper.

The sofa was covered with a colorful quilt. There was a throw rug on the floor and covered cushions scattered on the chairs. The coffee table was adorned with a vase full of real flowers, and there was an assortment of ornaments on the bookshelf and the table. And, the place smelt different. He was amazed at how she had given it a whole new look with just a few items.

'I like it,' said Harry. 'You're amazing.'

'Come and see the bedroom,' said Jessika, taking his hand.

When he'd left that morning the duvet had been enveloped

within a black and silver cover. Now the bed was under a spread of wildflowers that made Harry feel like he was standing outside in a field. Then he noticed that the sheets were bright yellow, and not his standard faded white.

'You know how to make an impression, Miss Walsh, and I'm impressed.'

'Thank you, Mr Fuller.' Jessika stood on her tiptoes and kissed him.

'Why don't you slip out of that suit and get into something more comfortable. Dinner will be ready in a few minutes,' she said, over her shoulder as she headed towards the kitchen.

While Harry was changing into jeans and a tee-shirt, he heard the sound of pots being moved around coming from the galley kitchen that opened off the living area. Harry could cook, and they'd discussed taking it in turns, but he was looking forward to eating Jessika's cooking. He knew he had one up on Carl in that department. Jessika was a great cook, unlike Nina, who was still learning under Carl's tutelage, and not making much progress according to her tutor.

'How was your day?' Jessika asked, when he joined her in the kitchen.

'Not as quiet as I hoped it would be after last night.'

'Just as well I was there to drive you home.'

'Yeah, well I don't want to do that again in a hurry. I woke up with a thick head this morning.'

Jessika shook her head. 'I'm not surprised.'

'Did you hear about the fire at Gladesview House?'

'Yes, I heard that on the morning news. What a shame about Bishop Knight, and that was such a lovely old place.'

'You've been there, have you?'

'My name's Walsh, remember? Half my uncles are priests and my grandfather's brother was a bishop.'

Harry stared at her. A window opened in his mind and he

saw a name written on a certificate of ordination.

'What's wrong, Harry? You look like you've seen a ghost.'

'Bishop Patrick Walsh?'

'How did you know that? He's been dead since we were little kids.'

'Well, in addition to the death of Bishop Knight in the fire at Gladesview House, Carl and I are investigating what looks like the murder of a priest: Fr Skinner.'

'Not the St Frank's Fr Skinner?'

Harry nodded. 'You knew him?'

Jessika slumped into his arms.

'Honey, he was such an old sweetheart. A lot of people Dad defended over the years ended up in his care. Why would anyone want to kill Fr Skinner?'

'That's what we need to find out.'

'Do you have any leads?'

'All we know at the moment is that it looks like the killer has big feet, and that he abandoned the priest's car in the street next to the cathedral. Hopefully, Forensics will get something out of the car we can go on.'

'Dad only mentioned last week that he'd heard that Bishop Kerry was forcing Fr Skinner to retire from St Frank's. What a shame.'

Harry kissed her.

'That's enough work talk. What have you got in those pots?'

Jessika lifted the lid of the larger pot. The smell of curry filled the kitchen.

Taking a deep breath, Harry told himself he'd made the right decision in agreeing to Jessika moving in with him.

Three hours later, spent from love making under the wild-flowers, Harry knew he'd made the right decision, and, for the first time in a long time, he went to sleep without thinking about work.

CHAPTER 6

THE SOUND of high heels approaching made Carl look up from his notes, shortly before eight am.

A tall woman with shoulder length dark hair, dressed in a navy suit, white blouse and five inch heels, walked into the Incident Room. She didn't look anything like a police officer to Carl.

'Inspector West?'

'Yes.'

'DC Templar. I was told I'd find you here.'

Carl relaxed, thankful she wasn't the press intruder he'd feared.

'Welcome aboard, Lisa. Take a seat. The others will be here shortly.'

When DS Fuller, SC Head and PC Priest joined them in the Incident Room, Carl introduced Lisa and welcomed the two uniformed officers, who had been seconded to his team for the investigation.

The team sat in a semi-circle of chairs facing Carl.

'Let's start with the Gladesview House fire. Any luck with the neighbours, Charlie?'

'We've door knocked the surrounding streets. Same story everywhere. No-one had any idea there was a fire until the fire trucks arrived, and no-one saw anything or anyone suspicious before that.'

'Did you find out if they had any security besides the fire alarm?'

'Nothing else. I gather they only had the fire alarm because the law requires them to be fitted in aged-care facilities. According to Fr Harris, he's the administrator at Gladesview, they didn't think they needed any security beyond locks on the doors to keep the older priests with dementia in at night. They hadn't really thought about being broken into, let alone being set alight.'

'Thanks, Charlie.' Carl picked up a paper from the table behind his chair. 'According to Dr Jonas, Bishop Knight appears to have died from smoke inhalation. There is nothing from the post-mortem suggesting that he might have been killed prior to the fire, so for the time being, it appears he's probably an unintended victim. We'll have to wait for the toxicology report to be sure, and we won't have that for several days.'

Carl picked up a second report. 'Forensics agree with the fire investigator that the fire started in the corridor outside the bishop's room, and that it was not accidental, which means we're dealing with an arsonist. Unfortunately, they aren't able to tell us much more, given the extent of the damage, and the volume of water used to put out the fire.'

'So where does that leave us for motive?' asked Harry.

'I think that leaves us in the Church Archives, for now, Harry. We need to find out if there is anything in the background of any of the residents that might provide a motive for a revenge attack on a bunch of geriatric priests.'

'That might not be our only option, sir,' said DC Templar.

Carl noted her initiative and hoped it meant she wasn't just trying to big note herself to create an impression. 'Want to expand on that for us, Lisa?'

'What if it's the building someone wanted to destroy? It could be a blunt attack on the Catholic Church itself, given all the bad publicity they've had it recent years.'

That made sense to Carl. 'What do you think, Charlie? You're our resident Catholic expert.'

Charlie smiled. 'She could be right, and then again, so could you. As I mentioned yesterday, Bishop Knight was accused of covering up for pedophile priests before he retired.'

Carl thought he detected a note of resentment in Charlie's voice.

'We'll need to interview the night nurse. Any news on when we'll be able to do that, Charlie?'

'Not before the end of the week, at this stage,' said SC Head.' She's still on the critical list, as are three or four of the priests.'

'God, that's all we need, multiple deaths. Can you imagine the media that's going to create?'

'Take a deep breath, Boss. We haven't crossed that line yet,' said Harry.

Carl watched DC Templar look at DS Fuller with a look of bemusement on her face.

'Lisa, I want you to chase up...What was name of that priest we spoke to yesterday, Harry?'

'Monsignor Rivers.'

'Yeah, that guy, over in the Church Offices, and get access to the records of all the Gladesview House residents. And, let me warn you, their records will most likely be paper. You'll have to cross reference them with the records of whatever bishop was in charge at the time, if you turn up any incidents. I hope you like research assignments. Could be slow work.'

'Sounds like fun, sir.'

They all laughed, including DC Templar.

I think she'll fit in, thought Carl. 'Right, now let's look at our murder.'

Carl put down the Gladesview reports and picked up the file he'd marked as St Frank's.

'We know Fr Skinner was murdered. Someone snapped his neck, so there is no doubt about the killer's intentions. The questions are: Who? And why? From what we know so far, Fr Skinner seems to have been some sort of living saint, at least as far as prison chaplains are concerned. I have to admit though, I'm a bit mystified as to why someone would want to kill a living saint, so this could be interesting.'

'Any luck with the door knocking around St Frank's, Jane?'

'The only people living around there are the men in the shelter. We took statements from them yesterday afternoon. They were all pretty shaken. Sounds like they held Fr Skinner in high regard, and were really grateful for the opportunity he had given them, but none of them heard or saw anything.'

'Are they all accounted for?'

'Mr Sturm told us that he had signed them all in for the night, but only he and the two he watched the late news with really have alibis. Everybody else was supposedly in his room alone, reading or in bed.'

'Do any of them have big feet?' asked DS Fuller.

'Only Mr Sturm that I noticed,' said PC Priest.

'Yes, I noticed that myself, but I think we'll need a bit more than that to convince anyone he's the killer,' said Carl.

'What about the car, sir? Did Forensics find anything?' asked PC Priest.

'We found his car abandoned by the cathedral,' said Carl, for DC Templar's benefit. 'I'm still waiting for that report. Apparently, we aren't the only people keeping them employed.'

'I wonder if this priest has a skeleton in his closet,' said SC Head. 'He's the only priest I know of who's spent almost his entire ministry as a prison chaplain. Doesn't that strike you as strange, Inspector?'

'What was that fancy word the monsignor used yesterday, Harry?'

DS Fuller looked at his notes. 'Personal charism.'

'Bullshit!' said SC Head. 'I know plenty of gifted priests that the bishop has moved along, no matter how well they were doing in a particular post. I'd say someone wanted Fr Skinner out of the way for him to have spent most of his life in that role.'

'What about his great record of service as chaplain, and his continuing service at St Franks?' asked Carl.

'I reckon anybody would become a great chaplain with thirty plus years' service, Inspector. Something isn't right here.'

'We looked at his Church file yesterday. There was nothing incriminating in it that I recall,' said Carl.

'What did it say?' asked DC Templar.

'It listed the two places he'd worked before moving to the prison chaplain role, told us he had lived at St Frank's for years, that his sister had been his housekeeper until she died last year, that he'd had a heart attack a couple of years ago, and lived on a very small income,' said DS Fuller, reading from the notes on his iPad. 'Oh, and that he was ordained on the same day as Bishop Knight.'

'I suggest we start by finding out if anybody remembers him at those two places, Inspector,' said DC Templar. 'I'm with the senior constable. Something is not right in this story.'

'We're talking about postings to parishes more than forty years ago. Long time to wait to get revenge, if it's about something that happened back then,' said Carl.

DC Templar shrugged her shoulders. SC Head shifted in his seat.

She's got that same attitude that Nina has, thought Carl.

'If that's the connection, Boss, we'll be looking for someone who was a child back then,' said DS Fuller, finally naming what they were all thinking.

Silence descended on the Incident Room.

'Why did you go and say that, Harry?' said Carl. 'You know what that is going to mean, don't you?'

'Pain for a lot of people,' said DC Templar. 'I've just come from a child abuse investigation. That's what made me think we might be looking at something like this.'

'I didn't want to go there, but I guess it's an option we'll need to consider if nothing else presents itself,' said Carl. 'You had better take a close look at that hard drive, Harry, especially the pictures and the internet search history.'

Carl looked at his watch. He had an appointment with Chief Inspector Rankin at nine, not that he had much to report.

'Jane, while we're waiting for Forensics, I'd like you to work with Lisa in the Church Archives. The sooner we get through those files the better.'

Carl turned to SC Head. 'Charlie, can you find out who the parish priest is at North Summit, and ask him if he has any parishioners who remember the days of Fr Skinner? We'll go for a drive, after I've met with the chief, if there's anyone up there to talk to.'

'What about Lawton, Inspector?'

'We'll worry about that if you draw a blank at North Summit.'

By the time Carl had briefed Chief Inspector Rankin, Charlie had spoken to Fr Peter Steele, the current parish priest of North Summit. Fr Steele had been unaware that Maurice Skinner had served as the local priest until Charlie asked him. After a brief discussion, the priest had given Charlie the names and telephone numbers of three elderly women who had lived in the parish all their lives, and were old enough to have been adults at the time Maurice Skinner had been the parish priest.

Charlie telephoned each of the women and asked them if they remembered anything about Fr Skinner, who had been their parish priest around forty years ago. After discussing how terrible it was that he had been murdered, the first two women Charlie called said that all they could remember was that he didn't stay very long, and that his departure had something to do with his mother being ill. They told him that they had been surprised when he didn't come back, and claimed that he'd been a lovely priest, and very popular with their sons who had been altar boys at the time.

The third woman Charlie called, Mrs Mary Cameron, said she had been waiting for his call and asked him to come and see her, as she didn't think she could tell him what he needed to know over the telephone. Charlie told her they'd come and see her straight away.

North Summit, a small rural village located in the hills that ran along the eastern edge of the metropolitan area and extended into the northern part of the state, was a two hour drive from the city. Carl and Charlie arrived in their unmarked silver Ford just after midday, with Charlie in the driver's seat.

Carl had decided to call on the parish priest before visiting Mrs Cameron. It didn't take them long to spot the steeple of the Catholic church, poking through the trees on the hillside that rose behind the buildings on the main street.

Built out of local stone, the church building resembled St Frank's in appearance but at least its gravelled car park looked like it received regular use. To the left of the church building stood a house built of the same stone, with a garden that opened onto the grounds of the church.

While Charlie knocked on the front door of the house next to the church, Carl stood behind him on the garden path looking at the flower beds. Their magnificence elicited a memory of Nina's father's garden, which unearthed a reminder of the senseless death of Nina's parents. Carl focused on the activity up by the front door.

The door of the presbytery was opened by a middle-aged man dressed in a black cassock.

'Afternoon, Father. Charlie Head. I spoke with you earlier.'

The priest stepped out onto the porch, closing the door behind him and extended his hand.

'Peter Steele. I've heard a few things about you Charlie, none of them good, mind you.' A broad smile spread across the priest's face.

'You must know my sister, then, Father. No-one else would dare speak badly of me,' said Charlie.

'And, who's your friend, Charlie?'

'Father, this is Inspector West. He's leading the investigation into Fr Skinner's murder.'

Carl shook hands with the priest.

'Did you know Fr Skinner?' said Carl.

'Oh, I knew who he was, Inspector, but I can't say I knew him. He wasn't what I'd call the fraternal type. To be honest, I don't recall seeing him at any of our gatherings in recent years. I think I've seen him more times on TV than in real life.'

'Charlie tells me you weren't even aware that he'd been the parish priest here.'

Fr Steele shook his mop of greying hair and smiled. 'I've been here for ten years, Inspector. The previous parish priest was here for fifteen years before that, and I didn't get much of a handover. He died on the job. In all the time I've been here, Fr Skinner's never come up in conversation with any of the parishioners and, to be honest, I'd never looked into the records for that time until Charlie here called me this morning.'

'And, what did you find?' asked Carl.

'Not much really. Looks like he baptised a few kids, married one or two couples, buried a few parishioners and then moved on. He doesn't appear to have spent more than a couple of years here.'

'Is that unusual?'

'I'd say so, Inspector. Usually we get appointed for at least five years, with an option to stay on for another five. But who knows what they were doing in those days? They had more priests then, and it was way before I signed on to be a priest.'

'Where will we find Mrs Cameron?' asked Carl, she's asked us to visit her.

Fr Steele pointed across the street. 'You'll find her in that house with the blue roof over there.'

'Thanks, Father,' said Carl.

Carl shook hands with the priest and made his way through the priest's garden back towards the road. He felt sorry for the priest, who would have to deal with the fallout, if Mrs Cameron told them what he suspected she had on her mind.

CHAPTER 7

As they approached the house, Carl noticed a movement in the lace curtains hanging in the window of the front room. When they stepped onto the porch, the door was opened by a diminutive woman with a sun wrinkled face and silver hair pulled into a tight bun.

'Mrs Cameron?' said Carl.

'Yes.'

'I'm Detective Inspector West and this is Senior Constable Head, who called you earlier this morning. May we come in?'

Mrs Cameron stepped back into the hallway, holding the door by its round china handle.

'Please, come in. I suspect you gentlemen could use a cuppa after your trip up from the city. Do you prefer coffee or tea?'

'A cup of tea would be nice,' said Carl.

'Tea will be fine for me, thank you,' said Charlie.

'Well, go through to the kitchen then. It's down the end there. We can have our chat where it's nice and cosy.'

Carl and Charlie walked down the corridor into a warm kitchen with a large table and four chairs.

'Make yourselves comfortable. I'll put the kettle on.'

Carl surveyed the country style kitchen and thought of his

grandmother making him lunch. The kitchen had been the main room in his grandparents' house when he was a boy. He'd spent many happy moments in a warm kitchen just like Mrs Cameron's. He wondered what secrets had been shared in this kitchen over the years.

After serving tea and biscuits, Mrs Cameron sat at the table with them.

'I suppose you're wondering what it is that I couldn't tell you over the phone,' said Mrs Cameron, sipping her tea.

Charlie took out his notepad and placed it on the table.

'As I'm sure Senior Constable Head explained to you, Mrs Cameron, we're investigating the murder of Fr Skinner,' said Carl. 'At the moment, we're looking into his background, so anything you can tell us about his time here as the parish priest would be helpful.'

'Yes, Inspector, and I guess if you're asking questions about his time here all those years ago, you must be wondering if he's one of those priests that did things to little boys. Am I right?'

'We have to explore all possibilities,' said Carl. 'I'm afraid we're having a problem identifying a motive for why anybody would want to kill him, given his work with prisoners, so yes, that has crossed my mind.'

Mrs Cameron looked down at the table in front of her.

'There hasn't been a day go by since we signed their bloody agreement that I haven't regretted it.'

Carl exchanged a pained look with Charlie, as Mrs Cameron struggled to regain some level of composure.

'Take your time, Mrs Cameron,' said Carl, looking around for a box of tissues, which he spotted on the bench behind him.

Mrs Cameron took a handful of tissues and wiped her eyes.

'I'm sorry. I'm not usually like this.'

'No need to apologise, Mrs Cameron,' said Carl. 'Tell me about this agreement. Who was it with?'

'Bishop Walsh.'

'What sort of agreement are we talking about?'

'An agreement not to say anything about what that bastard of a priest did to our son.'

Carl had to lean in to hear what she said.

'What exactly did he do to your son?'

Carl waited, dreading what he was about to hear, and watched Mrs Cameron's face as she summoned the courage to continue.

Mrs Cameron looked Carl in the eyes. 'He used him for sex, Inspector. A seven-year old boy. Can you imagine that? He didn't even know what he was doing.'

Carl thought she was going to explode but she took several deep breaths, and the blush of color in her face subsided.

'How did you find out?' said Carl.

'John spent a lot of his free time with Fr Skinner after he became an altar boy. He was an only child and, after all, it was only across the street. When Fr Skinner first arrived, he seemed like such a wonderful young priest, a real change from grumpy old Fr Malcolm. All the boys wanted to be altar boys. Why would I suspect anything? He was a priest. Anyhow, one night, we were sitting here talking. He must have been nearly ten by then, I guess. Anyway, we were talking about what he did when he was with Fr Skinner, and he told me about the games they played in the bath. He didn't even realise what he was doing was wrong.'

'What did you do then?'

'I told my husband, Roger. He went straight over and confronted Fr Skinner. He denied it, of course. Said John was making up stories.'

'So what led to the agreement with Bishop Walsh?'

'Well, after Roger had been to see the priest, he belted the truth out of John. My husband could be strict like that. Not like how they are these days, with little kids telling their parents what to do. It wasn't like that here.' Mrs Cameron looked up. 'Where was I? Oh, yes, that's right. Roger belted him but John didn't change his story, so my husband was convinced that John was telling the truth. Roger was so mad he got into the car and went to the city, and confronted Bishop Walsh in the middle of the night. That was on the Thursday. By Friday morning, Fr Skinner had disappeared. Father Spence came to replace him on the Saturday, and stayed for years. He was a lovely priest.'

'Why didn't you or your husband report it to the police?' asked Carl.

'Oh, Roger threatened to go to the police, Inspector, but things were different then. Everybody believed whatever a priest said. No-one listened to a little boy, apart from his parents. This was years before they started having Commissions of Enquiry into the Church. They wanted to do what was best for the Church, and a scandal like that was best kept secret. The bishop told Roger to think about the damage such a claim could do to the Church, and asked him to bring John to see him.'

'And did your husband do that?'

'Yes, we all went to see Bishop Walsh at his fancy house on the Saturday.'

'Was there anyone there apart from the bishop?' asked Carl.

'The bishop's brother, Mr Terrance Walsh.'

She obviously doesn't think much of him, thought Carl.

'He was a well known lawyer in those days. Always in the papers. Anyway, he was the one who had drawn up the agreement for us to sign.'

'So, what happened at this meeting?'

'Bishop Walsh asked John to tell them about what he had been doing with Fr Skinner.'

'Did you witness the interview with your son?'

'Yes. Roger refused point blank to leave John alone with them.'

Carl decided not to ask her for the details of what her son had told the bishop.

'Tell me about the agreement.'

'The bishop offered to pay off our mortgage and to put money into a trust account for John's education, provided we agreed to keep quiet. You have to understand, Inspector, we didn't have much money. We were barely making the payments on our mortgage as it was, so we signed. The money stopped coming when John finished school.'

'Do you still have a copy of the agreement or a record of the payments?'

'I'm sorry, Inspector. Roger burnt it all before he died. He was so ashamed he'd accepted the money, especially after what happened with John.'

Carl checked to confirm that Charlie was still taking notes. He was.

'Tell us about John. What happened to him?'

Mrs Cameron took several deep breaths.

'I used to think he was an angel when I saw him dressed as an altar boy. He looked so beautiful in red and white. He was such an innocent little boy.' She stopped talking and reached for the tissues. 'I'm sorry.'

'Take your time, Mrs Cameron,' said Carl.

'You know, at first, it seemed like nothing had happened to him. He continued as an altar boy and had a wonderful relationship with Fr Spence. But, by the time he went to high school, something had changed. My little angel turned into a very angry teenager.' She looked up from her hands. 'To be honest, Inspector, he was hell to live with. He was always fighting with his father, and he didn't have any friends to speak of. Roger and I were both relieved when he joined the army.'

'Where is he now?' asked Carl.

'I don't see him very often. He lives in the city but he hasn't told me where. I don't even know what he does for a living. He hasn't been the same since he came out of prison.'

Carl waited. Long experience had told him that silence was often the best questioning technique for getting information from people who wanted to tell you something.

'He got mixed up with people selling drugs when he came out of the army, Inspector. He was a body guard for some big-time dealer, and ended up shooting some policemen. Fortunately, he didn't kill them but he spent ten years in prison.' Mrs Cameron paused and looked at Carl. 'I only see him on my birthday these days. He bought his girlfriend, Sharon, last time. She seemed like a nice girl. They didn't stay long.'

'Do you have a telephone number we could use to contact him?'

'Yes, he's given me that at least.'

Mrs Cameron got up and left the kitchen. She returned with the notebook she kept her list of telephone numbers in opened to the page with John's number on it, and handed it to Charlie, who copied down John's mobile number.

'Thank you, Mrs Cameron,' said Charlie, giving her back the notebook.

'I'm sorry I have to ask you this question, Mrs Cameron, but do you think John might have killed Fr Skinner?'

Mrs Cameron gazed out the kitchen window for a long moment.

'It's possible, Inspector. He hated the man, and blamed him for the way his life turned out. I tried to persuade him to report Fr Skinner while he was in prison, but he wouldn't hear of it. Said he didn't want to relive the horror and shame of having to talk about it. I prayed he'd learn to let it go. Maybe that was silly. I know I should have spoken up when the Commission started, but I didn't want to drag John through it again.'

Carl thought he could understand that, especially coming from a mother.

'Do you have a photograph of John?'

'Nothing recent. That's him in uniform there, on the bench.'

Charlie picked up the framed photograph and handed it to Carl.

'He looks like a strapping lad.'

'He's a big boy alright, Inspector. I must admit that the bishop's money came in handy when he was growing up. His sporting gear cost us a small fortune. He was a good footballer. Played for the army as well. Won heaps of medals.'

'Do you mind if I take a copy of this?'

Mrs Cameron shook her head. 'If you think it will help.'

Carl took out his iPhone and took three photographs of John's picture, before he was happy with the result.

'Was John friendly with the other altar boys when Fr Skinner was here?' asked Charlie.

'There was a small tribe of altar boys back then. Not like today. Poor Fr Steele doesn't have one. There was one boy that John was friendly with. Damien Harris. They were best mates in primary school but Damien's parents sent him to boarding school down in the city, instead of to the local high school. He ended up becoming a priest. Michael and Sarah were so proud of him.'

'Ah, Fr Harris,' said Charlie. 'I know him, but I didn't know he was from here.'

'We used to see him all the time, until his parents died. That was terrible. Their house caught fire while they were asleep. Be ten years this Christmas. He stopped coming up to say Mass after their funeral.' Mrs Cameron's gaze drifted out of the room into the distance through the kitchen window.

Carl pushed back his chair and got up from the table. 'Thank you, Mrs Cameron. I know this can't have been easy for you. It's always painful bringing these things back into focus.'

Mrs Cameron stood and escorted them out to the front porch of the house.

'I only hope it wasn't John that killed him, Inspector. From what I've read about these priests, I understand there is usually more than one little boy involved.'

North Summit was one of those sleepy little country villages that had given up its resident policeman more than fifteen years ago. The nearest policeman, like the local ambulance, was twenty minutes away in Ashcroft. These days the ageing community had more call for the ambulance than the policeman.

Carl and Charlie drove along the main street looking for somewhere to have lunch. As the North Summit Hotel was the only place serving meals, they settled into a corner table with a bottle of mineral water and a steak sandwich each.

The small number of locals at the bar, enjoying a quiet ale and chatting, may have wondered what a policeman was doing having lunch with a man in a suit in the far corner of their drinking hole, but they were too polite to ask or intrude.

'How well do you know this Fr Harris, Charlie?' Carl asked, slicing his steak sandwich with the well-worn knife that had been placed on the table next to his plate.

'I've known him for years, Inspector. He was our parish priest for a stretch, until around ten years ago,' said Charlie.

'Is this Fr Harris the same Fr Harris you interviewed about the fire at Gladesview House?'

'The very same. I see him quite a bit actually. He's the St Vinnie's chaplain.'

'Has he ever mentioned anything about Fr Skinner being his parish priest when he was a boy?'

Charlie finished his steak sandwich and washed it down with a glass of the mineral water.

'As I said when we were talking to Mrs Cameron, I wasn't aware that he was from here until she mentioned his name. He never talks about himself much. He's always on about how we can help this family or that family. He's one of those priests that sees himself as a man of service.'

'How long has he been at Gladesview?'

'He ended up there after he left our parish. That's also when he took on the role of St Vinnie's chaplain. He went on some sort of sabbatical when he left us, and was off the scene for about a year, maybe longer, before he took on the role at Gladesview House. He was rather unwell at the time he left our parish. They said he was suffering from depression after the death of his parents. Burnt out, if you ask me.'

'Why do you say that, Charlie?'

'He's one of those priests for whom nothing is too much trouble. He'd do anything for you, and I think a few people took advantage of him, including the bishop.'

'Which bishop would that have been?'

'Bishop Knight.'

'Don't you think it's a bit strange he ended up being responsible for Bishop Knight's welfare?'

'Nothing surprises me when it comes to Church politics, Inspector. You should hear some of the stories my sister tells. The force has nothing on the Church when it comes to internal politics.'

'Did you ever think about becoming a priest, Charlie?'

Charlie leant back in his chair and smiled. 'I think every good little Catholic boy, especially those of us that were altar boys, thinks about becoming a priest at some point. I know I did for a while, but that was before I was old enough to understand that there were other things a man could be interested in.'

Carl laughed, as a wide grin spread across Charlie's face.

'I still don't understand why anybody would choose to become a priest,' said Carl, finishing his meal with a glass of mineral water. 'Come on, we'd better head back.'

Once they were back on the road, Carl took out his smartphone and called Harry. When Harry answered, Carl asked him to see what he could find out about John Cameron in the records database. Then he called DCI Rankin and told him what Mrs Cameron had divulged.

'You think this John Cameron could be our man, Inspector?' asked Charlie, when Carl ended his call.

'Too early to tell, Charlie, but I want to have all the background facts before we speak to him.'

'Guess we should speak to Fr Harris as well. He might be able to tell us who the other altar boys were.'

'You're starting to sound like a detective, Senior Constable. Sure you don't want to make the switch?'

'This is a nice change, Inspector, but I like the community policing aspect of the job too much to want to do this all the time.'

'What do you mean by that, Charlie?'

'In your role, Inspector, you're always dealing with the bad guys or with the family of victims. In Patrols, we get to deal with the good guys as well. I like seeing the good side of people. It helps balance all the other crap we have to deal with, and besides, I love my wife and kids. I like spending time with them.'

'How old are those kids of yours now?'

'Jamie will be fifteen in a couple of months and Megan's just gone seventeen.'

'Another couple of years and they'll be leaving home.'

'Might have been like that when we were young, Inspector, but it's not like that anymore. I can't see them leaving home any time soon, especially if they go to uni. It's way too expensive for young ones to leave home these days.'

'That worry you?'

'Not much I can do about it.'

'What was it like when they were little?'

It was dealing with little kids that concerned Carl. He thought he'd be okay when they got older.

'It was bloody chaos when Megan was born.' Charlie laughed. 'Having a kid in the house that only tells you she's not happy by screaming her lungs out; well let's just say that bit wasn't much fun, especially when I was on night shift.'

'I can imagine.'

'But, apart from that bit, it's been great. Kids are work but they're also a lot of fun. I'd do it all again.'

'What'd it do to your relationship?'

'I reckon it brought us closer together as a couple. We had to work as a team, especially when Helen went back to work after Jamie started school. But it can go the other way too. A few of our friends split up after having kids. I guess it helps if you love each other and you want it to work.'

'I suppose you're right.'

Carl looked at the passing countryside and wondered what becoming a father would do to him, and his relationship with Nina.

CHAPTER 8

It was almost four o'clock when Carl arrived back in the office. That gave him fifteen minutes to prepare his thoughts before fronting the media session DCI Ranking had organised for four fifteen, in time to make the evening news.

Carl wasn't happy. He'd wanted to wait until they had something concrete to announce but the media had been pressuring the Commissioner for answers, particularly on who had killed one of their favourite characters - the priest who rescued prisoners.

Consequently, when DCI Rankin had briefed the Commissioner on Carl's interview with Mrs Cameron, the Commissioner had seized the opportunity to move the spotlight from his office to the bishop's. He'd ordered the chief inspector to call an immediate media conference, and discreetly explode the priest's saintly image.

There were around twenty reporters and their associated camera crews in the media room on the ground floor of Police Headquarters. Carl recognised some of the reporters he had become familiar with over the years, and noted a sprinkling of new young faces among the veterans, as he took his place behind the podium next to DCI Rankin.

The buzz of voices fell silent when the technician in charge signalled they were ready to roll, and the chief inspector stepped up to the bank of microphones. The podium area was immediately flooded with light as the cameras were aimed at the speaker.

'Thank you for coming at such short notice,' said the chief inspector.

Carl smiled as DCI Rankin looked at the red light on the back wall, recalling the reminder they had received on their way into the room about looking at that light so that the cameras would capture a clear image of their faces for the TV news audience.

'As you know, we're seeking your assistance to help us solve the murder of the St Frank's Mens Shelter chaplain, Fr Maurice Skinner.' DCI Rankin paused for what Carl knew was the obligatory count of three to gain their attention. 'Detective Inspector West, who is leading the investigation, has just received some information that may influence the direction of our enquiries. I'll hand you over to Detective Inspector West.'

The chief stepped back, which was Carl's cue to step up to the microphones.

Carl looked into the sea of expectant faces as he prepared to drop their bombshell.

'Most of us know of Fr Skinner through his work, over many years, with prisoners as the prison chaplain, and more recently as the chaplain at St Frank's, which he helped to establish as a place of refuge for older prisoners upon their release.'

Carl spotted the face of Channel Seven's veteran police reporter, Mary Prescott, sitting in the front row. They'd often exchanged information over the years. He saw the recognition in her face that he was about to say something no-one was expecting.

'It would appear that Fr Skinner may have committed some transgressions of his own, and it's possible that his murder is connected with his actions as a young priest, some forty to fifty years ago.'

Carl noticed they were all staring at him now. Some of them with gaping mouths.

'We'd like to talk to anybody who was an altar boy at North Summit or Lawton during the time Fr Skinner served those communities as their parish priest. If you were an altar boy or you know someone who was an altar boy in those parishes in the late nineteen sixties, please call crime stoppers on the number on your screen.'

'Are you saying Skinner was a pedophile, Inspector?' a voice shouted from the back of the room.

Carl looked into the faces.

'What I'm saying,' said Carl, speaking slowly, 'is that I want to speak to anybody who might be able to shed some light on that possibility. It was a long time ago, so we're talking about a group of men in their late fifties or early sixties, who might be able to help us with our enquiries.'

Carl felt a tap on his shoulder, the signal that it was time to hand the microphones back to the chief.

Carl stepped back and let DCI Rankin wrap up the official part of the session with the media.

After fielding a few questions on other cases, including the investigation of the fire at Gladesview House, the chief inspector thanked the media for their attendance and closed the session.

Carl exited the room with DCI Rankin, using the door behind the podium, while the members of the Media Unit escorted the media from the room through the main doors into the lobby.

'That should create a bit of a buzz after the evening news,' said DCI Rankin.

'Let's hope it flushes out a few people to add credibility to

Mrs Cameron's information, Chief. It's a pity her husband destroyed the evidence.'

'Harry find anything on the database?'

'We've got a set of prints and some mug shots of Cameron but, like the photo I got from his mother, they're dated. Harry's spoken to Forensics about the prints.'

'Have you tried his number?'

'Harry's gone to check the address that goes with the number. If that draws a blank, I'll try a cold call but I thought it might be best to wait until tomorrow, now that we've put the story into circulation.'

'Keep me posted, Carl.'

The Chief Inspector's smartphone rang. He stopped to answer it as Carl stepped into the elevator to go up to his office.

'Good afternoon, Your Grace.'

The elevator doors closed. Carl thanked God it wasn't him talking to Bishop Kerry.

Harry was at his desk, scrolling through the photographs taken from Father Skinner's hard drive.

'Thought you were checking out that address for Cameron?'

'No-one home. One of his neighbours told me she hadn't seen him since he left for work yesterday morning, and that someone else had been around asking for him.'

'Did this neighbour know where he works?'

'Black Truck Couriers, apparently. And, Boss, funny thing is, there's a Black Truck Couriers van in the parking bay for his apartment number.'

'Did you call them?'

'Had to leave a message, but I wonder if he was actually going to work when he left yesterday, seeing that his van is still there.'

'Did you get a description of the person asking for him?'

Harry opened the notes app on his iPad mini.

'A middle-aged guy in a suit, open neck shirt and plenty of gold chains. Didn't like the look of him and his aftershave stank.'

'Yeah, well that could be a lot of people.'

'And a tattoo on the back of his left hand.'

'Any theories?'

'Given that Cameron hasn't been home, and his truck is still there, I guess our boy could be in some sort of trouble.'

Something was clamouring for attention just beyond Carl's conscious awareness, and then it broke through.

'Shit! Isn't Black Truck Couriers the company Frank Jordan worked for?'

'I think you're right, Boss.'

'I need to talk to DI Reid.'

'You'll have to wait until he comes out of his meeting with the Commissioner.'

CHAPTER 9

JOHN CAMERON SAT EATING his breakfast at the kitchen table of the cramped apartment that he had called home for the last ten years. The apartment was on the fifth floor of a block of sixty identical dwellings, constructed by an unimaginative property developer twenty years before John had moved in. For the last five years, he had shared the place with Sharon, but she'd left a week ago after being on the receiving end of one too many of John's alcohol-infused violent outbursts.

Sharon had packed a bag and fled to the women's shelter in the city. He'd been served with a court order telling him to stay away from her, which he hadn't bothered reading. She'd always come back after a few weeks in the past. He'd thrown the envelope onto the table in the main living space, which was still littered with her stuff.

John told himself that, if things were different, he'd clean the place up for her expected return. It was too late to worry about that now.

John finished eating the poached eggs and toast he'd cooked for breakfast, and made himself a cup of tea. He looked at his watch. It was ten to seven. He realised he needed to get a move on. Today was the day of the appointment he wouldn't be keeping, which meant he'd be in deep shit once he didn't show up. Maybe it was just as well Sharon isn't around, he thought, sipping hot tea from the cup. At least he wouldn't have to explain to her why he needed to disappear or why certain men would be knocking on the door looking for him. Hopefully, she'd be safe where she was. She'd been one of the good things that had happened to him in life, and he was not happy that he had driven her away.

'Why can't I hold on to the women that love me? Why do I always have to scare them away? Couldn't I have just one person in my life who understands me?' he said, to the empty room. 'What sort of God are you, anyway? Why do you always ignore me? Why do you have to keep punishing me?'

He threw the empty tea cup into the wall opposite him and watched it explode into a spray of white pieces.

He thought he'd feel different, after killing the bastard he'd blamed for everything that had gone wrong in his life since the day he'd felt Fr Skinner's cold hands on his seven-year old penis. He had endured three years of being the priest's sexual plaything before letting something slip to his mother. When his father had confronted the priest, and then the bishop, the priest had gone to visit his dying mother, and never returned. At least, that was the story. It was years later, after his father had died, that his mother had confessed to him that the bishop had paid them ten thousand dollars to keep their mouths shut. Ten thousand dollars had been a lot of money to a struggling couple back then.

John had been told to simply forget about it, and to get on with his life. But the way John saw it, the priest had abused him for his pleasure and his parents had used his story to get rich.

He'd tried to put the memory of what the priest had done to him out of his mind, and sometimes he'd succeeded. But it wouldn't stay away. As time had marched on, John had morphed from an angelic altar boy into an angry, rebellious teenager with no friends. The only girls that he'd had sex with during high school had been the ones having sex with anybody and everyone. John had graduated from high school without ever having a girl-friend, and barely enough grades to qualify for the certificate.

After school, he'd applied to join the police force but had failed the psychology tests. They'd told him he was not suited to being a policeman, and the psychologist had advised him to seek help for anger management.

The army hadn't been as discerning as the police, and he'd spent six years in an infantry battalion getting his anger manage-ment under control at the government's expense. He'd enjoyed the camaraderie of being part of a body of men dedicated to a common task, and after six years' service thought he was ready to start a normal life. At least, he'd gotten to a point where the night-mares had stopped and he had some friends, including a girlfriend.

Following his discharge from the army, he took employment as a body guard to a guy he knew as Joe Black, who controlled the supply of cocaine into the country from South America. Joe Black was loaded and John had enjoyed the high life, driving around in a Mustang, living in a luxury apartment and travelling all over the world with Joe. Unfortunately, Joe had consumed too much of his own product and had no real head for the finer points of the business. When Joe's empire imploded and Joe ended up dead, John wound up in prison, after wounding two members of the vice squad who had ambushed him on the way home from Joe's funeral.

By the time he'd served ten years, John was forty, and when he'd stepped back into society on parole, he was friendless again. None of his army mates had wanted to know him. All of his associates from the Joe Black world were either dead or well hidden.

Unfortunately, he'd discovered one thing in prison that had a lasting impact on his life, and that was that the Catholic prison chaplain was Fr Skinner. Once he'd recognised the priest, the nightmares had returned and, no matter how much he'd meditated or prayed, they had refused to leave him alone.

Like a lot of people released from prison, he'd found it extremely difficult to find employment. He'd spent three years living in hovels on unemployment benefits, before he got a break and scored a job driving a bus for a charity that transported elderly citizens between their homes and shopping centres. It was that job that had allowed him to upgrade to the apartment he was about to abandon, and which had led to his current job driving a courier van.

With hindsight, John could see that taking the job with the courier had been both a blessing and a curse. A blessing because it had brought Sharon, who worked as a dispatcher for the courier, into his life. She had been the first person he'd been able to open up to about his nightmares. But it had also led to him crossing paths with Ron Zeitz, who had been part of the Joe Black empire.

Ron was now running a business of his own, based on the new wonder drug known as ice. John didn't particularly like Ron but the cash money Ron paid him to pick up and deliver packages, which never appeared on his delivery manifest, had allowed John to squirrel away a sizeable retirement nest egg.

John knew he should have stuck to their original agreement, but sometimes, especially after he'd consumed too much alcohol in an attempt to drown out the demons that invaded his sleep, John made rash decisions.

It was after one nightmare fighting night that he'd listened to young Glen Trimmer, the son of one of his army mates who had worked with him protecting Joe Black. Glen had told him what he'd recently learnt about the role Ron Zeitz had played in the demise of Joe Black, including the death of his father, and how Zeitz had set up the ambush that had led to John's arrest.

It was within that happy coincidence of addled mind meeting desire for revenge that John had agreed to Glen's plan, and had switched the contents of one of Ron's packages for a lower grade product. While Glen got the high-quality product, a considerable sum of money went home with John in a brown envelope, and Ron got a customer relations problem.

A couple of days after the switch, John had been visited by Paolo Scaletta, one of Ron's henchmen, who had given him a week to set things right or face the consequences. He'd called Glen for help, but Glen hadn't returned his calls. That was when John realised he'd made a serious mistake, and gone on the bender that led to Sharon fleeing into the night.

The night after Sharon left, there'd been a story about St Frank's Shelter for recently released prisoners on the TV news, highlighting the approaching retirement of the saintly Fr Maurice Skinner. It was then that John realised that if that bloody priest had left him alone when he was a kid, he wouldn't be in his current predicament, because he wouldn't have been having the nightmares, and if he hadn't been having the nightmares he wouldn't have needed to drink himself stupid. That night he'd decided it was time for the bastard to pay, before it was too late.

No doubt that story would be on the TV news tonight. John hoped he'd still be alive to see it.

John left the breakfast dishes on the table and the shattered tea cup on the floor. He didn't see any point in cleaning up. No matter what happened, he wouldn't be coming back.

After using the bathroom, John picked up the bag he had packed and went downstairs. He stood in the shadows at the bottom of the stairwell and scanned the back car park. The meeting with Paolo was set for eight o'clock in the car park behind the railway station. He had no intention of keeping that meeting. In fact, he had no intention of turning up for work, so he didn't go to his van, which was parked in his allocated parking bay. After scanning the rear car park, John took the exit to the small car park in front of the building, and got into the car he had taken from the priest's place. He'd parked the ancient Golf in the bay that belonged to apartment 27, which had been vacant for weeks, when he'd arrived home the previous night. John planned on being well clear of the area by the time Paolo realised he wasn't coming.

Driving off in the priest's car, John was aware that he'd have to ditch it as soon as possible. He had no idea when the priest's body would be found but he hoped it wouldn't be until after eight. He glanced at the bag on the seat beside him, which contained his laptop, the five thousand dollars he'd been paid for switching the packages, his personal care pack and a change of clothes. He told himself he'd worry about more clothes if he got out of town alive.

John drove to the street behind the cathedral, which he'd decided was the ideal place to hide a priest's car. He parked the car and carefully wiped down the steering wheel and any other parts that he thought he might have touched. He left the keys in the ignition. They were of no further use to him. He grabbed his bag, opened the door and climbed out into the street. He shut the door and wiped over the door handle. Then he walked along the footpath to the nearest bin, where he dropped in the old tee shirt he had used to wipe off his finger prints. John didn't know much about forensic science but he thought he knew enough to believe he'd covered his tracks.

After disposing of the car, he walked into the city and went into the first barber's shop he could find that was open.

'Morning, sir, what can we do for you this morning?' asked the barber, ushering John into a chair.

'I'll have a number three all over, including the beard,' said John.

Sometimes, barbers are as talkative as taxi drivers, but wise operators took their cues from the guy in the chair. John didn't offer any conversation starters. He didn't want to say anything that the barber might remember later. The barber cut his hair in silence.

By the time the barber had finished, John looked like a different man. He looked at least ten years younger, and as if he'd just changed out of his uniform into a pair of blue jeans and a dark green sweatshirt.

John paid cash for the haircut and then walked to stop U3, where he caught the G45 bus which serviced the southern suburbs. He got off the bus when it stopped at its terminus and walked to the adjoining railway station, which was on the line that serviced the towns on the south coast. After waiting for ten minutes, he caught a south bound train, paying the ticket collector with cash. He hoped he'd outsmarted Ron Zeitz. He knew he'd be well out of town by the time the police started looking for him, if they ever figured out it was him they were looking for. But he knew Ron Zeitz's men would already be looking for him, and they'd do things to him that the police never would.

When the train pulled into the station for the small coastal town of Carrick, a favoured holiday destination for families taking a break from the city, John got off and made his way to the holiday apartment overlooking the Southern Ocean that he'd booked online.

It was the only place he could think of where he thought he'd be safe, and he'd never told anyone that this was where he went when he needed to get away from the pressures of life. Carrick was where his grandmother had lived, and she had always loved him, so he always felt safe there.

Lost in his own world, John paid no attention to the young woman going into the apartment two doors down, as he opened the door to the apartment he always stayed in.

CHAPTER 10

Ron Zeitz preferred to sleep until at least nine in the morning, so whoever was ringing him at this ungodly hour had better have a good reason, he thought, as he retrieved his vibrating iPhone from the antique dresser beside his bed. He looked at the display. The caller was Paolo. Then he remembered that Paolo was meeting John Cameron at eight.

Ron glanced at the other side of the bed before answering. There was no sign of Susie, who went to bed hours before he did, apart from a discarded tee-shirt. Ron assumed she was downstairs having breakfast, which meant he wouldn't have to get out of bed to take the call.

'This had better be important, Paolo,' said Ron.

'Sorry, mate, I know it's early, but I thought you'd want to know the little prick didn't show.'

Ron had some trouble picturing John Cameron as a little prick. There was nothing little about John Cameron.

'Where are you now?'

'I'm outside his apartment. His truck's still in the car park.'

'And?' said Ron, wishing Paolo would get to the point.

'The woman from the place next to his came out when I was

knocking on his door. She told me not to bother, I'd missed him. Said she'd seen him leaving just after seven.'

'Have you tried calling him?'

'He's not picking up.'

'Leave him a message that things will happen to his woman if he doesn't come and see me. In the meantime, keep looking. He can't have gone far if his truck's still there. And, Paolo, make sure he's still breathing when I get to see him. I want to beat the crap out of him myself.'

Ron ended the call and dropped his phone onto the bed. This was not how he had intended to start the day. He hadn't wanted to think about John Cameron until after breakfast.

He had no idea who was behind what he thought of as John's mistake, but he didn't think John was smart enough to have thought about the product switch on his own and, as far as he could tell, John didn't have any connections in the trade, so someone had to have put him up to it. John would have done it for the money without thinking it through, was how Ron saw it. And now, in Ron's assessment, John had failed to think things through to their logical conclusion again.

Ron had hoped John would keep the appointment, even if he couldn't deliver the goods, because Ron had plans for John Cameron. At that very moment though, if John had walked in, he would have gladly beaten the living daylights out of him.

Obviously, John was smart enough to realise he was in trouble and was running scared, thought Ron, as he took a few deep breaths to calm himself down. Ron smiled as he realised John being scared was something he could turn to his benefit. He hoped Paolo could find him or that John came to his senses once he got the message, otherwise he would have to move to plan B. And being a schemer, Ron Zeitz always had a plan B.

Deciding there was no way he could go back to sleep, Ron ambled to the bathroom and stepped into the shower to start his day, an hour earlier than he'd planned. As he stood in a stream of warm water, he decided he'd go for a walk with Susie after breakfast. She liked it when he went for walks with her, and a walk along the beach would clear his head, so that he could start moving things into place for plan B, just in case.

Susie liked to be seen in all the right places and Ron indulged her, just like any other fifty year old would with a lover half his age. A photographic artist, Susie had been introduced to Ron at a gallery party for a showing of her work. Ron had purchased one of her pieces and invited her out for a drink and, after a few more outings, had invited her home for sex. As far as Ron knew, Susie had no idea how he actually made his money and he had no intention of telling her. They had entered into an unspoken agreement, based on him spending his money on her for as long as she was prepared to pleasure him with her nubile body.

Ron had told Susie that he ran a security business and was a successful investor, with a number of commercial properties. Some of that was true. Ron did own a couple of commercial properties. He had to have the stuff made somewhere and a factory in an industrial zone was as good a place as any, and better than some half-baked backyard setup in someone's shed.

To keep Susie in the dark, Ron generally didn't conduct business from home, and he made it clear to Susie that business was business and she was something else. Most days, Ron spent his mornings with Susie. They made love after breakfast, they walked on the beach, they went shopping and had lunch at a seaside restaurant. Then he headed into the office to make sure things were ready for each night's trade through the nightclubs, where he controlled security and access. Consequently, Ron's empire moved a lot of product through the nightclubs spread across the city.

Generally, Ron didn't get home until late, when he'd find a naked Susie asleep in their king size bed. Most nights she'd snuggle up to him when he got into the bed and, with a little encouragement, satisfy his carnal desires before going back to sleep. Ron thought he'd hit the jackpot the night she'd agreed to move in with him.

Keeping a woman long term had not been one of Ron's strong points. Divorced twice, he'd had a string of girls between wives and while married. After his second divorce, which had cost him a small fortune, he'd decided to stay away from marriage and had not intended to get involved with anyone else. He'd set out on a quest of one night stands. Of course, that was before he'd met Susie or discovered that life without a partner was lonely. Susie had been a constant in his life for two years, and he hoped she'd stay forever. He was prepared to give her whatever she wanted so that she would. He'd even convinced himself that he'd consent to getting her pregnant, if that was what it would take. If he'd asked Susie, he would have known that was not going to happen, but there were some questions Ron wasn't brave enough to ask her.

After he'd been for a walk with Susie and watched her eat lunch at a seaside bistro, Ron drove himself to his office in a black Range Rover with Zeitz Security Services emblazoned in silver lettering down both sides.

Ron's office was located in a nondescript building on the western fringe of the city, from where he coordinated his team of nightclub security guards, and the distribution of the product responsible for most of his income, despite what he told the taxation authorities. The upmarket residence he'd driven away from, however, was on the foreshore of the beachside suburb favoured by people with money. He'd spent a couple of hundred thousand dollars doing the place up in the years since he'd bought the house for next to nothing, before the suburb had gentrified. Ron liked to think he picked winners.

Ron did not consume his own product and he did not associate with people that did. He'd seen what being addicted to the stuff led to when he'd worked for Joe Black. After he'd taken over Joe's empire he'd treated it as a business, and he regarded himself as a businessman. He didn't see himself as a criminal, despite the illegal nature of his main business activity. In his mind, he was simply supplying a product for which there was an insatiable demand, and if the government had decided the stuff was illegal, that was their problem. That definition of the product was simply part of the framework within which he operated as far as Ron was concerned.

Ron insisted on supplying a quality product. His factory had a quality control system that would not have been out of place in a pharmaceutical operation. Ron believed that if people died from using what he supplied, it wasn't because there was anything wrong with the product, it was because they were bloody idiots who couldn't regulate their own impulses.

There were, however, some quality control problems, particularly in getting product to his distribution network outside the nightclub scene, that were causing Ron a few headaches. His life would have been easier if he hadn't created a network to service the clients who did not frequent nightclubs, but there were too many of them to ignore. To move product around in daylight, Ron had recruited a team of drivers who were prepared to accept and deliver packages, as part of their normal delivery rounds for some other business, for a cash payment. The quality of some of these drivers, like John Cameron, whom Ron had personally picked because of his past association with Joe Black, had turned out to be less than satisfactory, and he had lost several shipments. Some of his distributors were accusing him of swindling them by supplying crap product.

One of those drivers had already paid with his life and, it looked to Ron, like another would be suffering the same fate if John Cameron didn't come to his senses and tell him what he wanted to know.

CHAPTER 11

GLEN AND RORY TRIMMER were men on a mission. They were doing their best to create the impression that someone was mounting a credible bid to take some of Ron Zeitz's empire away from him. While their product was crap by Ron Zeitz's standards, and their distribution network consisted of a mob of drug dependent dealers who'd pass anything to the willing in exchange for cash, the quality of their people watching operation was in a class way beyond what Paolo Scaletta regarded as surveillance.

Unsure of John Cameron's loyalties, Rory had placed him under surveillance from the day Glen had made contact with him and told him about how Zeitz had set him up with the police. Rory knew about Sharon's flight to the women's shelter and John's trips to St Frank's. He knew about the ancient blue Golf that John had driven home the night after the second of those trips, and about the train trip to the holiday apartment in Carrick. He also knew Scaletta was looking for John.

The one pleasing thing that Rory had learnt about John that morning was that he had not kept his appointment with Scaletta. That meant that, although John was on the run, he had not betrayed them to Zeitz. Although Rory still held doubts about bringing John into the game, he was starting to understand why Glen thought it was a good idea.

Rory looked at his watch and wondered where the day had gone. It was nearly four o'clock. He switched on the radio to find out what was going on in the world, and half listened to a story about the latest terrorist attack somewhere in the Middle East, details of the Opposition's latest proposal to save him from what the Government was doing to the country, and a story about an old-folks home for priests being burnt down overnight. Then the story of Fr Maurice Skinner's murder came over the airwaves, and Rory immediately understood what John had been doing at St Frank's.

'Glen, did you hear that?'

Glen looked up from his laptop. 'What? I wasn't listening.'

'Remember I told you Cameron went to see some old priest last night?'

'Yeah.'

'What do you think he was doing there?'

'Confessing to wife bashing, I suppose.'

Rory shook his head. 'No, he was killing the priest. It was just on the news. They said that old priest that runs St Frank's was found dead this morning, and that the police are treating it as murder.'

'No shit! This is fucking beautiful! We have Cameron right where we want him.'

'What? In Carrick.'

'No, you dickhead! Where we can use him.'

Rory laughed. He liked teasing his older brother.

'They were saying that old priest was some sort of folk hero. I wonder why Cameron went and killed an old geezer like that?'

'Who cares why he did it? All I know is it's going to be a lot easier to get him to help us deal with Zeitz. Where's that girl you have watching Cameron?'

'She's booked herself into an apartment down in Carrick. Same place he's staying. Wonder why he chose that place. If I wanted to hide from Scaletta I'd go somewhere interstate, not down the coast to some place where everyone goes for their holidays.'

'Let's be thankful he doesn't think like you. Give your girl a call and remind her she's not on holidays. I don't want him slipping away from us now that we've got him in a corner, and keep an eye on his woman. She could come in handy as a bargaining chip.'

'You sure? They've had a big bust up. She's moved into a women's shelter.'

'Don't let that fool you. He might hit her, but he'd do anything to stop anyone else from hurting that stupid tart.'

Rory hadn't seen Glen this excited since the day they'd bumped into John Cameron, after learning that Ron Zeitz had been responsible for the death of their father, who had worked for Joe Black when they were kids.

'Yes, this could work. Do you remember how pissed off Cameron was when we told him about Zeitz?'

'Do you think he was pissed off enough to help us?' asked Rory.

'I intend to find out, now that we've got something on him we can use to help him make up his mind.'

'How are we going to do that?'

CHAPTER 12

JOHN CAMERON STOPPED and finished his cigarette before entering the shopping mall, which was a short walk uphill from the apartment. He gazed at the town as it made its way up the hill away from the beach. He couldn't recall there being many shops, let alone a shopping mall, in the seaside town he had visited as a child when his grandmother was alive. The place has certainly developed a bit over the years, he thought, as he window-shopped his way around the mall until he found a menswear store.

He went into the shop and looked at the range of clothes on display in the Big Men section. At six foot three, with a bulked-up frame from working out five days a week in the gym, it was the only section in which he could hope to find anything that would fit him. John considered the limited selection of clothes before him. Black appeared to be the color of choice for the larger man in Carrick.

As making a fashion statement was the least of his worries, he selected two pairs of black jeans in his size, half a dozen black tee-shirts, which turned out to be their entire stock for his size, six changes of underwear, six pairs of black socks, a black sweatshirt, a black baseball cap and a grey fleecy-lined wind-cheater. He knew it got cold in Carrick at this time of the year, and he planned on staying for a while.

He tried on a pair of the jeans, one of the tee-shirts, the sweatshirt and the wind-cheater. Satisfied they fitted, he approached the shop assistant and waited for him to finish serving the young woman who had entered the store a few minutes after him.

'Do you have any tracksuits and sports shoes for a guy my size?'

'You'll need to go across to the Sports Store for those, sir,' said the assistant, pointing to the shop opposite Carrick's Menswear Store. 'Staying in town for a while? It's pretty quiet here this time of year.'

'Yeah, that's the way I like it,' said John. 'Don't know how you guys cope with the summer crowd.'

'That's when we make the money that lets us stay open for the rest of the year.'

The assistant scanned his purchases and slipped them into four large red plastic bags, with Carrick's Menswear emblazoned across them in black lettering. 'Will that be cash or card, sir?'

John paid in cash and walked over to the Sports Store, where he bought a black tracksuit with a narrow red stripe down the arms and legs, three pairs of sports socks and a large pair of cross-trainers, before heading back to the apartment.

After depositing his clothing purchases, John walked up the street to the supermarket to buy cigarettes, breakfast supplies and laundry liquid. He liked to wash new clothes before wearing them.

While the washing machine in the apartment was busy working on his clothes, John listened to his voice mail messages, and concluded that Paolo Scaletta was pretty pissed off with him for not showing for their appointment.

In addition to Paolo's voice messages, there was a text message from Sharon asking if he was okay.

He ignored Paolo's messages but sent Sharon a reply, saying he wouldn't be coming to work for a few days and reassuring her that he was okay, and telling her not to worry. He didn't know if that was wise but he didn't want her fretting about him. He knew he'd caused her enough grief, and God only knew how much more he might be causing her before this mess was over, if he survived or even if he didn't.

Too late to worry about that now, he thought.

John switched on the TV in the apartment to watch the six o'clock news, and sat through seven minutes of world and national news, plus a round of adverts, before the story of Fr Skinner's murder aired. When there was no mention of any suspects, John felt a wave of relaxation rippling through his body, releasing tensions he had been ignoring, as it spread from his head to his toes. He listened to the usual police plea for anybody who might have seen anything or seen someone driving a light blue Golf, like the one pictured, to contact Crime Stoppers before switching it off.

Looking at his reflection in the mirror, John laughed. He knew no-one had seen this guy driving anything.

At six thirty, he made his way to the bistro, conveniently located next door to the apartments, and ordered a meal. As he was sipping the beer the waitress had served him after taking his order, he noticed the young woman he had seen in the menswear store earlier in the day eating a meal at a table across the room from him.

She's cute, I wonder what she's doing here on her own, he thought, taking in her form.

After sharing the bistro with the young woman and three other patrons, John went for a walk along the beach. After ten minutes of walking, he sat on a rock and enjoyed a cigarette. Then he returned to the apartment and turned in for the night.

For the first time in years, he slept in.

As he was eating breakfast, he realised he had not had his usual nightmare, even though he had only consumed a couple of beers the night before.

Perhaps I really have freed myself by killing the bastard, he thought.

'Fuck, I should have done it years ago!'

He looked around. There was no-one there to hear him but there was a no smoking sign. He picked up his cigarettes and headed out for a walk along the esplanade to enjoy a smoke. As he stepped out onto the footpath, a silver Ford with tinted windows pulled into the car park adjacent to the holiday apartments. John stood where he was. He'd seen that car before.

The Trimmer brothers got out of the car and walked towards him.

'Hello, John,' said Glen.

'Hello, boys,' said John. 'I was just going for a walk.'

'We need to stretch our legs. We'll come with you.'

John offered them his cigarettes. 'Smoke, boys?'

'Don't you know those things aren't good for you?' said Rory.

'Lot of things aren't good for you, according to someone,' said John, lighting up a cigarette. 'Guess you got to die from something. I figure it may as well be from doing something I enjoy.'

They walked along the footpath and then down the boat ramp onto the beach.

'What brings you boys to Carrick?' asked John, as they walked along the shoreline into the wind.

'You,' said Glen.

'Thought as much. How'd you know I was here?'

'Never mind how. We're here now and we need to talk,' said Glen.

They headed up the beach to a large flat rock out of the wind and sat down.

'We know you killed that priest,' said Rory. 'That Fr Skinner that's been on the news.'

John didn't say anything. He simply stared out to sea, while he drew on the cigarette between his fingers. When he had exhausted its supply of smoke, he dropped it onto the sand.

The Trimmer brothers waited.

'Should have killed that shithead years ago.'

John turned and looked Rory in the eyes. 'Why are you telling me?'

'Would you prefer I told the police?' said Rory.

'We could all tell the police some interesting stuff.'

'That's why we'd rather do business with you, John,' said Glen. 'We're of no use to each other if we're inside.'

'The last time I did business with you guys wasn't exactly a picnic for me.'

'We sure pissed off Zeitz though, didn't we?' said Glen.

'That might be so, but it's me he's blaming for it, and now he's got that clown Scaletta threatening to do all sorts of things to me.'

'Is that why you're down here, John?' asked Glen. 'Are you running?'

'I needed somewhere to think.'

'Yeah, well while you're down here with your tail between your legs, thinking about shit, Scaletta is fucking with your woman.'

'Sharon? He'd better leave her out of this.'

'Too late for that. You should have thought about that before running.'

'If he touches her, I'll kill him!'

The Trimmers waited.

'What exactly do you boys have in mind?'

THROUGH HIS BINOCULARS, DC Nigel Beard watched the young woman leave the house. She was dressed in tight blue jeans, a red windproof jacket and a black woollen hat. A black camera case on a strap hung from her right shoulder. His eyes followed her across the road and down onto the beach, where he knew she would spend the next few hours taking photographs of breaking waves. Nigel didn't understand how anybody could find that interesting, especially in the wind that was blowing in from the sea, but he had watched her do it every afternoon that week.

Nigel placed the binoculars on the window ledge and made a note in his log, before turning his attention back to the terrace house with the dark green door and bay windows that she had come from. In addition to watching the scene at the front of the house through binoculars, Nigel was also monitoring the rear entrance to the property through a camera, trained on the roller door of the garage, which provided a digital feed to his screen from its position high up on the light pole across the street from the rear of the house.

From his vantage point in the holiday apartment building on the promontory, Nigel could survey both the house and the beach simply by swivelling his elbows. He preferred watching the woman. She was the sort of girl a young detective with too much time on his hands dreamed of bedding. Nigel knew he wouldn't be doing anything, apart from looking and dreaming. He was too shy to talk to beautiful girls like the one he was watching on the beach.

A movement in the street caught Nigel's attention. He watched as a white van slowed, and then edged forward as if the driver was searching for a house number. It stopped in front of the house with the dark green door. Nigel picked up his own camera, the one with the telephoto lens, and snapped the number plate. He watched as a big man, dressed in black, got out and opened the rear door of the van. Nigel snapped a sequence of shots as the man took a package from the van and walked up to the door of the house, and rang the bell. When there was no answer, the man placed the package on the mat, turned around and walked back to his van. Nigel's attempt to capture his face with the zoom lens was thwarted by the angle from his third floor window, a black baseball cap and a pair of aviator sunglasses.

A couple of seconds after the van had accelerated away there was a series of loud bangs, and the front of the house was engulfed in a cloud of white smoke. When the smoke cleared, Nigel could see that the door was on fire and the glass in the bay windows had shattered. He switched his attention to the woman on the beach. She was running towards the house.

Under strict instructions not to break cover, Nigel stayed where he was, reluctantly giving up any opportunity to comfort the girl. Instead, he called DI Reid and reported what he had seen, and waited to see what would happen next.

The curtains hanging in the bay windows were ablaze by the time the woman reached the house. Nigel watched her grab the garden hose and direct a stream of water onto the flames. As she fought the fire, an elderly man emerged from one of the adjoining houses and dragged his garden hose over to help her. It took the unlikely pair of firefighters around five minutes to extinguish the flames. It was another five minutes before a patrol car and a fire engine arrived.

Nigel recognised PC Lily Chan and drank in her form through the field glasses. Nigel might have only been dreaming about bedding the young woman he was watching on the beach, but he had every intention of bedding Lily Chan, once they had progressed beyond the awkward getting to know you phase of their budding relationship. PC Chan looked in his direction and touched her cap. Then she approached the woman standing in front of the house. Nigel made a note but not in his log.

About ten minutes after the police and the fire brigade had arrived a black Range Rover, with Zeitz Security Services emblazoned in silver lettering down both side, pulled up behind the patrol car. Nigel noted Ron Zeitz's arrival in his log.

This was the most excitement Nigel had witnessed since taking up his position in the observation post earlier in the week. And, going by the log entries, no-one else had seen much over the week they had spent observing the Zeitz house. The stake out had been such a yawn that Nigel had started to doubt DI Reid's information. Now he thought they were actually on to something.

From Nigel's vantage point it looked as if someone had fire-bombed the house. He surmised that the explosion had probably sprayed petrol or some other flammable liquid everywhere and that an incendiary device had been used to ignite it, which was why it had appeared that the door was on fire, though through his binoculars he could see that the door was not badly damaged beyond blistering to the paintwork. He realised it could have been a lot worse if it hadn't been for the quick thinking of the girl and the neighbour.

Nigel glanced at the beach, where the girl had been photographing waves breaking on the shoreline before the explosion. It was deserted, except for a man he could see walking away from him along the edge of the breaking surf.

Nigel looked at him through his binoculars. The man appeared to be holding a mobile phone to his left ear. Nigel snapped a shot of him with his camera but doubted whether the image would be of much use to them.

As he pulled in behind the police car in front of his house, Ron swore to himself. He realised he should have used the back entrance. There was a policeman stretching crime scene tape across his front yard. When he walked up to the tape, he noticed a fireman taking photographs of the blistered door, burnt out windows and the black soggy mess on his porch. Four other fully kitted firemen were standing around their truck, stowing gear they hadn't had to use.

'Can you stand where you are for the moment, sir?' said the policeman.

'Where's Susie?'

'Are you Mr Zeitz?' asked the policeman, after tying off the end of the tape and walking over to where Ron was waiting.

God, they're bloody observant aren't they, thought Ron. Who else did he bloody think I'd be?

'Yes.'

'She's next door with your neighbour, talking to my partner,' said the policeman, pointing to the house of the neighbour that Ron knew as retired banker Jim Collins.

Ron looked up at his house.

'You won't be able to go in that way, Mr Zeitz, until Forensics have been, and they haven't arrived yet,' said the policeman.

Ron walked over to Jim Collins' house and rang the doorbell. The door was opened by Jim Collins.

'G'day, Ron,' said Jim. 'I think you might owe me a beer.'

'What happened?'

'Looks like someone tried to set fire to your place, mate. You're lucky Susie was only on the beach taking pictures and not down the street shopping. She almost had the fire out before I could help her. The fire brigade only had to mop up when they got here.'

'Is she okay?'

'Come in, she's in the front room giving a statement to the police.'

When Ron entered Jim's front room Susie looked up. Her eyes told him he was in trouble.

'Are you okay, Susie?' said Ron.

'What's going on, Ron? Why would anybody try to set fire to our house?' said Susie.

Ron sat down beside her on the couch. 'I don't know, baby. Hopefully the police can find out. Are you hurt?'

'I'm not hurt. I'm scared.'

Ron put his arm around her.

The policewoman introduced herself as Constable Chan, and asked him who he was.

'I'm Ron Zeitz. I live next door.'

'Do you have any ID?'

Ron pulled out his wallet and showed her his driver's licence.

'Thanks, Mr Zeitz. I like to know who I'm talking to before I start asking questions.'

'No problem. I understand where you're coming from, Constable.'

'Do you have any idea who might want to burn your house down?'

Ron had a lot of ideas but he shook his head, deciding it would be a lot safer to let the police run around after shadows while he found out who was behind the firebombing of his house, and took care of it.

'What line of work are you in, Mr Zeitz?'

'Nightclub security.'

'Does that mean you control who gets into nightclubs and who gets thrown out?'

'You could say that.'

'So, you could have upset a few people, then?'

Ron told himself to be careful; this constable obviously wasn't just a pretty Asian face.

'Maybe, but we've been doing it for years. We haven't changed anything about the way we operate, so why would someone suddenly decide to do this now?'

'Well, somebody has, Mr Zeitz. The question now is who? Susie told me you have security cameras covering the front and back entrances. Do you record the images?'

Ron cursed Susie under his breath for divulging too much information, but then he realised they'd notice the camera on the front veranda without too much trouble when their crime scene investigators arrived.

'Yes. The recorder is in the garage.'

'How many hours does it hold?'

'It's digital, so we always have the last five hundred gigabytes. It erases the older stuff to record the current.'

'When Forensics arrive, we'll want a copy of today's recording, if you don't mind?'

Ron was almost going to say that he did mind, but realised he'd have to explain that to Susie, and that wasn't going to happen. 'Sure, no problem.'

Ron listened as PC Chan read through the statement Susie had given her and asked if she had anything else to add. Susie confirmed that the constable had recorded her statement correctly.

The crime scene investigators collected samples from the debris and removed the remains of the device from the front veranda. They viewed the recording made by the security camera, located in an edge of the ceiling of the front veranda, and asked Ron if he recognised the man who had delivered the package. When Ron replied that he had no idea who the guy was, they made a copy of the disc and told him he could go ahead and get the place secured.

By early evening, the front windows had been boarded up and Ron had contacted Paolo Scaletta, and told him that the guy who had delivered the firebomb to his front door looked a lot like John Cameron. Then he told Paolo that he wanted him to move to plan B.

CHAPTER 14

SHARON WILSON EXITED THE WAREHOUSE, where she worked as a dispatcher for Black Truck Couriers, through the small door that opened onto the street at the rear of the warehouse. She locked the door and stopped on the footpath to light a cigarette. Then she headed towards her bus stop, located around the corner at the far end of the street, far enough away for her to enjoy her smoke before she caught the bus home.

Since John's text message had told her that he would be out of town for the next few days, Sharon had decided to move back into their apartment. She hoped he'd be calmer by the time he returned. She hated staying at the women's shelter. It was too depressing, and there were too many noisy kids in the place. Besides, she knew that deep down John loved her, despite his demons.

As she walked along the street away from the warehouse towards the bus stop on the main road, thinking about what she'd eat that night, a white van pulled up so close to her that it almost knocked her over. Before she could react, the side door of the van slid open and two strong hands pulled her inside. Sharon heard the door slam shut as she was pulled down onto the floor of the van. Then everything went dark, as someone pulled a cloth bag over her head.

'Keep your mouth shut, Sharon, and you won't get hurt,' said a male voice she did not recognise.

She felt someone, smelling of stale perspiration mixed with cheap aftershave, holding her in place as the van moved forward. She wondered what was happening to her, and who this man was that knew her name.

After a rough ride that left her buttocks sore, despite her human restrainer, the van came to a halt. Sharon heard the door slide open, and then she could see the inside of the van.

'Okay, Sharon, we're going to get you out now and have a little talk,' said the man who had driven the van.

Sharon looked at the man speaking to her. She had no idea who he was. He extended his hand and waited for her to take it, and then pulled her up to her feet and out of the van.

Sharon blinked in the bright lights and realised they were inside a warehouse, not that much different to the one she had just left.

'Where are we?'

'Where we are isn't important. What's important is where's John?' said the man standing in front of her.

'How the fuck would I know?'

Sharon felt a sharp pain in her right cheek. He'd hit her.

'Don't get smart with me, bitch!'

Sharon looked him in the eyes. 'At least John has to get pissed out of his mind before he hits me. What do you think gives you the right to hit me, Shithead?'

He glared at her, and raised his hand to hit her again.

In one swift movement, Sharon lifted her bony knee and crushed his testicles against his pubic bone. Two strong arms wrapped around her shoulders and pulled her away, as the man in front of her doubled over in pain.

'I think we'd better go inside and put a table between you two before someone gets seriously hurt,' a surprisingly calm voice said from behind her.

Sharon let herself be led into an office by the owner of that voice and sat in the chair he indicated she should use, while he stood in the doorway and waited for his partner to recover. She looked at the man standing in the doorway. He was bigger than John. His partner, who had driven the van and hit her, was smaller in stature but with well-developed muscles. She wondered what sort of trouble John had gotten himself into for these two to have abducted her from the street.

After a few expletive filled minutes, the smaller man came in and sat down opposite Sharon.

'Why don't you tell me what's going on? That way I might be able to help you,' said Sharon.

The man looked at her. She watched as a smile slowly spread across his face.

'I need to find John.'

'Why?'

'He owes someone a lot of money. Do you know where I can find him?'

'I haven't seen him for a few days. I don't know where he is.'

'Don't you live with him?'

'He had one of his episodes. I had to move out for a few days.'

Sharon noticed the tattoo on the back of his left hand and wondered what the intricate symbol represented.

'When was the last time you heard from him?'

'Yesterday. I called him when he didn't turn up for work.'

'Where was he?'

'He didn't say. He only sent me a text to say that he would be away for a while.'

Sharon watched a smile spread across his face and wondered what she'd said.

'Do you have your phone with you, Sharon?'

'It's in my handbag.'

The man standing in the doorway went out to the van and retrieved Sharon's handbag, which he handed to his partner, who checked to see if it held anything she could use as a weapon, before passing it to Sharon.

'Call John for me.'

Sharon took the new iPhone John had bought for her birthday from her handbag and called John's number.

'It's gone through to voice mail.'

The man extended his hand across the table. Sharon passed him the phone.

'John, this is Paolo. I'm with Sharon. I suggest you call back real soon.'

He placed the phone on the table between them. They waited.

Ten minutes passed before the phone rang. The man who had called himself Paolo picked it up.

'Hello, John. I want you to say hello to Sharon.'

He handed the phone to Sharon.

'John, what's going on?'

John asked her where she was and why she was with Paolo.

'I don't know, he wants to know where you are.'

Paolo reached over and took the phone from her.

'John, I want you to listen very carefully. Are you listening?'

Sharon watched Paolo roll his eyes while he listened to whatever it was that John was saying.

'Calm down, you idiot. I haven't done anything to her, yet. If you'd come to see me when you should have this wouldn't be happening, so don't give me any of that crap. If you don't want anything to happen to her, get your sorry arse back here.'

Paolo handed the phone to Sharon. 'He wants to talk to you. He needs some assurance that you're okay.'

'John, I don't know what you've gotten us into but can you do whatever it is he wants so I can go home.'

After listening to John expressing his concerns and saying he was sorry to have dragged her into this, she said, 'I'm okay. Just come and get me.' Then she handed the phone back to Paolo.

'Tomorrow night. Be in the city and have your phone with you. Make sure it's on and answer when I call on this number.' Paolo tapped his fingers on the table as he listened. 'I'll give you the details when I call. Don't worry about the package, just turn up.' Paolo gave John another chance to speak. 'Sharon won't be going anywhere until you show.' He ended the call.

'Does that mean I won't be going home tonight?' asked Sharon.

'You'll be staying here.'

Sharon looked around the office. The only window opened onto the interior of the warehouse where the van was parked.

'Here? Is there a toilet? I need to pee.'

Paolo stood and opened the door in the wall behind him, revealing a small kitchen.

'There's a bathroom over there.'

Sharon entered the kitchen and walked over to the door on the far side. It opened into a cramped bathroom with a shower recess and a toilet. She switched on the light and shut the door. The place was covered in dust. Desperate for a pee, she lifted the lid and used the toilet without sitting. Then she looked around for a way out. The only window was above the toilet. She stood on the toilet seat. The window was locked, screwed into position with a small opening for ventilation. There was no way she'd get her body through that tiny gap. Reluctantly, she opened the door and went back into the office.

'Now what?' she said.

'Now, we wait.'

'What, we're going to sit here until tomorrow night?'

'You are.'

Sharon wondered what he meant, until she spotted the roll of duct tape and the pistol.

Paolo pointed the pistol at her.

'Take your top off, bitch!'

Sharon slowly removed her jacket and blouse.

'All of it.'

She undid her bra, exposing her white breasts to the harsh yellow light in the office, and glared at him.

He waved the pistol at her skirt. 'And, everything else.'

She slipped out of her skirt and knickers, and stood naked before them wondering whether they were going to rape her before tying her up.

Paolo picked up Sharon's smartphone from the table. 'What's the code?'

'Five six four six.'

He keyed in the code and pressed the icon for the camera.

'Smile for John.'

He took two photos and then checked the resulting images. Obviously satisfied with the results, he told her to get dressed.

When they left her in the dark, bound and gagged with duct tape, on the cold hard floor of the small kitchen, Sharon was grateful they had let her put her clothes back on. After she heard the van leave and the roller door close, she tried to free herself from the tape binding her hands and feet behind her.

It didn't take her long to realise that she wasn't the first person they had tied up with duct tape. She couldn't free her hands, no matter how much she tried, and she couldn't stand up. She was effectively hobbled, with her hands tied to her feet behind her back. The only way she could get comfortable was to lie on her side.

She wondered what John had done and what the mysterious package was. Whatever it was, she wasn't impressed with being held captive for twenty-four hours while they arranged some meeting to sort out their issue.

Knowing that they thought John cared enough about her to respond to their demands was no consolation either. The floor was cold. It was dark. She was hungry. She wanted to kill him.

She couldn't even cry.

As she realised that she really was at their mercy, she hoped John would turn up for the meeting and that someone would come back for her. She didn't want to die alone in the dark, trussed up like a sacrificial lamb.

Sharon slowly became aware of an aching sensation throughout her body and realised she must have fallen asleep. The possibility of spending the night sleeping on the cold floor of the tiny kitchen, with her body locked in one position, had not been one she had considered feasible. In fact, simply lying on the floor for hours had been agony, and she had directed a stream of blame thoughts in John's direction. If she had been able to speak, she would have spent the night cursing him for landing her in her current predicament.

From the sounds of the traffic going past the warehouse, she guessed it had to be morning. She couldn't see a thing inside her tiny dark prison. The left side of her body was numb. It felt like she'd been lying on her side forever. As her senses tuned into her surroundings, the cold dampness of her dress, mixed with the smell of stale urine, reminded her that there were some things she simply couldn't hold forever, no matter how much she'd tried.

With an effort, she managed to roll over onto her other side but it wasn't long before the numbness returned to her arms and legs. It wasn't only her limbs that hurt. Her head was pounding. She was dying for a cigarette, and the inside of her mouth was dry.

She vowed to herself that even if John kept his word, and they let her go, she'd leave him for good this time. Then she wondered whether they would really let her go. She might not know who Paolo was, but she knew she'd never forget his ugly face. She wanted to kill him for making her take her clothes off at gunpoint so he could photograph her naked. She'd never felt so demeaned in her life.

Her silent rage was interrupted by a noise in the warehouse. It sounded like the roller door going up. Then she heard the unmistakable sound of a vehicle entering the building. She waited, not knowing what to expect.

Light flooded into her prison and one of her tormentors, not the one that had called himself Paolo, came in and pulled the duct tape from her mouth.

It hurt. She wanted to scream at him but no sound came from her throat.

He squatted down beside her and showed her a plastic bottle with a tube at one end.

'Breakfast, sweetheart. Suck on this,' he said, and pushed the tube into her mouth and squeezed the bottle.

Sharon felt a sweet tasting liquid ooze into her mouth. It seemed like the most refreshing thing she had ever tasted.

'It's a green smoothie,' he said. 'I hope you like banana and kiwi fruit.'

Sharon took a big suck on the tube.

'Take it easy or you'll choke yourself.'

Sharon sucked on the tube until the bottle was empty and then glared at him.

He took a tissue out of his pocket and gently wiped around her mouth, like a parent attending to a child who had dribbled her drink. Then he replaced the duct tape with a fresh strip and left her alone in the dark.

Sharon heard the vehicle start up and leave, and then the sound of the roller door closing. She wondered why they had fed her. Maybe, she thought, they're not as bad as they made out and they really will let me go after John gives them what they want.

CHAPTER 15

DI Reid and DS Strong watched the security camera recording of the man dressed in black delivering the package to Ron Zeitz's house.

'What do we know about the delivery van?' asked DI Reid.

'Reported stolen yesterday. Looks like our man only drove it a few blocks before abandoning it. Forensics are giving it the once over. We should have their report in the morning,' said DS Strong.

'That suggests he might not be acting alone. There could have been someone waiting to pick him up. Anyone see him when he ditched the van?'

'It was found in a shopping centre car park,' said DS Strong.

'Any security cameras?'

'No. It's one of those small local centres.'

'What did young Nigel have to say for himself?'

'Said the van arrived a few minutes after the woman left the house to take photos on the beach. Nigel's wondering whether someone else was watching the place. Told me he saw a man walking away along the beach after Zeitz arrived, and that he seemed to be using a mobile phone.'

'Did he get a shot of this guy?'

DS Strong flicked through the images on her screen.

'Here. But as you can see it's from behind, and too far away to be of much use.'

DI Reid stood back from the screen and scratched his head. He'd persuaded the chief to invest a lot of resources in this operation. He hoped he'd get something out of this incident before the chief lost patience and pulled the plug on him.

'I wonder if we're dealing with a turf war. If our information is correct, I guess he must have competitors like everybody else in the business. Where's this Zeitz guy now?'

'Staying at the Hilton. I gather his girlfriend is pretty shaken up, despite her heroics. Can't say I blame her.'

'What do we know about her, apart from the fact she takes photographs that cost a fortune?'

'I've got DC Paterson looking into her background in case she's the target instead of Zeitz,' said DS Strong.

DI Reid didn't think that was at all likely but knew that angle had to be covered. 'Keep me posted on what he comes up with. While we're waiting, get that video out to the media to see if anybody out there recognises our man in black, and then set up an interview with Ron Zeitz and his girlfriend for tomorrow morning. Get them to come in here. Perhaps we can prompt his memory.'

At the end of the day, Carl decided he'd catch up on his email in an attempt to stay ahead of the administrative tasks that came with managing a team of detectives, while he waited for Nina.

When Nina finally walked into his office at six-twenty, the expression on her face told him something was up.

'What's happening? You look like you've just won the lottery.'

'Someone firebombed Zeitz's house,' said Nina.

'What, the one you have under surveillance?'

'Yep!'

'Guess that explains why I haven't been able to talk to your boss. Anybody get hurt?'

'No, but the windows caught fire. Luckily for Zeitz, his girlfriend was down on the beach in front of the house. She and one of the neighbours managed to put the fire out before it did too much damage.'

'Did you manage to get any shots of the perpetrator?'

'Nigel had a field day. You know what he's like with a camera. Makes Mike Jonas look like an amateur. And Zeitz has a security camera covering his front door, so we have plenty of photographs of the guy who delivered the bomb. Too bad we can't release any of Nigel's images, but I've sent the video from Zeitz's camera to the media. Should make tonight's news. Unfortunately, Nigel didn't get a clear shot of the guy's face. Baseball cap and sunglasses used to maximum effect.'

Nina walked around the desk and tousled his hair. 'How was your day? I hear you've been for a drive in the hills, and word in the corridors is you've denounced Fr Skinner as a pedophile.'

'Bad news travels fast, I see.'

'Well, is it true?'

'According to the woman Charlie and I spoke to today, it's true. She claims Fr Skinner molested her son years ago, when he was an altar boy, and that they signed some sort of agreement with the Church to keep quiet about it.'

Carl picked up his smartphone from the desk, opened the photo app and handed the device to Nina.

'This is the boy as an adult. He was only seven or eight at the time. This photo was taken when he was in the army around twenty years ago.'

'Oh my God!'

'What?'

'This is the guy that delivered the bomb.'

'You sure?'

'I've spent the last hour looking at pictures of him, Carl. This is him. What did you say his name was?'

'John Cameron.'

Nina handed back his phone and sat on the edge of the desk.

'That's the name of one of the drivers at Black Truck Couriers we've been wanting to interview.'

'Don't get too excited. Harry's been out to his place. Apparently his van's there, but he isn't. And, according to one of the neighbours, he hasn't been home since yesterday morning, when she thought he'd gone to work.'

'Black Trucks told us he had rung in sick.'

'And, we aren't the only ones looking for him. Where's Bob?'

'He should be out of the Commissioner's office by now. I'll call him.'

CHAPTER 16

HAVING RETURNED to Carrick on the three o'clock train from the city, John Cameron was enjoying a cigarette and watching the waves crash onto the beach. The trip back on the train had given him time to get over the adrenalin rush of the raid on Zeitz's house, but he hadn't felt this excited since his days in the army. He needed to calm himself down, and he knew watching waves roll in and out was one way he could do that.

His smartphone vibrated in this pocket. He was expecting a call from Glen Trimmer, so he let Sharon's call go through to voice mail. He wasn't sure he wanted to talk to her in any case, now that he'd become part of Glen's plan for getting even with Ron Zeitz.

John finished his cigarette, then curiosity got the better of him and he listened to Sharon's voice message. He almost dropped the phone when Paolo's voice burst into his ear. It didn't take him long to work out that if Paolo was calling on Sharon's number that meant he had her phone and, if he had her phone, he probably had her as well. He listened to the message again, and clearly understood that Paolo was with Sharon.

Glen's words about Scaletta fucking with his woman reverberated through his mind.

'Fuck!'

The ocean ignored him and continued to send its waves onto the rocks, and wait for them to retreat back into its depths.

John hated Scaletta almost as much as he hated Zeitz, but he understood Scaletta was using Sharon to get to him. He hoped she wouldn't get hurt because of him. He'd never be able to forgive himself for that.

John spent a few minutes breathing deeply. He wanted to be in control of himself when he made the return call.

I'm fucked either way, he thought, as he pressed the call button next to Sharon's number. Might as well see if I can get her out of this if I can, I owe her at least that much. I don't care what they do to me but she doesn't deserve this.

John could feel the menace in Paolo's voice when he answered the call, and the absolute fear in Sharon's when she spoke to him.

He couldn't stop himself from threatening to kill Scaletta if he so much as hurt Sharon but, from Paolo's calm response, John knew he wasn't holding the winning cards in this particular hand. So he listened, and agreed to show up for the meeting in the city planned for the following evening.

When Paolo ended the call, John wondered why they didn't want to meet with him straight away, before realising that Zeitz would be dealing with a distraught girlfriend, and the police, thanks to his little parcel bomb.

As he walked back to the apartment building, Glen Trimmer called to congratulate him on a job well done. The tone of the conversation changed when John told Glen about Sharon.

'That could work in our favour, mate,' said Glen. 'We'll know precisely where Zeitz will be when Scaletta rings you tomorrow with the details. Stay where you are, I'll send a car to pick you up in the morning, early, and I'll get someone on to locating Sharon.

Scaletta isn't that smart, so we should be able to work out where he's holding her.'

John was eating his evening meal in the bistro when he heard the ping announcing the arrival of an email on his smartphone. His appetite dissipated when he opened the jpg file attached to the message from Sharon, and found himself staring at an image of her, stark naked and with fear in her eyes. Looking at the plea for help in Sharon's face, he hoped the Trimmer boys really did have guns.

He purchased a bottle of Jim Beam on his way out of the bistro and headed for the darkness of the beach.

Most of the Jim Beam was gone by the time John returned to his apartment and sat down at his laptop to write Sharon a letter. Not knowing whether he'd be alive after the encounter with Zeitz, John wanted Sharon to know how sorry he was for dragging her into his mess. He also wanted to tell her that she was the best thing that had ever happened to him, and give her the details she'd need to access the thousands of dollars he'd saved for their old age together.

John wasn't sure how he was going to get the letter to her, as he didn't have access to a printer and he didn't want to email it to her while Scaletta had her phone. He decided to sleep on it and work it out in the morning.

He felt good for having written the letter, and celebrated by draining the remaining Jim Beam.

CHAPTER 17

Ron Zeitz wanted to increase security at his house before spending a night there, so once the place had been boarded up, he and Susie packed their overnight bags and headed for a hotel in the city. Aware enough to realise that Susie was too frightened to be left alone, Ron called his office to tell them he wouldn't be in. Then he spent the evening trying to convince Susie that he had no idea why anybody would want to firebomb their house, and discussing the extra measures he would take to ensure their safety.

By the time he went to sleep, Ron thought he'd done enough to put her mind at ease, especially after the hot sex session she'd turned on for him once they were in the king-sized bed on the twenty-sixth floor of the Hilton.

When Ron awoke the next morning, he was alone in the bed. At first, this didn't concern him. He was accustomed to Susie's early rising habits and assumed he would find her down in the restaurant having breakfast. After a quick shower, he made his way down to the restaurant in the lobby and asked the maître d' where Susie was sitting.

'Miss Morte has not come down yet, Mr Zietz,' said the maître d'.

Ron walked away from the restaurant, pulled out his phone and called her number. The call went through to her voice mail.

'Susie, it's Ron. I'm about to have breakfast in the lobby. Come and join me.'

Then he returned to the restaurant for breakfast, expecting Susie to join him at any moment. As he enjoyed the hot breakfast selection alone, Ron told himself that she had probably gone up to the gym or the pool for a session before breakfast. She often did things like that at home.

When he had finished breakfast and there was still no sign of her, not even a text message on his phone, an uneasy feeling crept into his awareness. He looked at his watch. It was almost ten. They had an appointment with the police at eleven. It was not like Susie to keep him waiting, for anything.

It was only when he returned to their room and noticed that her things were gone, that he realised something definitely was not right.

From his time in the military, Ron had learnt the importance of organisation and discipline. The inner circle of his security business was composed of men who had served their country under arms. These were men who understood loyalty and the value of silence. They also understood the meaning of discipline, and had no qualms despatching anyone who failed to live up to his commitment to the group. Ron wasn't the only one making a fortune out of his business operations, since he'd learnt to maximise loyalty by linking reward to performance.

To date, as far as Ron could tell, his business had operated without attracting the attention of the police, despite the small glitch that had led to the death of Frank Jordan, and which looked like leading to the demise of John Cameron. Although the police had been asking questions about Frank Jordan, no-one in his organisation had been questioned, and he'd made sure the other Black Truck drivers knew what would happen to them if they said anything.

Ron stood outside the imposing building that housed Police Headquarters, and watched people coming and going as if it was a shopping mall. He'd never been inside the building before, despite a life of criminal activity spanning more than twenty years. In fact, Ron had never been interviewed by a police officer until the previous day, when PC Chan had asked him a few questions about the fire.

Suppressing his misgivings about being at Police Headquarters, Ron entered the building, determined to be a cooperative, if clueless, victim of crime.

After announcing himself at reception, Ron sat in the waiting area until a female detective arrived to escort him into an interview suite.

'Mr Zeitz?'

'Yes.'

'Detective Sergeant Strong. Is Ms Morte with you?'

'I'm afraid Susie isn't up to coming in, Sergeant. It's all been a bit too much for her.'

'I guess that's understandable, Mr Zeitz. It's not everyday someone explodes a bomb on your front doorstep. If you'll come with me, I'll take you to meet Inspector Reid, who's leading the investigation.'

Ron wondered why an inspector would be in charge but decided to keep his opinion to himself, as he had no way of knowing how the police handled things.

He took a moment to admire the sergeant's curves, before standing to accompany her along a corridor and into a room with a table and four chairs, where she introduced him to Detective Inspector Reid.

'Take a seat Mr Zeitz,' said DI Reid. 'I was expecting Ms Morte to be with you. Where is she?'

'She didn't feel up to coming in, Inspector.'

DI Reid exchanged a glance with Nina, who shrugged her shoulders. With his back to DS Strong, Ron sat down in the chair opposite the inspector.

'Now that you've had a night to sleep on it, Mr Zeitz, any ideas on who might have wanted to set fire to your house?'

'Not really, Inspector. It's not like I've made a habit of making enemies.'

'I understand you told Constable Chan you didn't recognise this man,' said DI Reid, sliding a photograph of the man in black, taken from the security camera footage, onto the table in front of Ron.

'His face is pretty well obscured with that hat and those glasses, Inspector. He could be anybody.'

'Doesn't remind you of anybody in particular? He's certainly not someone I'd forget if I'd seen him before.'

Ron stroked his chin with his hand and studied the photograph.

'I see what you mean. He's certainly a big boy with a good physique. Perhaps you should show this photo around some of the gyms.' Ron looked directly at the policeman. 'But, as I said, I don't know who he is.'

DI Reid leant back into his chair and crossed his arms.

'Mr Zeitz, I understand that you supply security services to several nightclubs in the city, is that correct?'

Ron nodded. 'I've been doing that for years.'

'How many people do you have working for you?'

'Around forty guys.'

DI Reid leant forward and rested his arms on the table.

'That's a sizeable operation, Mr Zeitz. Are you sure one of your people hasn't upset someone influential?'

'I run a tight ship, Inspector. I don't tolerate stupid behaviour and neither do my managers. If someone had fucked up, believe you me, I'd know, and that person would no longer be working for me.'

DI Reid smiled. 'Mr Zeitz, do you visit the venues your company protects or do you leave the hands-on stuff to your managers?'

'Most nights I pass by each of the venues to make sure things are running smoothly. I guess I don't have to tell you guys that young kids drink too much, and that we need to be on top of things to stop the alcohol-fuelled fighting some of the young bucks are keen on.'

'Yes, we've all spent too much time coping with that,' said DI Reid. 'Do you think any of those young hot heads would want to set off a firebomb on your doorstep? Looks like it was a fairly simple device, something any smart-arse university student could put together.'

'Who knows, Inspector? It would have to be someone who had gone to the trouble of tracking me down as the owner of the security firm. It's not like I participate in any of the physical interventions required to hose these guys down when they're all fired up and want to take on the world.'

'How hard would that be, tracking you down?'

'It wouldn't be too hard, Inspector. After all, my firm's called Zeitz Security Services and my address is in the phone book,' said Ron.

'Perhaps it would help if you gave me a list of the nightclubs you service, so we can have a look at their CCTV recordings to see if we can spot this guy.'

'I'll get the office to send you the contact details for each of the venues. They all have CCTV coverage of the area immediately outside their entrances, which is where most of the trouble occurs, but I'd say they'd only have recordings for the last week at most. Worth a try, I suppose. Do you have an email address?'

DI Reid handed him his card, and waited while Ron called his office and asked his personal assistant to send through the list.

'If you've seen today's paper, Mr Zeitz, you'll know we've released this photo to see if it triggers anybody's memory.'

'No, I haven't seen today's paper yet, Inspector. I'll pick one up when I leave, and I'll ask my people if they recognise him. I don't want him coming back for a second visit, otherwise I'll have to sell the place. Susie would never move back in if it happened again.'

'Before you go, Mr Zeitz, perhaps you could give us a hand on another case we're investigating that involves some of the city's nightspots,' said DI Reid.

'Suppose that depends on what you want to know.'

'I was wondering whether you'd seen these guys around the nightclub scene.'

DI Reid nodded at DS Strong, who placed a photograph of Frank Jordan on the table in front of Ron.

The inspector watched Ron closely as he viewed the photograph, and noted the brief squint in his eyes when he first registered the face.

'Can't say I've seen him before,' said Ron.

DS Strong picked up the photograph of Frank Jordan and placed a photograph of the Trimmer brothers on the table.

DI Reid watched Ron's eyes expand slightly as he looked closely at the photograph.

'Can't say I've seen either of them around, Inspector. Why do you want to know?'

'Well this one,' said DI Reid, pointing to the photograph of Frank Jordan, 'is a guy named Frank Jordan. He was a driver with Black Truck Couriers. He was found in his truck with a bullet in his head a couple of weeks ago. From what his family have told us, he was a bit of a party boy. Always out at the nightclubs. As you'd understand, we're trying to work out his movements on the day he was killed.'

'And the other guys?'

'They're what we refer to as persons of interest. Their names are Glen and Rory Trimmer. They've come to our attention as small-time ice dealers. Word on the street is they're trying to infiltrate the nightclub scene, which is why I thought you might have seen them. Anyway, if you do happen to notice them around any of your venues, I'd appreciate a call.'

DI Reid picked up his card from the table, where Ron had dropped it, and handed it to him. 'When are you planning to move back into your house, Mr Zeitz?'

'Once I've got the security system connected to a monitored service and they've installed shutters on the front windows. Susie won't stay in the house overnight without those extra measures.'

'I see in this report you already have a steel reinforced front door. What prompted you to install that?'

'When I was renovating the place, the guys who installed the doors had a special going on them. They put one out the back as well, the door that opens into the house from the garage. Seems like they were a good investment, as things have turned out.'

'Yes, well let's hope you don't have to rely on them again, Mr Zeitz. Thanks for coming in. If you think of anything else, my number's on the card.'

As Ron stood to leave, DI Reid asked, 'I don't suppose Ms Morte is in any sort of trouble that might have led to this attack?'

'I can't see how, Inspector. All she does is take photographs and spend my money.'

'I've seen some of her work. She has a real talent, if you don't mind me saying. Is she working on anything in particular at the moment?'

'Apart from the breaking waves exhibition she's preparing, Susie's been working on a project for that priest that was killed the other night. She's doing the photographs for the calendar they're planning to use in their next fundraiser. She's like that. Lives off my money and does their work for free.' Ron's face lit up with a smile. 'I'd be very surprised if anybody wanted to blow up Susie, Inspector. I think we'll find it's all been some kind of mistake. That clown obviously made his delivery at the wrong address.'

'Well, I hope you're right,' Mr Zeitz, 'but I guess we won't find that out for sure until we find him.'

DI Reid shook hands with Ron and watched him swagger out alongside DS Strong, as she escorted him back to reception.

'Too bad I couldn't get a court order to listen in on his phone service. I'd love to hear what he has to say and to whom after that,' said DI Reid, as DS Strong rejoined him in the interview room.

'Not convinced he was being honest with us, sir?'

'You should have seen the look on his face when you showed him the photo of the Trimmer boys. I'd bet London to a brick he knows who they are, and I reckon he recognised Jordan as well. I wouldn't be surprised if he knew who the bomber was either.'

'What makes you think that?'

'Body language. Eye movements to be precise, but that's not the sort of stuff that holds up in court I'm afraid, Sergeant.'

'No, sir.'

'Where's young Nigel?'

Before DS Strong could answer, DI Reid's mobile phone rang.

'Ah, we were just talking about you, Nigel. Wondering where you were,' said DI Reid.

The inspector listened and then ended the call.

'Not sure what's going on, Sergeant, but it looks like Ms Morte has been home and collected her things. Nigel says she just got into a taxi with a couple of suitcases.'

'Well, that would explain why she wasn't here, but I thought Zeitz said she was too scared to go home until their security had been upgraded,' said DS Strong. 'Though, I suppose she could simply be getting her things for a protracted stay at the Hilton.'

'Two suitcases doesn't sound like she's heading for the Hilton to me.' DI Reid shook his head. 'I reckon Zeitz might be sleeping alone tonight. By the way, has Wayne come up with anything on her yet?'

'Not yet. Said he'd only done a Google search to date and all he could find was stuff about her photographs,' said DS Strong, as she picked up the photographs to take back to the Incident Room.

'Okay. I'll flick you the list of venues and you can start on getting copies of what CCTV they have.'

'You don't really think we're going to spot this guy do you, sir?'

'No, but I want Zeitz to think we believe him for the time being. Any news on Cameron?'

'Nothing yet, but every patrol car in the state has his mugshot, thanks to his mum.'

Ron hadn't thought of Jack Trimmer in years, not since the day he'd knocked Jack off his motorbike to stop him derailing his carefully planned takeover of Joe Black's empire. He'd forgotten all about Jack's bimbo wife and her three kids.

Those boys must have still been in short pants back then. He wondered whether they were the brains behind the scheme that had cost Frank Jordan his life, and caused John Cameron to betray his trust. He didn't know what the smooth-talking inspector had in mind when he showed him the photographs, but he was glad he had. Now he had something specific to ask John Cameron, and he was confident of getting the right answer, thanks to a bargaining chip with Sharon written all over it.

As he walked across the plaza to where he'd parked his car behind the cathedral, a small nagging thought made it into his awareness. One of those Trimmer boys looked like Susie, a bit too much like Susie for Ron's liking. He wondered whether she was Jack's little girl, and whether she was in on her brothers' little scheme. Fuck, he thought, I hope not. I really like Susie.

Ron stopped so abruptly that the woman walking behind him, with her eyes on her smartphone as she texted, collided with him.

'Sorry, love,' she said, recovering and moving around him.

Ron ignored her and pulled out his own phone and tried Susie's number again.

Where the fuck is she, he wondered, as his call went through to her voice mail again.

'Hi Susie, it's me. I'm going to the office. Give me a call when you get this.'

It occurred to him that, although Susie had been living with him for a couple of years, he really didn't know all that much about her, apart from the fact that she was famous and great in bed. He'd never really asked her about her family, and she hadn't volunteered all that much information about them, apart from saying she was not on good terms with them.

The feeling that something wasn't right about Susie wouldn't go away. The more he thought about it, the more he realised she looked like Jack's bimbo wife. He couldn't wait to confront her. Pity, he thought, she's such a great fuck but, if she had played him for a fool, she'd have to pay. He knew he'd have to let Paolo take care of her. He didn't think he'd be able to do it himself, and he knew Paolo would enjoy fucking her before he slit her throat.

He climbed into the Range Rover and called Paolo.

'Hi, Paolo.'

'How was the interview?'

'The police were very helpful. See what you can find out about a couple of young bloods by the name of Trimmer. The cops think they're pushing ice. They could be behind the little scheme that's causing us so much grief. Ask around and get back to me.'

'Where do you want to meet with Cameron?' said Paolo. 'I've sent him some pictures, so I'm sure he'll show this time.'

Ron didn't want to imagine what sort of pictures Paolo was talking about, he preferred not to know how some things were done.

'Behind the Merlin. Tell him to be there at nine. I've got an appointment with the manager at nine thirty, so tell him not to keep me waiting.'

Ron ended the call and drove to his office.

CHAPTER 18

HAVING SPENT the day examining the files and photographs extracted from Fr Skinner's hard drive, Harry arrived home with tight shoulders and sore eyes. Jessika knew exactly what he needed. She massaged his shoulders and used the power of sex to release his bodily tensions.

Harry awoke from his sex induced coma feeling very relaxed, and wondered what he was doing lying in the bed. The alarm clock was only displaying 18:45. Then he remembered, and wondered where Jessika was. She wasn't in the bed with him. The sound of activity coming from the direction of the kitchen answered his question. He got out of bed, slipped on some clothes and joined Jessika for the meal she had prepared while he was sleeping.

'Feeling better, Detective?'

'Yes, thank you.' He kissed her and sat at the table.

'You've been working too hard.'

'Someone has got to do it.'

'Can't you get your new constable, what's her name, to do it?'

'Lisa. The boss has sent her and Jane over to search through the Church Archives. There's only me.'

'You guys are under resourced, aren't you?'

'Fact of life these days. Do anything exciting in that law firm today?'

Jessika served the meal: spaghetti bolognese with red wine. One of her favourite combinations. 'We got another domestic violence case today. That's the third one this month.'

'Serious?'

'Serious enough for her to be hospitalised. At least the animal that did it has been arrested, thank God.'

Harry took a sip of his wine. 'I don't get domestic violence. Why do some guys think it's okay to beat up their wife or their girlfriend? I could never do that.'

'That's nice to know, Harry. You know Dad would kill you, if I didn't first.'

Harry smiled and then frowned as a thought hit him. 'Do any of these idiots threaten you?'

'Most of them are all meek and mild by the time we see them. Not that it stops them doing it again.'

Jessika forked a mouthful of the spaghetti into her mouth. 'Are you making any progress in finding out who killed Fr Skinner?'

'We're looking for a guy whose mother reckons Fr Skinner abused when he was an altar boy.'

'I was meaning to ask you about that. Dad said he'd heard something about that on the news last night. Do you really think Fr Skinner was a pedophile? He was such a nice old man.'

'Who knows? Perhaps we'll find out when we find this guy.'

'Does this person have a name?'

'John Cameron. But keep that to yourself, we haven't gone public with that yet.'

Jessika put down her fork. 'That's interesting. That's the name of the partner of one of my domestic violence clients.'

'Which one?'

'Sharon Wilson.'

'I wonder if she knows where he is. We've checked his apartment and called Black Truck Couriers, where he works. No-one knows where he is.'

'Who did you speak to at Black Trucks?'

'I didn't. Someone in DI Reid's team did. Apparently, they want to interview him about some drivers delivering drugs.'

'Sharon works at Black Truck Couriers. She answers the phone.'

'Guess I had better pay her a visit in the morning, then.'

CHAPTER 19

THE MERLIN NIGHTCLUB operated in an imposing grey granite building on North Terrace, at the northern edge of the business precinct. The premises had started life as a gentlemen's club. Its current clients were a far cry from the high society men of that era, who had preferred to meet and conduct business in private places. Now the Merlin was one of the city's hot nightspots for young people looking for sex and other forms of entertainment. The place opened at ten and raged until dawn, seven nights a week.

Access to the small car park at the rear of the building was from the lane that ran behind the buildings that fronted North Terrace. The Merlin's CCTV cameras covered the front entrance on North Terrace and the area immediately around the rear exit into the car park. They did not reach into the shadows beyond the first row of car parks, which contained the manager's parking space.

Ron Zeitz edged his black Range Rover into the shadows at the far end of the parking area, well outside the range of the security camera his firm had installed, and parked so he and Paolo could watch the entrance to the car park from the lane. He glanced at the clock in the dashboard display before killing the engine. It was five minutes to nine.

'Text him and tell him we're here.'

Shortly after Paolo had hit send, the dark shape of a huge man appeared in the dimly lit space between the buildings that marked the entrance into the car park. Paolo exited the Range Rover and intercepted John as he approached the car.

'Up against the wall and spread your legs.'

Feeling the sharp end of Paolo's pistol in his belly, John turned and did as he was asked. Paolo gave him a quick pat down to check whether he was carrying a concealed weapon. Then he opened the rear door of the Range Rover and directed John to get in.

John glared at Ron Zeitz, who was illuminated by the interior light until Paolo climbed in beside him and shut the door. He didn't like the smug look on Zeitz's face. Prick thinks he's got the upper hand, thought John.

'Where's Sharon?'

'Nice to see you too, John.'

'Yeah, now where's Sharon?'

'We'll talk about Sharon when you've told me who paid you to switch the packet,' said Ron.

John looked out through the windscreen of the Range Rover, and then looked directly at Ron.

'What guarantee do I have that you'll keep your word after I tell you?'

'You'll just have to trust me, John. If you don't talk, I'm sure Paolo will enjoy fucking her before he slits her throat.'

Paolo poked the barrel of his pistol into the side of John's head. 'You know what happened to Jordan. I'll enjoy blowing your brains out too, if you don't talk.'

John ignored him. 'How do I know he hasn't done that already?'

'We aren't the ones who break our word, mate.'

John looked out through the windscreen again and then at Paolo, before relaxing back into the seat of the Range Rover.

'So, John, what will it be? I don't have all night. Who are you working for?' said Ron

'Those guys out there,' said John.

Ron turned in his seat and stared into the dimly lit space in front of the car. At that moment, the two men approaching the car from the lane raised their automatic pistols and opened fire, shattering the windscreen of the Range Rover, and ending the lives of the three men behind it.

CHAPTER 20

AT TEN O'CLOCK on Wednesday night, Carl and Nina were watching the weather girl deliver the forecast at the end of the 9:30 edition of the late-night news when Carl's smartphone rang. He took one look at the call display and answered the call.

'What's happening?' said Nina, after he ended the call.

'There's been a shooting in the car park behind a nightclub in the city. Three fatalities. One of them has been identified as that security guy you were talking about.'

'Ron Zeitz?'

Carl nodded. 'And, one of the others is John Cameron.'

Nina raised an eyebrow. 'Who's the third guy?'

'Someone called Paolo Scaletta.'

'Don't know who he is.'

'Guess we'll be finding out soon enough. That was DI Reid. He wants us to join him. I'll call Harry. We can pick him up on the way.'

When they arrived in the city, Carl drove to the eastern end of the lane leading to the Merlin's car park. It was blocked by a patrol car with flashing red and blue lights. The uniformed constable blocking the entrance directed them to the western end of the lane, which was being used as the entrance to the crime scene and as the car park for police vehicles. The constable at the western end lifted the crime scene tape to let Carl drive in and park at the end of the line of vehicles crowded into the lane.

The cold night air hit them as soon as they climbed out of the car but at least the rain, forecast by the weather girl on the late edition news, had not yet materialised. Carl opened the trunk and took out three disposable scene-of-crime boiler suits, before they trudged down the lane to the car park.

The space behind the Merlin was brightly lit by a set of portable floodlights, powered by a noisy diesel generator spewing noxious fumes. The lights illuminated a black Range Rover surrounded by shattered glass and spent brass shell casings. The doors on the driver's side were open. Every window in the vehicle was shattered, as if the assailants had attacked from all sides.

Inside the vehicle, three bodies slumped in the seats. One in the driver's seat and two in the back. A pool of coagulated blood had collected under the open driver's door.

DI Reid was standing with Dr Jonas, the pathologist, behind the bank of lights, waiting for the Forensic's scene of crime photographer to complete his task of capturing the grisly details before the bodies were moved.

'Looks like we've found your John Cameron for you, Carl,' said DI Reid, as Carl, Nina and Harry joined him. 'Too bad he's in no position to answer any of those questions you wanted to ask him.'

'I wonder what he was doing here? Isn't he the clown you think delivered the bomb to Zeitz's front door?'

'I had my suspicions that Zeitz knew the bomber,' said DI Reid. 'Fat lot of good it did him, though.'

'Anybody see anything?' said Carl.

'Not that anyone is saying. Can you believe it? We're in the middle of the bloody city!'

'Do we have any idea why Zeitz was here in his flash company car?' said Carl.

'The Merlin's one of the places on the list he sent me. His firm do security here. Apparently, he had a nine thirty appointment with the manager of the club. He's the one who called us. Claims he found this when he came out to meet with Zeitz.'

The repetitive beat of a dance music track briefly competed with the hum of the generator, as someone opened and closed the rear door of the Merlin.

'What's it look like to you, Mike?' said Carl.

'We have three bodies with multiple gunshot wounds. Going by the number of shell casings, I'd say we're dealing with someone armed with an automatic pistol,' said Mike.

'He must have emptied a couple of magazines,' said Harry.

'Or there was more than one shooter,' said Nina.

'The spread pattern of the shell casings suggests two shooters to me,' said DI Reid.

'Surprising that no-one heard anything,' said Nina.

'You been inside this place, Sergeant?' said DI Reid. 'You need earplugs to hear yourself think.'

A uniformed constable approached the group of detectives. DI Reid beckoned him over. 'What did you find, Constable?'

'The security camera covering the car park doesn't penetrate this far back, sir.'

'Anything from Traffic Control?'

'They picked up a black van exiting the eastern end of the lane at nine sixteen. It's registered to Black Truck Couriers. We're looking for it now.'

'Let me know when you find it.'

The photographer lowered his camera and joined the detectives out of the glare of the lights. 'Time to move the bodies so we can bag up the evidence, Inspector.'

DI Reid deferred to Dr Jonas. 'All yours, Mike.'

Dr Jonas walked into the lane in search of the team from the Coroner's Office waiting to take the bodies to the morgue.

'Are any of Zeitz's people here, Bob?' said Carl.

'Three guys securing front of house. Said they were dropped off in the street out the front at nine-thirty by their squad leader.'

'So, we have three guys killed in a back car park in the middle of the city and no witnesses,' said Carl.

'Interesting that Zeitz parked in this section of the car park, don't you think, Inspector?' said Harry, 'especially since he'd know that the camera didn't cover this section.'

Carl looked at Bob Reid. 'What are you suggesting, Harry?'

'I wonder what else goes on in this car park at night that Zeitz knew about.'

Carl shrugged his shoulders.

Nina took out her iPad and keyed in a note.

'There's something I want to show you before they move the bodies,' said DI Reid.

They walked over to the Range Rover.

'That's Ron Zeitz up front, the big fellow in the back is your boy, Cameron, and that one on the far side is Scaletta. Look at his right hand.'

Carl peered into the back of the vehicle. John Cameron's body reclined in the seat, as if he had leant back and gone to sleep, even though his eyes were wide open. He had been hit in the head and neck by several bullets. The other body rested against the door. Carl looked at its right hand. It held a pistol, still pointing in the direction of the body of John Cameron.

'I'd say Cameron might not have been here voluntarily, Carl,' said DI Reid.

The Coroner's van backed into the entrance of the car park,

and the task of transferring the bodies into body bags and taking them to the morgue got underway.

When the Coroner's team departed with their cargo, the Forensics team closed the doors of the Range Rover and dragged it onto the back of their flat-top truck for its trip to the warehouse that served as their laboratory for examining motor vehicles. Then they retrieved the spent shell casings and swept up the broken glass, and washed away the pool of coagulated blood.

While Forensics worked on clearing the debris from the car park, the detectives started the long process of interviewing the nightclub's staff and the security detail from Zeitz Security Services.

By the time Carl and Nina dropped Harry off on their way home, the forecast rain had been falling for hours.

'Try and get some sleep, Harry. See you at eight.'

CHAPTER 21

DROPPED off by Jessika in front of Police Headquarters, Harry was unable to avoid the throng of reporters standing around waiting for the inevitable media conference that a triple murder warranted. He was surrounded by microphones before he got anywhere near the front door.

'Tell us what's going on, Harry?'

Harry pushed his way through. 'Sorry guys. You'll have to wait for the conference.'

'Come on, Harry. You were there last night. Who did it?'

Harry stopped and looked at the young woman blocking his path, with whom he'd spent several sexually charged evenings in the days before Jessika had inserted herself into his life. 'If I knew that, Sam, we wouldn't be here doing this, would we?'

Samantha Jolley, star reporter for Eye Witness News, flashed him a smile designed to arouse sleeping dragons, and stepped out of his way to let him enter the building.

The briefing didn't get underway until after nine, when the inspectors finally emerged from their closed-door meeting with

DCI Rankin. By that time the room had filled with the detectives and uniformed officers assigned to assist with the case.

DI Reid stood in front of the assembled officers, with the chief inspector's words still ringing in his ears. The chief had reminded him that he'd gone out on a limb to authorise the surveillance of Zeitz, and made it clear that he expected an arrest; not more bodies.

Carl sat in the front row next to Harry, Lisa and Jane.

'Sorry to keep you waiting, folks.'

DI Reid put his hands in his pockets. 'As most of you know, we've had Zeitz Security under surveillance for the last week as part of the Jordan case. They were starting to look so clean I was about to change focus. Then we had the firebombing of Zeitz's house.' DI Reid smiled at the young detective in the dark suit sitting next to Nina. 'DC Beard here, got a few good shots of the bomber, and thanks to DI West, we identified him as a John Cameron, who'd done time for armed assault. Last night, this same John Cameron got himself shot in the car park behind the Merlin, along with Ron Zeitz and someone by the name of Paolo Scaletta.'

'About time someone took out that scumbag,' said DC Paterson.

'Want to explain yourself, Wayne?'

DC Paterson, a veteran detective in a crumpled suit, who had been with DI Reid's team for a couple of years but with the force for nearly twenty-six, leant back in his chair. 'Came across him when I was with Vice. Right little thug. Used to be a debt collector for Arthur Redmond. Remember Redmond, Inspector?'

'Isn't he inside?'

'Yeah. Went down just over three years ago,' said DC Paterson. 'Do we know whether Scaletta was with Zeitz or Cameron, Inspector?'

'Too early to say. He was in the back of the car with

Cameron. Had a pistol in his hand, so it's possible he was working for Zeitz.'

'Well, if he was with Zeitz, Inspector, I'd say that rumour you picked up about him dealing is probably spot on,' said DC Paterson.

DI Reid nodded and took his hands out of his pockets. 'At present, we have no witnesses to the shooting, despite interviewing everybody who was at the Merlin at the time. That doesn't mean nobody actually saw what happened but, until someone changes their mind, that's not going to help us. So, we'll have to make a few assumptions to get the game started. Any suggestions?'

'There must have been something going on between Cameron and Zeitz,' said Nina.

'Why's that, Sergeant?'

'Two reasons. One, he firebombed Zeitz's house and, two, he was in Zeitz's car.'

'I want to know what that something might be, Sergeant,' said DI Reid. 'Any ideas on what the connection between them is?'

Nina shook her head.

'Harry, you looked up Cameron's record. What's on his file?' said Carl.

Harry opened his iPad. 'Did ten years for wounding with intent. Took out two officers in a shoot-out with the Vice Squad around twenty years ago, when he was a body guard for a local drug lord, the late Joe Black. Other than that, he's clean apart from a couple of restraint orders.'

'Cameron was on our list of drivers from Black Trucks,' said Nina, looking up from her iPad.

'Speaking of which, have we located that van?' said DI Reid.

'Forensics are working on it. It was found in Cameron's parking space at his apartment building this morning by Community Liaison,' said DC Paterson. 'They're still trying to locate his girlfriend. She wasn't home and she hasn't shown up for work this morning.'

'I might be able to help with that,' said Harry. 'Let me make a call, I think I can find out where she's staying.'

'Who are you going to call?' said DI Reid.

'Walsh and Garcia. They do a lot of domestic violence work,' said Harry.

'How on earth do you know that, Harry?' said DI Reid.

'Sleeping with the enemy,' said Carl.

It took DI Reid several attempts to regain sufficient control of himself, let alone the room, before he could continue.

'You're a brave man, Harry, is all I can say,' said DI Reid. 'Now, where was I?'

'The van, Inspector,' said Nina.

'Any chance someone might have seen who left the van there, Wayne?'

'There are sixty apartments in the building Cameron lives in, and another sixty in the one behind it overlooking the car park.'

'Let's hope someone was looking out the window last night, then,' said DI Reid. 'Sergeant, we'll need statements from Cameron's neighbours. Have we had any luck contacting Susie Morte?'

'I traced the taxi she caught yesterday,' said DC Beard. 'It took her to the airport but when I called the airlines, none of them had a record of a ticket being issued in her name.'

'Better get down there with a photo. I assume you've got one of her we can use.'

'Yes, sir,' said DC Beard, who had more photos of Susie Morte than he would be admitting to DI Reid.

'Does this Scaletta have any next of kin?' said DI Reid.

'We're still looking. There might be something on his file,' said Nina.

'Okay. Sergeant. I want a search of Cameron's apartment,

Zeitz's house and whatever hole Scaletta crawled out of. While you're doing that, I'll be interviewing Zeitz's business associates.'

'There was a media circus outside when I came in, Inspector. Are you releasing a statement?' said Harry.

'The Chief Inspector will be talking to the media as soon as Charlie reports in that he's broken the news to Mrs Cameron. Have we got the happy snaps from Forensics?'

'Electronic file came through just after eight, Inspector,' said Nina.

'What else have they given us?'

'Four mobile phones, three wallets and a Glock.'

'Carl, can I have Harry to use his charm with the phone companies?'

'Sounds like a good idea to me,' said Carl.

'Okay, Sergeant, get the search teams organised.'

The murder of Fr Skinner was starting to look like a sideshow in comparison with what the media had dubbed the Merlin Massacre. It was certainly no longer page one news, despite Carl's request for long ago altar boys to come forward.

After the presentation to the media naming the Merlin victims, Carl met with DC Lisa Templar and PC Jane Priest to discuss the progress of their search of the records in the archives of the Catholic Church.

'Find anything of interest?' said Carl.

DC Templar opened her notebook. Carl noted that her neat handwriting was nothing like the scribble he and Harry employed.

'According to Fr Harris, there were only eight residents in Gladesview House, besides Bishop Knight. Two of them, Fr Peter Wilson and Fr Brendan North, are contemporaries of Fr

Skinner and Bishop Knight. The others are in their eighties. In fact, one Fr Flaherty, is in his nineties. There's nothing in their records. They're all pretty sketchy, like Fr Skinner's, and not one complaint.'

'What about Bishop Knight's file?' said Carl.

'According to his file, he resigned due to poor health. Complications from type two diabetes. There was nothing in the file about accusations of covering up child abuse by priests. In fact, he was setting up an enquiry just before he resigned. Maybe that's where SC Head's rumours came from,' said DC Templar.

'If you don't mind me saying so, Inspector,' said PC Priest. 'I reckon their personnel records are crap. They certainly wouldn't cut it here. Have you seen what's in our files?'

'Yes. I had the pleasure of reading Lisa's file earlier in the week.' Carl smiled at DC Templar, who fiddled with her pen as a blush swept across her cheeks. 'And, I agree with you. There was more in that file covering her short time with the force than the one detailing more than fifty years of service for Fr Skinner.'

'I guess as a government agency we have to comply with higher standards,' said DC Templar. 'I suppose their more recent records are more detailed.'

'Let's hope so,' said Carl. 'Did you come across any references to Bishop Walsh?'

'Not in the files we've looked at. The Monsignor told us we'd need a search warrant to access his archive,' said Lisa.

Carl reached into his inside coat pocket, pulled out an envelope and placed it on the desk. 'The Commissioner gave this to DCI Rankin first thing this morning. I have no idea how extensive the bishop's archive is, however, you can tell me all about it when you find out.'

Carl handed the envelope to DC Templar. 'Focus on the records from the period of Fr Skinner's time as a parish priest. Give me a call if you have any trouble getting access. And let me know if you find anything mentioning John Cameron or any other altar boy from North Summit. The Commissioner is keen to move the media attention back onto the Church, so be thorough.'

Shortly after DC Templar and PC Priest had left his office, Carl's smartphone emitted a ping, alerting him to the arrival of an email. Forensics had lifted a fingerprint from the keys in the blue Golf and matched it with a fingerprint for John Cameron in the police database.

While he was pondering the implications of the message, DS Fuller appeared in his doorway.

'Boss, the hospital just called. Two of those old priests from Gladesview House died this morning.'

'We need to speak to that nurse.'

'She's still in intensive care.'

'Find out when we can interview her.'

'And, Boss, we have another problem.'

Carl raised an eyebrow.

'I got Sharon Wilson's mobile number from Jessika.'

Hearing Jessika's name reminded Carl of what he'd said at Harry's expense in the Incident Room. 'Sorry, about that comment earlier, Harry. It slipped out before I knew what I was saying.'

'Think nothing of it, Boss. I thought it was funny. Besides, watching DI Reid almost wet his pants trying to keep a straight face was priceless,' said DS Fuller. 'Mind you though, Jessika will make you pay for it, calling her the enemy. She wasn't impressed when I told her.'

'Guess I'll have to find some way to make it up to her. Anyway, what's the problem with the number? Have you spoken to this Sharon Wilson?'

'Her iPhone's in one of the evidence bags from the Merlin.'

'You're kidding me. Who had it? Cameron?'

'No. The notes say it was found on Scaletta.'

'Can you access the phone?'

'It's an iPhone 6. Even Apple can't open it.'

Carl scratched his head. 'Bloody privacy laws. How the hell are we supposed to do our job?'

'I've got the providers doing location traces on all four phones. Hopefully we'll be able to work out where she's been and if she was with Scaletta at some point. I'm also getting the call records for each phone. I still need to get the details for Scaletta, but Black Trucks had Cameron's number and DI Reid had Zeitz's.'

'Did Jessika know where she was staying?'

'At the City Women's Shelter, but the woman in charge told Jessika that Sharon had checked out yesterday and was planning to go home. Apparently Sharon told her that her partner, our mate Cameron, was out of town so it would be safe for her to go home.'

'Something's not right here, Harry. If she isn't home and she's not at work. Where is she? And why did Scaletta have her phone?'

DS Fuller had turned to leave when Carl remembered the email. 'Forensics have put our mate Cameron inside Fr Skinner's Golf. Fingerprint on the keys.'

'Pity he can't tell us how it got there.'

Harry studied the positioning data for the four smartphones, for the week leading up to when they had been found in Zeitz's car at the Merlin. Reading one sheet at a time, he used colored pins to mark the trail of each phone on a wall map of the metropolitan area.

The trail left by Sharon Wilson's iPhone intersected with the positioning data from Paolo Scaletta's Samsung at a GPS co-ordinate close to the location of Black Truck Couriers' office. When he checked the times recorded for each position, Harry realised the data trails collided late in the afternoon of the day Sharon was meant to be returning to the apartment she had shared with John Cameron. It looked like she had met up with Scaletta when she had left work that day.

Harry wondered what sort of meeting had occurred between the bearers of the phones. Had it been friendly or otherwise, and had anyone witnessed it? He scribbled a note in his notebook. They'd have to interview anybody who had been in that location at the time to find out.

From their point of intersection, the two devices had travelled together to a location in the light industrial zone on the northern fringe of the metropolitan area, according to the pins on the map. Both devices had stayed at that location for fifty-seven minutes. Then they'd travelled in unison to various locations around the city, including overnighting at the address at which Scaletta had resided, before finally ending up in the car park behind the Merlin.

Harry was puzzled. The data suggested that Sharon had met up with Scaletta after work, visited a location north of the city and then spent the night with him. He wondered if she had been in the car park behind the Merlin as well. He decided to call Jessika.

'How well do you know Sharon Wilson?' Harry asked, when Jessika came on the line.

'I've only met her a couple of times. Why are you asking?'

'I'm trying to work out what her phone records are telling me. Do you think she's the type that would spend the night with another man?'

'Harry, part of the problem with working with people like

Sharon is that they stick with their man, no matter what he's done to them.'

'Okay, thanks. By the way, I'll probably be late home tonight.'

'Dad did warn me this would happen. I'll try and wait up for you.'

'That would be nice.'

'Could be more than nice if you're not too late, Detective.'

Harry looked at the wall map, without seeing it, as the thought of Jessika rubbing her lithe body against his occupied his imagination. He hoped he wouldn't be too late. The sound of a door shutting bought him back to reality, and he turned his attention to the sheet holding the positioning data for John Cameron's phone.

When he'd plotted the data for Cameron's phone on the wall map, Harry realised that apart from his brief visit to the Zeitz house for the firebombing, Cameron had been in the vicinity of St Frank's on the night of Fr Skinner's murder, and on the preceding night, and that he had travelled to Carrick on the South Coast the day after. The data also told him that Cameron had returned to Carrick after the firebombing and spent the night in a building on the foreshore.

According to his phone, Cameron had returned to the city on the morning of the massacre and spent the day in the CBD. At 20:15 he had travelled to the vicinity of his apartment and then made his way to the lane behind the Merlin, arriving at 21:00. The timings connected to the data points suggested to Harry that Cameron had travelled from the city to his apartment and then on to the Merlin by car. That could explain why his van was seen being driven away. He wondered whether Sharon had been the driver, and why she'd left her phone behind with Scaletta.

The positioning data for Ron Zeitz's phone aligned with his known movements since the time of the firebombing.

When he'd plotted the positions of the smartphones, Harry

turned his attention to their call logs, to see if there were any calls between them.

There were numerous calls between Scaletta's and Zeitz's numbers, and several calls between Scaletta's and Cameron's. There were no calls between Zeitz's and Cameron's or Sharon's numbers. There were several calls between Sharon's and Cameron's.

The timing of the last few calls from Sharon's iPhone to Cameron's caught Harry's attention. There was a short call to Cameron's number followed by a longer call from Cameron's to Sharon's ten minutes later. Harry guessed that Sharon had left a message and Cameron had returned her call. He checked Cameron's call log again and spotted the intervening call to 101, required to retrieve a voice mail message. The exchange of calls had happened during the fifty-seven-minute window Sharon's phone had been in the light industrial zone north of the city. The next call had been mid-afternoon the next day, when it appeared Sharon had called John from Scaletta's home. The last exchange between the phones had been a text message at 20:58, shortly before the massacre in the car park.

Harry rechecked the positions of the phones during that last exchange. They were almost on top of each other when the text message had been sent.

There was one other call to Cameron's phone, that he had received while in Carrick, which intrigued Harry. It was tagged untraceable. When he queried his contact at the telephone company, he was told it had been generated by a disposable number app and was a lot more difficult to trace, especially as the provider of the software was located offshore and the user had used a pre-paid phone.

Harry decided it was time for a second opinion, so he called Carl over to his wall map dotted with colored pins.

'Very artistic, Harry.'

'Well, the scientific aspect kicks in when you look at position and timing together. Look at the blue and green pins. See where they come together here? That's at 16:45 Tuesday, outside Black Truck Couriers.'

'Whose phones do they represent?'

'The blue one is Sharon Wilson's. The green one is Paolo Scaletta's.'

'Harry, are you telling me they travelled together from that time right up to the shooting?'

'Looks like it.'

'Why isn't Wilson in the morgue?'

Harry scratched his head. 'The other thing that's interesting, Boss, is that while Sharon was with Scaletta, she made a few calls to Cameron. There was an exchange of calls when she and Scaletta were at this location.' Harry pointed to the light industrial zone on the map. 'Then there was a call from Sharon mid-afternoon yesterday, while she was at Scaletta's place instead of being at work, here.' He pointed to a spot in the north-eastern suburbs. 'Finally, there was a text message from her phone, from within the Merlin's car park, to Cameron's phone, which appears to have been in the lane leading into the car park at the time.'

'Any other surprises, Harry?'

'Take a look at the red pins. That's Cameron's phone.'

Carl studied the map. 'Isn't this where St Frank's is?' Carl placed his finger on a red pin and looked at Harry.

'Would appear he was there on the night the priest was strangled, and the night before that as well,' said Harry.

'Maybe his mother was right. Not only does it appear he was there at the right time, it looks like he took the priest's car for a drive as well.'

'Yeah, and his phone was outside Ron Zeitz's place at the time of the firebombing. Looks like he's been a busy boy over the last few days.'

Carl looked at the pattern of pins. 'I take it that the white pins are Zeitz?'

'Yeah. No surprises there. The only calls are between him and Scaletta but we do have one mystery caller to Cameron's phone the night before the shooting, when he was still in Carrick.'

'Mystery caller?'

'No way we can find out who the number belongs to. I asked.'

Carl sat on the edge of Harry's desk. 'What's the connection between these people? We know that Zeitz knew Scaletta. We know that Cameron knew Sharon. How does Cameron connect to Zeitz and Scaletta?'

'I don't know, Boss, but I wonder if it has anything to do with Black Truck Couriers. If DI Reid is right about their drivers, who would have been a better contact for Zeitz than Sharon? She's their head dispatcher. If anyone needed a driver off the record, she'd be the first place to start. Maybe she's Zeitz's contact.'

'I wonder if we're making a few too many assumptions here, Harry. What if Sharon is only caught up in this because she's Cameron's girlfriend?'

'You think she was being used as some sort of hostage by Scaletta to get Cameron to meet him and Zeitz?'

'It's a possibility.'

Harry looked at the map. 'If her meeting with Scaletta wasn't consensual, she could be anywhere along that track of twin blue and green pins.'

'What's at that point where they spent fifty-seven minutes?'

Harry fed the details of the location into Google Maps. 'Looks like a warehouse in an industrial park.'

'Get a patrol out there to have a look around.'

SHORTLY AFTER THE mid-afternoon update on ABC News 24, the Crime Stoppers hotline received a call from Fred Hart, who managed the Surfers Apartments in Carrick. He'd called to report that the John Cameron named in the Merlin Massacre story looked like the man of the same name who had been one of his guests.

When the information came through to Carl in the Incident Room, he called Mr Hart and learnt that John Cameron had not checked out. The manager of the Surfers Apartments told him that Cameron had booked an apartment for ten days but hadn't been seen for a couple of days. Carl asked him to keep the apartment locked until he arrived.

'Harry, get your coat. We're going for a drive.'

It was early evening by the time they arrived in Carrick and located the Surfers Apartments.

Mr Hart was waiting for them in the reception area, which also served as his office.

Carl showed Mr Hart several photographs of John Cameron.

'That's him alright, Inspector. He's stayed here a few times over the years. Always wants the same room.'

'How long was he here this time?'

'Arrived early Monday afternoon. Came down on the train, like he always does. He made the booking online, Saturday.'

'Did he have any visitors?'

'Not that I saw.'

'Did you have any other guests while he was here?'

'There was a young lady that stayed for a couple of nights. She arrived the same day as Mr Cameron, about the same time actually. She didn't have a car either, so she probably came down on the same train as Mr Cameron, but she checked out Wednesday morning. The three couples staying now only arrived this afternoon.'

'Do you have her name and contact details? We might need to speak to her.'

'We always ask guests for their name and address, Inspector.' Mr Hart turned to his computer and bought up her account. 'She paid with a credit card.' He printed the record and handed the page to Carl.

Carl looked at the name: Janice George. It didn't ring any bells. He passed the page to Harry.

'Don't suppose you have any security cameras, Mr Hart?'

'No, nothing happens in Carrick, Inspector. They'd be a waste of money.'

Mr Hart handed them the key to apartment six and told them how to find it. Carl and Harry walked along the veranda facing the car park and let themselves into the apartment, which according to the manager had been serviced on Wednesday morning. Carl looked inside the wardrobe and inspected the clothes John Cameron had left behind.

'Looks like our man was into black.'

Harry unzipped the black sports bag sitting on the bench next to the TV.

'Boss, there's a laptop in this bag,' said Harry, 'and a shitload of cash.'

They took possession of the bag and its contents, bagged up the clothing Cameron had left behind, and headed back to the city to speak to Janice George.

When they arrived at the address the manager had given them for Janice George it was a boarded up second-hand book-shop, which looked like it had served its last customer several years ago.

'Better see what you can find out about this Janice George, Harry.'

CHAPTER 23

JESSIKA WAS READING a brief for an upcoming case when Harry got home, just after nine.

He collapsed onto the sofa beside her and undid his tie.

She kissed him on the cheek.

'Long day, Detective? Have you eaten?'

'Not yet but I can rustle something up.'

'Why don't you get out of that suit and have a shower while I cook you something?'

'You sure?'

'I've been waiting for you, Detective, and I don't want you passing out on me from lack of energy.' She undid the buttons of his shirt and tickled his belly. 'Go and get in the shower.'

Harry did as he was told, and discovered that having sex under running hot water only increased his appetite for more. It was well after ten when they sat down to eat.

'Did you have any luck contacting Sharon?'

'None, I'm afraid.'

'What made you think she might have spent the night with another man?'

Harry chewed a mouthful of steak and gazed at the semi-naked woman sitting across the table from him asking questions. 'I've got the GPS data showing me where all the phones found in Zeitz's car were for the week leading up to the shooting.'

'Why would that make you ask about Sharon?'

'You need to keep this to yourself, for the time being, but her phone was in that car.'

Jessika pulled her gown together and crossed her arms over her breasts. 'Who had the phone, Harry?'

'It was in Scaletta's pocket.'

'That doesn't make sense to me.'

'Well, it might if she knew him or was with him before the shooting.'

'What makes you think that could be possible?'

'That's where the GPS data comes in. It shows that Scaletta's and Sharon's phones were in the same places at the same time from Tuesday afternoon, from about the time she left work, right up to the time of the shooting.'

'But that doesn't mean the people were together, necessarily, does it?'

'Well, unless he found her phone in the street, and I guess that is a possibility, she must have given it to him at some point.'

'Why would she do that?'

'Good question.' Harry finished eating and sat back in his chair. 'Another good question is why did someone call John Cameron from Sharon's phone on Tuesday evening, when it was in the same location as Scaletta's, and why did someone send a text message from it to Cameron just before Cameron met up with Scaletta and Zeitz?'

'You have quite a puzzle there, Detective.'

'Yes, and all the people who could help me untangle it are dead, except for Sharon, and she's gone missing.'

'I'd probably disappear too, if I could, if my boyfriend had been killed like that. Maybe she knows who shot them. Then again, given the history between Sharon and John, maybe she did it herself.'

Harry realised he hadn't thought of that.

Jessika stood, her gown falling open and exposing her firm round breasts as she leant across the table, grasped Harry's hand and led him to their bed.

Once they had crossed the threshold and fallen onto the bed, all talk of missing persons or unsolved puzzles was forgotten, as detective morphed into lover and Harry made the most of Jessika waiting up for him.

CHAPTER 24

FRIDAY STARTED with a meeting in the Incident Room. DI Reid opened the session by requesting updates on the three searches executed the previous day.

'Let's start with the Zeitz place,' said DI Reid.

'Lots of nice stuff but nothing linking him to Scaletta or Cameron or anything outside his security operation,' said DS Strong. 'There was a wireless router connected to his modem but no sign of a laptop or a computer, and according to Forensics, there wasn't one in his car either.'

'Interesting,' said DI Reid. 'When I asked his office manager if we could get a copy of his hard drive, he told me Ron always had it with him.'

'Maybe it's still at the Hilton?' said DC Beard.

'No, I went there first. Nothing but clothes,' said DS Strong.

'Any sign of Zeitz's girlfriend?'

DS Strong shook her head. 'No.'

'Something's not right there, Inspector,' said DC Beard. 'Why would a woman pack her bags and take a taxi to the airport, and then not catch a flight?'

'Are we certain she went to the airport?'

'I have a statement from the taxi driver that dropped her off at the airport. Of course, he didn't take any notice of where she went after she got out of his cab.'

'They have CCTV down there,' said DI Reid.

'You should see the paperwork they want filed before you can see it,' said DC Beard. 'I'm booked in for a viewing at one o'clock.'

'Good work, Nigel. Keep me posted. What about Scaletta's place, Wayne?'

'For a scumbag, he lived in a flash apartment. Big screen TV and plush everything else. Obviously had more money than any of us is ever likely to see. We picked up three computers. Forensics are working on getting into them. I spoke to a couple of his neighbours. They said he was hardly ever home,' said DC Paterson.

'Who was in charge of the search of Cameron's place?'

'Me,' said DC Beard. 'The place is a mess. It looks like someone else has been through it searching for something, so I'm treating it as a crime scene. Forensics has a team there this morning. We should have their report later today, Inspector.'

'We've got Cameron's laptop,' said DI West. 'He left it in an apartment in Carrick, along with about five thousand dollars in cash.'

'That's a lot of cash for a courier driver to be carting around,' said DI Reid.

'I'd say he wasn't planning on coming back any time soon,' said DS Fuller.

'What makes you think that, Sergeant?'

'His phone places him at St Frank's around the time Fr Skinner was killed, and we have his prints on the keys found in the priest's car. Given what his mother told us, we have both motive and opportunity.'

'Bloody long time to wait for revenge, if you ask me, said DI Reid. 'Learn anything else from those phone records, Sergeant?'

'Are you aware, Inspector, that one of those phones belongs to Cameron's girlfriend, Sharon Wilson?'

'This is the woman we haven't been able to contact?'

'Yes.'

'Has anyone tried Black Trucks this morning to see if she's turned up for work?'

'Yes,' said DS Strong. 'Still no sign of her. They asked me to list her as missing. I've sent a patrol to get a statement.'

'So what can you tell me about those phones, Sergeant?'

DS Fuller walked over to the wall map he'd spent the previous day covering in colored pins. 'I've plotted the position of each of the phones for the week leading up to the shooting at the Merlin. The red pins are Cameron's phone. They show us he was at St Frank's as I mentioned, that he was at Zeitz's place at the time of the firebombing, and that he was at the Merlin. And, you can see from this loop that he was staying at Carrick.'

'Well, that suggests why Zeitz might have been interested in talking to Cameron but it doesn't give us a clue about why Cameron firebombed Zeitz's place,' said DI Reid. 'What about those pins that looked like twins?'

'That's the trail of Scaletta's and Wilson's phones. This point here is where they first crossed on Tuesday afternoon at 16:45, just after Sharon Wilson signed off at work. Then they travelled to what appears to be an empty warehouse, here.' DS Fuller pointed to the part of the map representing the northern suburbs. 'I had a patrol check it out yesterday. According to the manager of the crash repair shop next door, it's been vacant since the last tenant moved out about six months ago. There are two interesting things though, Inspector. While they were in that location, Wilson called Cameron and then Cameron called Wilson, and then there was a text message sent from Wilson's phone to Cameron's at 20:58, when all three phones were here, at the Merlin.'

'Any ideas, people?'

'Do you think it's possible that this Sharon Wilson is the shooter, Inspector?' said DS Fuller.

'What would be her motive?'

'She wouldn't be the first woman to shoot the guy that had abused her.'

'That might explain why she'd shoot Cameron, but what about the other two?'

'Maybe she blamed them for whatever it was that set Cameron off,' said DS Fuller.

'I reckon that's a long shot, Inspector,' said DC Paterson. 'Look at Sergeant Fuller's pins. I'd say Scaletta grabbed Sharon off the street and held her hostage so they could get to Cameron.'

'Why?'

'Look at the timings. The meeting of the pins is on the same day that Cameron firebombed Zeitz's house. He lied to us, Inspector. He knew Cameron was the firebomber.'

'So, why didn't he tell us?'

'Maybe he was afraid Cameron would tell us things he didn't want us to know.'

'This is starting to sound interesting, Wayne. Go on.'

'Well, they knew where Sharon was but they didn't know where Cameron was. I'd bet there is a phone call from Zeitz to Scaletta sometime that afternoon. Am I right, Sergeant?'

'There were several.'

'Too bad we can't get a transcript, but I'd say one of those calls was Zeitz telling Scaletta to pick up Sharon and then put pressure on Cameron. She's his weak spot and using weak spots is Scaletta's calling card.'

'That might explain why she's not at work. Scaletta stashed her someplace to get Cameron to the Merlin but then things didn't go to plan,' said DC Beard.

'That means she's still being held somewhere,' said DS

Strong. 'Otherwise we would have heard from her by now, surely?'

'Shit!' DI Reid looked at the wall map and then at DS Fuller. 'How many places did Scaletta visit between the time he met up with Sharon and getting himself killed at the Merlin?'

'If she's not in his apartment, I'd say our best bet is that warehouse. All the other spots Scaletta spent any significant time at are nightclubs,' said DS Fuller.

DI Reid turned to DS Strong. 'Sergeant, get some armed backup and go visit that warehouse. Take Wayne with you.'

DC Nigel Beard sat in the security control room at the airport staring at Sally Marsh's computer screen. Twenty-six year old Sally was busy showing him what their cameras had captured on Wednesday morning. Nigel was doing his best not to look at her uniform stretching bust.

'That's her getting out of that taxi,' said Nigel, pointing to an image on the screen.

They watched as the cab driver lifted two suitcases out of the trunk and Susie stood on the pavement next to her suitcases until the taxi had departed. Then, instead of heading into the airport building as Nigel had expected her to do, Susie headed towards the entrance of the multi-story car park.

'Might take a while to locate her in there,' said Sally. 'There are seven levels.'

Nigel looked through the window of the control room and watched people milling about in the concourse below, while Sally flicked through videos from the cameras on the different levels in the car park.

'There she is. She got out on the third.'

A view of the third floor elevator lobby of the car park

appeared on the screen. Nigel watched Susie drag her suitcases out of the elevator and walk across the camera's field of view before disappearing.

'Do you have any cameras covering the parking area?'

Sally shut the window she had open and clicked on another mp4 file. 'There she is, getting into that car. See, there.' Sally pointed at the screen.

They watched as the car reversed into the lane and turned away from the camera.

'Freeze it there. Let's see if we can get the registration number.'

Sally zoomed in on the image of the car. They couldn't read it.

Nigel gave her his thumb drive. 'Give me a copy. I can get that enhanced.'

Sally took the thumb drive and transferred the file.

'Do you have any shots of vehicles leaving the car park?'

'Sorry, that camera was down on Wednesday.'

***

'You're in luck, Harry,' said Sergeant Dean Lang, handing him John Cameron's laptop. 'Our mate Cameron relied on the world's most common password.'

'Thanks, Dean.'

Harry attached the power cord, keyed in password and waited for John's MacBook to fire up.

The email program loaded on log on. The last email John had received was from Sharon Wilson. It contained a short text: 'Sharon sends her love' and a jpg attachment. Harry opened the attachment and stared at an image of a naked, middle-aged woman with fear in her eyes. The paleness of her skin, in relation to the background, suggested to Harry that the photograph had been taken in poor lighting with a flash. He zoomed in and looked closely at the background. There were two shadows on the wall behind her, and one definitely wasn't hers. Harry couldn't tell where the photograph had been taken, except for it being in a room, perhaps an office, with a white door.

Harry dialled Nina's number.

'What's up, Harry?'

'Have you looked inside that warehouse yet?'

'The locksmith's working on the door, so we should be inside any moment.'

'I'm sending you an email with a photo of Sharon Wilson that I suspect Scaletta sent to Cameron from her phone. My guess is it was taken in an office. She looks terrified. Be careful. I reckon Scaletta had help.'

'Thanks for the warning, Harry. I need to go. He's got the door open.'

After browsing the emails in Cameron's inbox, Harry turned his attention to the document files. He sorted them by date modified and opened the most recent document, which turned out to be a letter John had written to Sharon on the night he had received the email with her naked image attached.

Harry couldn't help wondering how a man who expressed so much love could also be under a restraining order, because he had hit the woman to whom he was professing his gratitude for being part of his life. Half way down the page he came across a reference to Zeitz:

I'm sorry sweetheart but I made a big mistake and I can't see any way out of it now. I should have let bygones be bygones when I found out about Zeitz but 10 years in prison is a big chunk of your life, and he's the bastard that put me there. He's another one I wish I'd never met but we go back a long way. We first crossed paths in the army. He was the one that got me that job with Joe Black I told you about. Should have stayed in the bloody army. The only good

*thing about any of it was finally meeting you and now I've fucked
that up too.*

*You've probably heard about the priest by now. The night-
mares have stopped. Should have done it years ago. If I have to
spend the rest of my life in prison for doing that at least I'll be able
to sleep. I'm only sorry I won't be able to make it up to you by
being a better person.*

*I don't know what's going to happen. I don't trust Zeitz or
Scaletta. I'm only meeting them so they'll let you go. When they
do, there's a key in the freezer, it's in that container with the green
lid at the back. It's the key to a safety deposit box at B&A. The
number is on the key. You only have to show them the key and
your ID. It's in our names. I had planned to use that money for
our retirement. I want you to take it and go someplace away from
here.*

The letter ended. Harry guessed John had not finished it as
he couldn't find any sign that John had emailed it to Sharon.

As Harry was thinking about what to do his phone rang. The
display told him it was Nina.

'She's not here, Harry.'

'Could the photo have been taken there?'

'Yeah, there's an office with a white door. And, Harry, everything's covered in dust in this place except for the interior of the
office and the kitchen behind that white door. Whatever
happened here, someone's had a go at erasing every sign of it.'

Once she had seen the clean floor and compared the photograph
that Harry had sent her with the office setting, Nina was not
confident they would find Sharon Wilson alive. She called Operations and asked them to send a team from Forensics to examine
the warehouse. The floor might have been cleaned but Nina

knew blood was extremely difficult to remove, even when you could no longer see it.

With two uniformed officers securing the warehouse, Nina and Wayne visited the surrounding businesses. The owner of the crash repair shop adjacent to the warehouse told them that for anything that happened after four-thirty in the afternoon their best bet would be to talk to Metropolitan Security, who patrolled the area at night. They were turning to leave when his young apprentice, who had waited for his boss to finish talking, said that he'd seen a white van coming out of the warehouse on Wednesday morning when he was arriving for work.

When Nina asked him if he could recall what type of van it was, he said he thought it was a Mitsubishi but that he couldn't be sure, as he hadn't taken that much notice. He'd assumed it was someone looking at the warehouse. After all, there was a sign out the front advertising that the place was available for lease.

The next nondescript warehouse that Nina and Wayne walked into turned out to be the garage for the vehicles belonging to Zeitz Security Services. Nina caught a glimpse of the beehive of activity within the warehouse when the door leading into the warehouse proper opened to admit a man, dressed in the black uniform of Zeitz Security Services, into the reception area that opened onto the street after she had pressed the button on the desk.

'We're not open to the public,' he said.

'We aren't the public,' said Nina, showing him her badge.

He crossed his arms. 'What do you want?'

'We're looking for a missing person in connection with the murder of your boss. We have reason to believe she was in the vacant warehouse next to the crash repair place early Tuesday evening. Just wondering if you'd seen any activity around that warehouse over the last few days,' said Nina.

'Listen, love, if I could help you find the bastards that killed

Ron I would, but I haven't seen anything going on down there. The main entrance to this place is at the back of the building. I only go out this way at the end of the day.'

'You don't happen to know who owns that warehouse by any chance, do you?' said Wayne.

The man smiled. 'Now, I can help you with that, mate. Arthur Redmond. Guess I won't have to tell you his current address, will I?'

'No,' said Wayne. 'I helped him move in.'

Outside, Nina looked at the warehouse they had just come out of. 'I thought we had a camera on this place.'

'We do but it's at the other end of the building. DI Reid wanted to know what was going in and coming out. As you heard the man say, Sergeant, nothing comes in this way, so we didn't bother with a camera out here. Guess it might have been useful if we had.'

After interviewing someone in every other warehouse in the immediate area, they headed back to the warehouse to see if Forensics had arrived.

'What's this Arthur Redmond inside for?' said Nina.

'He was running an import business, bringing stuff in from China.'

'Given that half the stuff in the world seems to be made in China these days, what sort of stuff are we talking about?'

'White goods, lined with cocaine.'

'No wonder he could afford a warehouse.'

'He wasn't operating from here. We busted him down at the port in a joint operation with Customs.'

'I wonder why this place wasn't seized under the Proceeds of Crime Act,' said Nina.

'Beats me,' said Wayne.

'Why wasn't his mate Scaletta picked up?'

'We couldn't pin anything on him. Believe me, we tried.'

'Guess that explains how he had access to this place, if he used to work for Redmond.'

'Yeah, I wonder if he was still working for Redmond,' said Wayne.

'We need to catch up with Scaletta's associates and see if any of them want to talk, now that he's dead. Any ideas?'

'I know where to start looking.'

CHAPTER 25

CARL STOOD on the cracked slate tiles of the porch with Charlie Head, as the senior constable pushed the doorbell button. They heard the ding-dong of the doorbell, followed by the sound of footsteps approaching the door from within the house. The door was opened by a tall man dressed in priestly black and white dog collar. He smiled when he saw Charlie.

'Ah, Charlie. I've been expecting you'

'Afternoon, Father. This is Inspector West.'

'Hello, Inspector.' Fr Harris extended his hand.

The priest's handshake was weak, functional but without any power. Carl wondered what sort of man he was dealing with. 'Thanks for making time to talk to us, Father.'

Fr Harris stepped back and held the door open for them. 'We can sit in here.' He pointed to the first doorway leading off the hallway. 'I was speaking to Frank Mulligan yesterday, Inspector. He told me that if anybody is going to catch our arsonist it would be you.'

Carl smiled and thought that catching up with Fr Mulligan might not be such a bad idea.

The front room of the residence, furnished with plain wooden chairs set out in a semi-circle and decorated with St

Vincent de Paul Society posters on the walls, was clearly marked as a meeting room. Father Harris pulled three of the chairs out of the semi-circle into a corner of the room and they sat in a tight triangle.

'Let's hope I can live up to Frank's confidence, however, before we get to the fire, I'd like to ask you a few questions about Fr Skinner, if you don't mind?'

'I'm not sure I can help you much on that case, Inspector.'

'Charlie and I paid a visit to North Summit on Tuesday. We spoke to a Mrs Mary Cameron. Do you remember her?'

Fr Harris joined his palms together and tapped his joined fingertips on his chin. 'John's mother.'

'Yes,' said Carl.

'Was she the person behind your press conference announcement?'

'Yes.'

'That was a long time ago.'

Carl waited. Charlie took out his notebook and pen.

'John and I were altar boys. We must have been seven or eight when Fr Skinner arrived. I remember being jealous of John. His house was across the road from the Church, so he got to do all the special events like funerals and weddings. We lived out of town. My parents had an apple orchard.'

'His mother told us you were good friends in primary school. Is that true?'

A faraway look came into the priest's eyes. 'I was so angry when my parents decided to send me to boarding school but after a couple of years John had changed so much it was like I had never known him.'

'Did you have any idea why?'

'Not really. He wouldn't talk to me.'

'What was your relationship with Fr Skinner like?'

'Nothing special. I remember we all wanted to please him.

He was pretty scary if you made a mistake on the altar during Mass. He didn't like mistakes.'

'What do you mean by scary?'

'He would shout at you or biff you across the ears, and then he'd be all sorry and give you a hug. I didn't like hugs.'

'Is hugs all he gave you?'

'I don't know what Mrs Cameron told you, Inspector, but I don't recall anything apart from that. He wasn't in the parish all that long. He was gone before I left for boarding school, if I remember correctly.'

'Do you remember the names of any of the other altar boys from that time?'

'Not specifically, Inspector, but if you look at the student register for the local school for that period, I'm sure you'll be able to find them. There was a fair tribe of us, maybe ten or twelve boys. The senior altar boy was a lad called Michael Waybright. He was still living in North Summit the last time I was there. He owns the pub.'

'Mrs Cameron told us you stopped visiting after the fire at your parents' place.'

'I only ever went up there to keep my parents happy. They liked showing off their priest. There wasn't much point after they died in the fire.'

'Fair enough,' said Carl. 'Perhaps while we're talking about fires we should talk about Gladesview House.'

Fr Harris crossed his arms on his chest. 'Do you have any leads?'

'We're still waiting to talk to the nurse. Hopefully, she'll be well enough to see us tomorrow.'

'Yes, they won't let me in to see her either.'

'Do you mind telling me where you were in the early hours of Monday morning, Father?'

'Here, in bed.'

'Can anybody vouch for that?'

'Well, unless one of the neighbours saw me come home Sunday night, I suppose not. One of the side benefits of being a priest, Inspector, is living alone.'

'No housekeeper?'

'Mrs Carey only comes during the day. She certainly does not stay overnight. Besides, I eat at Gladesview on Sundays. At least, I ate at Gladesview on Sundays.'

'So, you were at Gladesview on the Sunday evening before the fire?'

'Yes.'

'What time did you leave?'

'About eleven, when Bishop Knight went to bed.'

Carl waited.

'He liked to beat me at chess, Inspector, and to talk.'

'What did he like to talk about?'

'He'd become something of a mystic after his health forced him to retire. He spent a lot of time meditating and studying scripture, and a lot of other stuff you wouldn't expect a bishop to read. I guess that's one of the benefits of no longer being the shepherd in charge of the flock. He was on what he called a journey of discovery.' Father Harris shook his head. 'He probably would have been labelled a heretic if he'd been preaching what we talked about.'

'You weren't offended?'

'It was just talk, Inspector. Some of it was laughable but it was always interesting. I don't get the time to research any of that new age stuff. Bishop Knight was intrigued by it. I was simply amused and sometimes challenged by what he'd say.'

Carl wondered what sort of conversations they'd had but couldn't see any value in continuing that line of enquiry.

'Father, who has a key to Gladesview?'

'Bill Giles, he's the maintenance manager, me, and Sister Murray, the matron.'

'Isn't that the name of the nurse in the hospital?'

'Yes, she was on night shift this week. She arrived at eight, when the kitchen staff were leaving.'

'She was there on her own?'

'After I left, yes. They're old, Inspector, not sick.'

'Three of them are dead.'

'The night nurse was there to handle medical emergencies, Inspector. Not a fire.'

'From all accounts it sounds like she risked her life trying to save them, Father,' said Charlie.

'Let's pray it doesn't cost her her own.'

Carl took a breath and thought of Sister Murray, and hoped she'd be well enough to speak to him soon.

'Had you received any threats from someone saying they'd burn the place down?' said Carl.

'Nothing, Inspector. I've even checked that with the bishop's office. Nothing. I've got no idea who would want to burn the place down. In fact, I was surprised to hear it was arson. I thought an electrical fault would be the likely cause, given the age of the wiring, but there you go. I'm no expert.'

'Our expert says the arsonist left his petrol can behind.'

Fr Harris uncrossed his arms and leant forward. 'Does that mean you might find fingerprints or something?'

'Not after the deluge the fire brigade let loose. Besides, the can was left inside the building. Ever seen a burnt petrol can, Father?'

'Unfortunately, I've seen a lot of burnt stuff, Inspector. As Mrs Cameron told you, my parents' house burnt down with them inside.'

The size of Bishop Walsh's archive was in stark contrast to the meagre files detailing priestly lives that Lisa and Jane had scrutinised in Monsignor Rivers' office. The storage unit dedicated to the diocesan archive of Bishop Walsh's administration, located in the basement of the Church Offices, was stacked with boxes marked with faded handwritten labels that looked like they had not been opened since they had been sealed and placed in storage.

'Whoever catalogued this collection had no idea what he was doing,' said Monsignor Rivers. 'You'd think it would be either chronological or alphabetic, not haphazard.'

'Might make a side project for your retirement years, Monsignor,' said Lisa.

'I was hoping to spend my retirement years by the seaside, not in this dungeon.'

Lisa laughed. After spending several hours with him, she had decided she liked Monsignor Rivers, despite the fact that he was a priest.

'Some of them have dates on them,' said Jane, 'but it does look like they were just dumped in here.'

'These boxes have nineteen seventy something written on them,' said Lisa.

'Fr Skinner left North Summit in nineteen seventy,' said Monsignor Rivers. 'Let's start there.'

'What exactly are we looking for?' said Jane.

'Anything that mentions Fr Skinner or anything with the name Cameron on it,' said Lisa.

They each took a box to the table located under the single fluorescent tube, which illuminated the area set aside for examining the contents of archive boxes, and started the search.

'I didn't realise there would be so many records,' said Lisa, 'especially after the individual files. Is there an archive like this for Bishop Knight?'

'That unit over there,' said Monsignor Rivers, pointing to the next storage unit. 'But it's all electronic now. Bishop Kerry's archive will be digital.'

'Too bad this lot isn't,' said Jane, as she pulled a bundle of papers out of the box she was searching.

After they had rifled through five boxes, without finding anything mentioning complaints against Fr Skinner or any correspondence concerning the Cameron family of North Summit, Lisa decided it was time for lunch. They closed the boxes and locked the storage unit, and then went upstairs to the sandwich bar which serviced the people working in the Church Offices. They bought sandwiches and coffee, and sat at a table by the window, as it was too cold to sit out in the courtyard where a couple of women were huddled over coffee cups, smoking.

'How do you feel about all this child abuse stuff, Monsignor?' said Lisa.

'It's not something I can explain, Lisa. I don't understand how anybody, let alone a priest, can abuse a child,' said the monsignor, 'but, if what we see on the TV is a true reflection of what's going on in the world, child abuse by priests is a small part of a much wider problem.'

Lisa nodded in agreement. 'You're not wrong there. I've just come off a case where the perpetrator of the abuse was a teacher in a public school.'

'Still, that doesn't absolve the Church for hiding it. That part makes my blood boil. To think so much of it could have been prevented if that hadn't happened.' Monsignor Rivers shook his head. 'To be honest, I'll be very surprised if we find anything in these archives, even if what Mrs Cameron told you is true. From the research I've done for Bishop Kerry, I suspect these files have been purged or that things were never recorded in the first place.'

'I guess we're all living by different rules these days,' said Lisa.

'Do you ever wonder about any of your colleagues?' said Jane.

'Do you wonder about yours?' said the monsignor.

'All the time.'

'Why's that?'

'Well, say you were sharing a parish with a priest who was abusing children, and you found out. You'd feel betrayed, wouldn't you?'

'Of course.'

'But your life wouldn't be threatened, would it?'

'No, I don't suppose it would.'

'It's not quite the same for us, and believe me, Monsignor, there are a lot of ways to make it look like an accident.'

'And, there I was thinking you were such a nice girl, Jane.'

'You wouldn't be the first person to be fooled, Monsignor,' said Lisa. 'Young Jane here is not someone to be messed with from what I've been told.'

Jane looked at Lisa. 'Who have you been talking to?'

'You have admirers in high places,' said Lisa. 'You could go far, if you play your cards right.'

'Yeah, right.'

'So what makes a man become a priest these days, Monsignor?' said Lisa. 'I've always wondered why anybody would choose that path.'

'It's definitely not the money,' said Monsignor Rivers. 'We believe we're called to serve, to do God's work. When you stop looking at the TV news and look behind the facade of The Church,' Monsignor Rivers twisted his fingers in the air to make quotation marks, 'there's a lot of good work being done.'

'I have no doubt about that, Monsignor, Charlie Head is always telling us about it, but it must be lonely,' said Jane. 'I can't imagine choosing to live alone.'

'We don't necessarily live alone. For example, I share a house with another priest and I have a lot of friends, but I know what you mean. There are times when I wonder what it would be like living with a woman in a committed relationship.'

'Not all beer and skittles according to my husband,' said Lisa. 'He keeps complaining that I've divorced him now that I'm married to the force.'

As they were clearing their table before returning to the basement, Lisa's mobile rang. She stepped away to answer it.

'That was Inspector West, Monsignor. More evidence has turned up linking our suspect to Fr Skinner's murder. He says we can pack up here.'

'Well, as I said, we were probably wasting our time in any case.'

'Thanks anyway, Monsignor. It's not every day we get this level of cooperation.'

At the end of the day, Carl called the team together in the Incident Room.

'The chief inspector believes we have enough evidence to convince the coroner that John Cameron killed Fr Skinner, so he's decided to close the case,' said Carl.

'Does that mean we'll be dragged into finding out who killed Cameron, Inspector?' said Lisa

'No. DI Reid's been assigned the Merlin case. We have our own triple fatality to resolve, thanks to the Gladesview House fire. Charlie, let's go over what we know.'

SC Head massaged the back of his bald head. 'Not much would pretty well cover it, Inspector. So far we have no witnesses and no evidence, apart from a burnt petrol can and three dead priests.'

'We have a few questions,' said Harry.

'Like what, Sergeant?' said Jane.

'One of the obvious ones is why was the fire started where it was? Did the arsonist choose that spot because of the wood paneling or was it because it was immediately outside Bishop Knight's room?'

'Oh, I see,' said Jane. 'Was he setting fire to the building or was he intending to kill the bishop?'

'I told you that you'd make a good detective, Jane,' said Carl.

A flush of color spread across Jane's cheeks.

'Does that mean we may have to go back to those archives?' said Lisa.

'Maybe,' said Carl, 'but I think we can start with the living. We need to talk to anybody who knew Bishop Knight.'

'That could take a while, Inspector,' said Charlie. 'He was the bishop for about fifteen years before he retired.'

'Any suggestions?'

'I think you should start with Monsignor Peterson, he was Bishop Knight's right hand man.'

'Was he at Gladesview?'

'Heavens no. He's as fit as a mallee bull. He only retired last year. Went to live with his sister at Carrick. She has a big house right on the foreshore. Her husband used to run the Carrick pub. Now there was a character. Poor bastard had a heart attack out fishing. Took us three days to find the body.'

'So there are some down sides to community policing, Charlie?'

SC Head nodded. 'Yeah, that's one weekend I'd like to forget.'

'Anybody else, Charlie?'

'Bishop Kerry. I'm sure he and Monsignor Peterson can suggest others,' said Charlie. 'What about Fr Mulligan? He's been around for a while, and he seems to know everybody.'

'Might pay to talk to the people that work at Gladesview House, Inspector,' said Lisa.

'I'm interviewing Sister Murray tomorrow morning. I'd like you to come with me. Might be better than having Harry scare her.'

'Thanks, Boss,' said Harry.

'What time?' said Lisa.

'Ten o'clock.'

Carl waited as she entered the details into her smartphone.

'What about the people that work at Gladesview who weren't there at the time of the fire?' said Lisa.

Carl picked up some papers on the table in front of him. 'Statements from those very people, Lisa. Charlie's colleagues have spoken to everyone. We need to read these.'

Harry stifled a yawn.

'Stop that, Harry. Or we'll all be doing it,' said Carl.

'Sorry, Boss. It's been a long day.'

Carl looked at his watch and wondered how much sleep Harry was getting. 'Okay, let's call it a day. We can review these statements first thing tomorrow.'

CARL WAS in the kitchen preparing their evening meal when Wayne dropped Nina home.

Nina gave him a peck on the cheek and collapsed into a chair. Carl poured her a shiraz and returned to his cooking.

'Harry tells me there was no-one at that warehouse.'

'Did he show you the photograph?'

'Not pretty.'

'I reckon it was taken in the office of that warehouse.'

'Find anything else?'

Nina kicked off her shoes. 'The place has been vacant for months. Everything is covered in dust, except for the office area. It looked like someone had cleaned it just before we walked in. It was spotless.'

'Bit suspicious.'

'I had Dean Lang look at it, that's why I'm late.'

'Did he find anything?'

'Nothing to indicate a crime.'

'Anyone see anything?'

'One of the lads from the crash repair shop next door said he'd seen a white van leaving the warehouse on Wednesday morning. No details apart from maybe it was a Mitsubishi.'

Carl washed some potatoes and then sliced them up.

'Are they trying to rent the place?'

'There's a sign out the front. Why do ask?'

'Did you speak to the agent?'

'I tried but the mobile number on the sign is disconnected.'

'Probably explains why the place is still vacant.'

'I've got Wayne looking in to it. Would you believe the warehouse belongs to Arthur Redmond?'

Carl stopped cutting up vegetables. 'How'd you find that out?'

'Wayne asked the guy we spoke to in Zeitz's garage.'

'Zeitz's garage? I didn't know that was out there. I thought his business was located in the western suburbs.'

'His office is but their garage is in a warehouse a couple of doors down from the place we were searching.'

'Don't you have that under surveillance?'

'Yes, but their main entrance is off the street behind the warehouse. I didn't even recognise it from the front.'

Nina drained her glass. 'How long before dinner? Have I got time for a shower?'

'Go for it. I'll be another twenty minutes or so.'

CHAPTER 27

CARL LEFT Harry in charge of the statement reading detail, while he and Lisa headed to University Hospital to interview Sister Murray.

'Done many arson cases, Inspector?' said Lisa, as she parked the car in the hospital car park.

'I don't like arsonists, Lisa. Fires have a nasty habit of destroying the evidence. You have to be lucky to catch them, unless they do something silly.'

'We certainly don't have much to go on,' said Lisa.

'We know whoever it was used a can of petrol and, according to Forensics, not just any can.'

'What do you mean?'

'Do you remember a petrol company called Golden Fleece?'

'Can't say I've heard of it, Inspector.'

'I had to look it up myself. According to Google, it became part of Caltex in the nineteen eighties.'

'That explains why I've never heard of it. Why did you ask?'

'The can left behind by our arsonist has Golden Fleece embossed on its sides.'

'How does that help?'

'Those cans are worth a small fortune as collectables. Someone is going to be missing that can at some point.'

'Let's hope they tell us.'

'We'll be doing more than hoping, Lisa. That can will be exhibit A at our next media conference, and I'll be asking people to check if they still have theirs. If we can find out where it came from we might be able to work out who took it.'

They took the elevator to the Burns Unit on the fifth floor, where they had to gown up before being admitted to Sister Murray's room. When they entered, there was a woman wearing a mask and gown like the ones they had just donned, sitting quietly next to Sister Murray's bed.

'You'll have to keep it short, Inspector,' said the nurse, beckoning to Sister Murray's visitor to come with her. 'These people are the police. They need to speak to your friend in private.'

The woman stood and made her way towards the door. 'Can I speak to you when you've finished, Inspector?'

'By all means.'

'I'll wait outside.'

Sister Murray smiled as Carl approached the bed. At least her face isn't disfigured, thought Carl, as he looked at the middle-aged woman in the bed. The rest of her body was hidden from his view by a sheet draped over a frame.

'Hello, Sister, I'm Inspector West and this is Detective Templar. We're investigating the fire at Gladesview House. We'd like to ask you a few questions.'

'I was wondering when you'd arrive.'

'We would have been here sooner but they wouldn't let us in,' said Carl, sitting in the chair next to the bed.

Lisa stood at the foot of the bed; pen and notebook in hand.

'Sister Mary, that was her just now, has told me about who has died, Inspector. It's just too horrible to think about.'

Carl nodded. 'We're treating it as homicide.'

'You mean the fire was not an accident, Inspector?'

'I'm afraid not.' Carl waited for Sister Murray to digest that news. 'Do you think you can tell us about the night of the fire?'

'Not much to tell really. I was reading. A Louise Penny novel. I like her Chief Inspector.' Sister Murray smiled at Carl. 'There's not much to do once they've gone to bed. Anyway, I'd nearly finished the book when I smelt smoke. At first, I thought one of the kitchen staff must have left something turned on but there was nothing burning in the kitchen. When I opened the door to the east wing it was like an oven. There were flames everywhere. It was so hot I couldn't get in there. I called the fire brigade. They told me the alarm had gone off and they were already on their way, so I woke up everybody I could get to and took them outside.'

'I understand you got most of the residents out,' said Carl.

'All except the three in the east wing. The firemen got Fr Kelly and Fr Porter out when they arrived with all their gear, but the roof had fallen in where Bishop Knight's room was and they couldn't get to him.' Sister Murray turned her face away from them. 'I couldn't save them. I tried. Now they're dead.'

Carl waited.

'I know it's not my fault, but it's hard to accept just the same.'

'Fr Harris told me he was at Gladesview on Sunday night. Do you remember when he left?'

'He left just after eleven, when Bishop Knight went to bed.'

'Did Fr Harris spend a lot of time at Gladesview?'

'He was there every day but Sunday was the only night he stayed late. He played chess with Bishop Knight.'

'Did you see anybody else after Fr Harris left?'

'No.'

'Hear anything unusual?'

'No, the place is as quiet as a tomb once they go to bed.'

'Any reason why Bishop Knight might not have woken up at the smell of smoke?'

'That's my only consolation, Inspector. He wouldn't have felt a thing. I gave him his sleeping pills just before midnight. They usually knock him out for at least four hours.'

The nurse walked into the room. 'Time's up, Inspector. You'll have to come again if you need to ask more questions.'

Carl turned back to Sister Murray. 'Thank you, Sister.'

The woman who had vacated the chair beside Sister Murray's bed was waiting for them in the corridor.

'Inspector, I'm Sister Mary Kite. I work at Gladesview House with Sister Murray.'

'Has one of my officers interviewed you, Sister?'

'Oh yes, I spoke to a nice young man earlier in the week but that was before Fr Kelly and Fr Porter died.'

'Is there something else you have thought of since then, Sister?'

'I probably read more murder mysteries than I should, Inspector, but I couldn't help thinking about the fire and trying to work out why anybody would do that. I know I'm not a detective and I hope you won't think I'm telling you how to do your job.'

'Go on, Sister, I won't be offended,' said Carl. 'In fact, with arson, I usually need a lot of help from people just like you,'

'Thank you, Inspector. What I wanted to say is, when I thought of all the places the fire could have been started, it struck me as a bit strange that someone chose to set fire to the place outside Bishop Knight's new room, a few days after he moved into it. Might be coincidence. I don't know, but maybe the bishop was the target and not the house.'

'Why had the bishop moved rooms?'

'Fr Skinner. I suppose you already know they were at the seminary together.'

Carl nodded.

'Well, Fr Skinner was moving into Gladesview. As a matter of fact, he was supposed to be moving in today. God rest his soul.' Sister Kite crossed herself. 'We'd done up two rooms in the east wing so they could be together. That's why I thought it might have been an electrical fault, until you said it was arson.'

Carl looked across at Lisa and raised an eyebrow.

'How well did you know Bishop Knight, Sister?'

'He was a very private man, Inspector. Spent most of his time either in prayer or with his head in a book. He talked to the other priests when he was in the common room, and he liked to play chess, which was why Fr Harris spent a lot of time with him, but he didn't talk to me beyond domestic matters. I'd have to say I didn't really know him. It was more like I knew who he was and what he liked to eat, that's all.'

'Was he like that with the other staff?'

'He was old school, Inspector. I'd see him talking to Bill Giles out in the garden for hours, so it wasn't like he didn't talk to the staff but, I'm a nun, Inspector, a mere woman.'

Carl wasn't sure whether the smile in her eyes was genuine or ironic.

'Are you suggesting that he might have had enemies on the staff?'

'Oh, he wasn't rude or anything, Inspector. It's just that we didn't exist except when he wanted something, and he was always very polite. Some might say he was a cold fish but I don't think anybody hated him, which is why I find it so hard to believe that anybody would have wanted to kill him.'

'When was the last time you saw him, Sister?'

'Sunday night. I'm in charge of the kitchen. He was sitting in the common room playing chess with Fr Harris when I left.'

'And where were you when the fire started, Sister?'

'Like all good nuns, Inspector, tucked up in my bed asleep.'

'Can anybody verify that?'

'Oh, dear me.' Sister Mary's eyes widened. 'I suppose, as they say in all the books, I don't have an alibi. You see, Inspector, I share a house with Sister Judith and she was at work.'

'Sister Judith?'

'Sister Murray.'

'Nothing of interest in these statements, Boss,' said Harry, when Carl and Lisa returned to the office. 'Get anything from your interview with Sister Murray?'

'Not really but we had an interesting conversation with a Sister Mary Kite,' said Carl.

'Ah, the head cook,' said Charlie. 'I read her statement. I don't recall anything interesting.'

'Seems she's had time to think about it since talking to whoever took her statement,' said Carl.

'What did she say?'

'She was wondering if there was any significance behind the arsonist's choice of ignition point.'

'We've all asked ourselves that question, Boss', said Harry.

'Yes, but we weren't aware that the bishop had only just moved into that room or that Fr Skinner was supposed to be moving in across the corridor today, were we?'

'There was something about that in the statement from the guy in charge of maintenance,' said Jane. 'I've just finished reading his statement. Here it is. Bill Giles. He told us they had finished renovating the two rooms at the end of the east wing the week before the fire.'

'Harry, do you have the reports from Forensics?' said Carl.

Harry sat at his desk and opened a file on his computer. 'What do you want to know?'

'Did they work out whether our arsonist entered through the bishop's window or do they think he used the door that opens from the back veranda into the east wing?'

Harry scanned through the report. 'It looks like the door wasn't forced. There's no damage to either the lock or the door frame, apart from charring. There's a note saying that if the arsonist used the back door it was either not locked or he had a key.' Harry looked up from the screen. 'The bishop must have been a heavy sleeper if the arsonist broke in through his window.'

'Sister Murray told us she'd knocked him out with sleeping pills around midnight. Any sign of that in the report?'

'We're still waiting for that bit.'

'What did people say about the bishop in their statements?' said Carl.

'All the bland usual stuff from what I read,' said Charlie. 'You know, holy man, well respected, no trouble to look after, friendly enough, lots of visitors.'

'I'd have to agree,' said Jane. 'Why did you ask?'

'We got a bit of a different picture from Sister Kite. How did she describe him, Lisa?'

'Bit of a cold fish,' said Lisa. 'I got the impression there might have been a bit of antagonism between her and the bishop.'

'Yes, and she divulged that she didn't have an alibi for the time of the fire,' said Carl.

'You're not seriously suggesting a nun burnt the place down because she didn't get on with Bishop Knight, are you?' said Charlie.

'We've got a motive, and she'd have access to a key. She shares a house with Sister Murray, and Fr Harris told us she had a key, which they could have copied, and she has no alibi,' said Carl.

'You're pulling my leg, Inspector, aren't you?' said Charlie. 'I've known Mary Kite for years. No way is she our arsonist.'

Carl winked at Harry. 'Stranger things have happened, Charlie. Look at all the trouble your Church is in because priests couldn't keep their hands off little boys.'

Charlie leant back in his chair. 'I still don't believe you, Inspector. Not Mary Kite.'

'I'm with Charlie,' said Lisa. 'Somehow I just can't see her as a killer.'

'Me neither,' said Carl, 'which means, until we find out why our arsonist wanted to burn the place down, the field of candidates is wide open. Mind you, Sister Kite did suggest that maybe the bishop was the target and the fire was simply the means.'

'Does that mean we need to go back into those archives, Inspector?' said Jane.

'Let's hope not, Jane.'

Jane's face lit up with relief.

'For now, we need to find out how many keys there are and who has them. I'm not confident Fr Harris' count can be relied on. Human nature being what it is, I wouldn't be surprised if everybody working there had a key.'

'And, Boss, unhappy thought that it is, and I'm sure Charlie will object, but we also need to consider the possibility that Sister Murray set the fire. She was there. She'd have had the opportunity.'

'No way!' said Charlie.

'You'd better come up with a good motive if you want us to consider that seriously, Harry. The woman almost got herself barbecued trying to rescue them,' said Carl.

'We need to get all possibilities on the table, Boss. I'm just saying we need to consider it.'

LOCATED in the hills forming the eastern boundary of the metropolitan area and easily accessible to hikers, Lang National Park is crisscrossed with walking trails and dotted with camping sites.

The park was a favourite weekend destination for Ralph and Hilary Whitelaw. They had walked in on Saturday morning and camped overnight in one of the park's many campsites. It had been a quiet weekend. Not many people hiked in the rain but the Whitelaws were in training for their next overseas adventure holiday. On Sunday, the weather gods had a change of heart and granted them an unseasonably warm day for their hike out of the wilderness back to civilization.

As the sun slowly slid towards the distant ocean, Ralph and Hilary were descending the path into the car park, where they had left their car on Saturday morning, when they became aware of something foreign in the air.

'God, Hilary, that smells something awful,' said Ralph.

'It wasn't me,' said Hilary, reaching for her handkerchief and covering her nose. 'Smells like something dead. I reckon it's coming from over there.' She stopped walking and pointed to a clump of trees to their left.

Ralph pinched his nose and stepped off the path to investigate. Hilary watched him disappear behind the trees.

Less than a minute later Ralph stepped out from behind the trees. His face was white.

'What's wrong?'

'We need to call the police.'

It was dark when Carl and Harry arrived at the car park preferred by the hikers that overnighted in Lang National Park. By the time they arrived the Whitelaws had gone home, after giving a statement to the uniformed patrol that had responded to their call and secured the scene.

The side of the hill on the southern side of the car park was illuminated by a large set of portable floodlights, powered by the same noisy diesel generator they had listened to behind the Merlin.

Dressed in their mandatory crime scene suits, Carl and Harry joined Mike Jonas in the glare of the floodlights. Adjusting their breathing to cope with the confronting smell of decaying flesh, they looked down at the slightly bloated body of a woman dressed in black clothing. Her wrists were bound behind her back with duct tape and tied to her ankles, which were also bound with tape, and there was a wide strip of the grey tape across her mouth.

'Any idea how she was killed, Mike?' asked Carl.

'Nothing obvious. I can't see any external wounds. She's been here a few days though, maybe close to a week.'

'Oh, shit!' said Harry.

Mike and Carl turned and looked at him.

'It's Sharon Wilson.' Harry pulled out his smartphone and

opened the email he had sent to Nina when she was at the ware-house looking for Sharon.

'This is the photo sent to Cameron,' said Harry, handing his phone to Carl.

Carl took a look and handed the phone to Mike.

'You could be right, Harry,' said Mike. 'Looks like her. We'll know for certain when we get her back to the lab. There's not much more I can do here.'

Carl and Harry made their way back to the car park with Mike, while Sergeant Dean Lang and his crime scene team completed photographing the body and its surroundings, before transferring the body into a body bag and searching the area for any evidence that might lead them to whoever had dumped the body where it lay.

'Wonder why they didn't notice on the way in on Saturday,' said Harry, 'if the body has been here for days.'

'It was raining Saturday morning, Harry. Don't you remember?' said Mike.

'I was in the office reading statements, trying to figure out who started the fire at Gladesview House.'

'How's that going, Carl? Making any progress?'

'I have a petrol can. All I have to do now is find out who left it behind.'

'Dean told me it wasn't just any old petrol can. What's so special about it?'

'Golden Fleece.'

'My dad used to collect their stuff. One of their petrol cans in good condition would be worth quite a bit these days. We made a few dollars when we auctioned his collection,' said Mike.

'I'm glad you added that last bit, Mike, otherwise I'd have to consider you a suspect,' said Carl.

'No, Carl, what you need to do is find out who's lost his

precious Golden Fleece can. Although, I guess in its current state he won't be wanting it back.'

'That's the plan, Mike. That can had its own spot on tonight's news. All we need now is for someone to realise his has gone missing.'

THE MILD WINTER WEATHER, which the city had enjoyed late into the season, came to an abrupt halt early Monday morning. The city awoke to the pounding of icy rain, driven by a southerly gale that felt as if it had blown in from Antarctica. The early morning storm brought down trees and power lines. With traffic lights out all over the city, the morning traffic flow descended into chaos.

The Incident Room slowly filled with officers who stood around in their overcoats, with hot coffees in their hands, waiting for the heating to make a difference to the ambient temperature of the room. It was nine o'clock before the equipment in the plant room was pumping out sufficient heat for people to take off their coats. By then, most members of DI West's and DI Reid's teams had arrived.

DI Reid was the last to arrive. He'd had to wait for the State Emergency Service to clear away the tree that had fallen across his drive way and crushed his neighbour's roof.

'Think we might have located Sharon Wilson, Bob,' said Carl. 'At least, we have a body that looks like it could be her.'

'Is that the body found in the hills yesterday?'

'Yep. Mike's doing the post-mortem at eleven.'

'Any sign of trauma?'

'She was trussed up with duct tape. Harry, do we have any of Dean's photos yet?'

'I'll throw them on the wall.'

Harry switched on the ceiling mounted projector, opened the file he had received from Forensics and displayed a full body shot of the corpse on the wall. The officers in the room looked at the image in silence.

'Mike said he couldn't see any external injuries when we spoke to him last night,' said Carl.

'I've seen that method of tying people up with duct tape before,' said DC Paterson.

'What's so special about it, Wayne?' said DI Reid.

'Wouldn't you agree that most people simply tie your hands behind your back and then tie up your legs, Inspector?'

DI Reid nodded his agreement.

'See how her hands are bound to her ankles? If you're tied up like that it forces you to either kneel or lie on your side. Either way, it's very uncomfortable. You can't sit in a chair tied up like that.' DC Paterson leant back and crossed his arms. 'Redmond's people used that method. That's got Scaletta written all over it.'

'What do you think, Harry?'

'Scaletta could have tied her up. They were in that warehouse together but I doubt very much that he dumped the body in the hills. Look at his GPS trail. He didn't go anywhere near where the body was found. Besides, he was shot on Wednesday night, right where his phone tells us he was.'

'Wayne, I want you to concentrate on Scaletta's known associates. Someone had to be helping him.'

'Look at the wall behind Sharon in this shot,' said Harry, as he projected the image of Sharon he had copied from the email in Cameron's laptop. 'See, there are two shadows. There is someone else, besides Sharon and whoever took this shot, in that room.'

'Yes, and we know that someone washed the floor where that photo was taken,' said Nina.

'Did Forensics find anything?' said DI Reid.

'Not from the floor but they did lift some prints from the chairs in the office. We've matched one to Scaletta. Guess we should see if any of them match the body in the morgue.'

'Anything else in that report?'

'Tracks on the warehouse floor indicating recent vehicle movement in and out of the place, but it appears we managed to obliterated any useful footprints when we stormed in,' said Nina.

'Okay, while we're on wives and girlfriends, any luck locating Susie Morte, Nigel?'

'Getting there, Inspector. The car that picked up Susie from the airport is registered in the name of a Rosemary Mortimer, of seventeen Longbottom Street, Morton Sands. So far we haven't been able to contact her but she's old enough to be Susie's mother. Maybe she simply went home to mum.'

'Wayne, weren't you doing a background check on our Ms Morte?' said DI Reid.

'Was I?'

'I asked you to,' said Nina.

'Let's get Jane to follow that up, Bob. Wayne's going to be busy talking to Scaletta's associates,' said Carl.

'I'll give you the details, Jane,' said Nina.

'Now, where's that letter Cameron wrote?' DI Reid searched through his papers. 'There's a paragraph in this letter that poses a few questions I want answers for. Here it is, and I quote. I should have let bygones be bygones when I found out about Zeitz but ten years in prison is a big chunk of your life, and he's the bastard that put me there. He's another one I wish I'd never met but we go back a long way. We first crossed paths in the army. He was the one that got me that job with Joe Black I told you about. Should have stayed in the bloody army.' DI Reid looked at the officers assembled in front of him. 'What do you make of that?'

'Joe Black was the biggest drug dealer in town until his death about twenty years ago,' said Carl. 'I'd just joined the force. There was one hell of a battle over the spoils when he died of an overdose, if I remember. That's when John Cameron first came to our attention, after he shot a couple of the Vice Squad boys who arrested him. I don't remember anything about Ron Zeitz being mentioned in connection to Joe Black. I wonder if any of those boys are still around to ask.'

'Not sure they'd want to talk to us, Carl. Quite a few of them ended up inside after that corruption enquiry,' said DI Reid.

'Guess that means we're going to have to go through the Black files, Bob. You've been looking into Zeitz for a while, when did he set up his security business?'

'It's been going for about twenty years, according to the guy I spoke to on Thursday. Told me he and Ron, and a couple of others, had set it up to give themselves something to do after they came out of the army. In fact, a lot of the people that work for them have seen military service.'

'Bit of an old boys' club, then?' said Carl.

'I got the impression they were providing a pathway for people to transfer their military skills to civilian service, within a company that understands them.'

'You should be doing their marketing for them, Inspector,' said DC Paterson, 'that was impressive.'

DI Reid rolled his eyes.

'Guess that makes sense. I wonder what the connection to Joe Black was. Were they part of his empire or one of his service providers?' said Carl, ignoring DC Paterson's snide remark.

'More to the point, Boss,' said Harry. 'What was going on between Cameron and Zeitz that led to them being shot last week? When I read that letter I wondered what Cameron was planning to do to Zeitz or Zeitz to Cameron.'

'Sounds like somebody else knows something about Zeitz and Cameron, Inspector,' said DC Templar. 'That sentence about leaving bygones. Seems to me that Cameron must have recently found out something about Zeitz in connection to his arrest. Question is, who told him, and why?'

'I've always assumed Black Truck Couriers were called that because they use black trucks. Does anyone know if that's correct or is there a connection to this Joe Black person? I mean, they've been around forever,' said PC Priest.

'Something else for you to research, Jane,' said Carl.

'Did we get any reported sightings from Cameron's neighbours? We must have interviewed them all by now,' said DI Reid.

'We got a couple of interesting statements, Inspector,' said Nina. 'A Mrs Yale, who lives in the same building as Cameron, claims she saw three men get into his van around eight thirty on the Wednesday night of the shooting. It was dark but she thought one of them was the man that owned the van. All she could remember about the other two was that they were smaller, and that they were carrying what she thought were sports bags. She lives on the third floor and was out on her balcony having a smoke.'

They waited while Nina flipped through the statements looking for the one she had marked with a green sticky note.

'Ah, here it is. This is from a Miss Joanne Rogers. She lives in the apartment next to Cameron's. According to her statement, she hadn't seen John since around seven on the Monday morning before the shooting, when she assumed he'd gone to work. She told us that a man came looking for Cameron on that same Monday morning, just before she went to work around eight fifteen.' Nina looked up. 'She's since identified that man as Scaletta. The other thing she told us was that she heard someone go into Cameron's apartment on the Wednesday night around ten o'clock. She assumed it was Cameron, as she heard a key go into the lock. She was already in bed, so she didn't see anyone. Reckons she could hear him opening and closing drawers and cupboards, and after about ten minutes he left.'

'Nigel, didn't you have Forensics look over Cameron's apartment?' said DI Reid.

'The only prints they could identify were Cameron's. Guess we might be able check the other set with the body in the morgue, if it's his girlfriend,' said DC Beard. 'I think our late night visitor might have been wearing gloves.'

'Where's your friendly, nosey neighbour when you need one?' said DI Reid.

'In bed, apparently,' said Nina. 'Or too scared to admit otherwise.'

'Sergeant, let's go back to the statement from Mrs Yale. She said she saw three men getting into the van, right?'

'That's right.'

'So, that means Cameron must have gone to the Merlin with whoever drove the van back to his apartment block, which means he was probably with the killers.'

'That might explain that untraceable call to Cameron's phone,' said Harry.

'God, whose side was Cameron on?' said DI Reid.

'Maybe the question is whose side did he think he was on?' said Carl.

'Well, it doesn't look like Scaletta's,' said DI Reid. 'According to the pathologist's report one of the rounds he dug out of Cameron's side came from the Glock in Scaletta's hand.'

'I wonder if there is any connection between this and Jordan's murder, apart from the fact that both Jordan and Cameron worked for Black Trucks,' said DC Beard.

'Maybe it's time to find out,' said DI Reid.

'Let's not forget that Sharon Wilson worked there, too,' said Harry.

'Oh, here it is,' said DI Reid. 'Ballistics are saying that the round that killed Jordan was fired from the Glock found with Scaletta.'

In Carl's opinion, there was nothing pleasant about a post-mortem examination of a body. He'd been present too many times to be intrigued by the procedure anymore. All he was interested in was the findings.

Given a choice, he would have chosen something other than watching Mike Jonas dismember another corpse but protocol required the presence of an investigating officer to maintain the integrity of the evidence chain.

'The only external signs of trauma are a slight bruising of the left cheek and both knees, bruising to the buttocks, and marks on the wrists and ankles caused by being bound with twisted duct tape,' said Mike. 'George, can you remove the tape from her mouth?'

Carl watched as Mike's assistant removed the large piece of grey tape from the face of the body.

Mike opened the mouth of the body on the table and probed with a blunt instrument. The smell of vomit escaped into the room.

'I'd say she choked on her own vomit,' said Mike.

Twenty minutes later, after examining her lungs, Mike confirmed his initial opinion.

At the conclusion of the autopsy, Mike announced that unless the analysis of the contents of her stomach and blood revealed anything else, drowning in her own vomit was the most likely cause of death.

'Guess that analysis might explain why she vomited,' said Carl.

'It might if she'd eaten something that induced the vomiting but it could have been triggered by fear.'

'When do you think she died?' said Carl.

'I'd say around five days ago. That would be some time Wednesday.'

'Let me know when you get the results of the analysis.'

Carl had seen and smelt enough.

CHAPTER 30

S IMON F LAHERTY and Peter Bolt had been at the heart of Zeitz
Security Services since its inception. Although the firm's trading
name suggested to the world that it was Ron Zeitz's operation,
the firm was actually a private company with three shareholders.
Being men of action, they'd held a shoot-out to decide whose
name would adorn the company's letterhead. When Ron Zeitz
had been the first to throw a dart into the bullseye of the board in
their local pub, their little dream had become known as Zeitz
Security Services.

Ron, Simon and Peter had become mates in the army.
Starting a security operation of their own had seemed like a good
idea when they were leaving the military. Initially, they had been
a three man operation providing bodyguard services. As demand
for their services increased, they had employed other soldiers, like
John Cameron, who were looking for a fresh start after several
years in uniform.

At the time Zeitz Security Services employed John Cameron,
they were the main supplier of security services to Joe Black, and
John ended up being Joe's personal bodyguard. Exploiting their
unique position in the Black empire, and Joe's indulgence in his
own product, Ron and his partners had expanded the horizon of

their business possibilities and quietly taken control of the Black operation, eliminating guys like Jack Trimmer who'd had their own plans.

Ron had regarded John Cameron's proximity to Joe and his close associates as a potential problem, and had quietly arranged for John to be in the wrong place at the wrong time, shortly after Joe's death. John's hot-headedness had taken care of the rest, and the world had moved on by the time he had been released from prison.

Following their takeover of the core business of Joe Black's operation, Ron and his partners repositioned the firm as a provider of security services to nightclubs and special events across the city. This put them into a position to control the flow of illicit substances into the venues they secured, and to charge premium prices for the products they supplied.

The firm had also set up a second distribution system using Black Truck Couriers, by inserting a team of their own drivers into that operation. Ron had recently expanded the team by recruiting Frank Jordan and John Cameron, who had both been part of Joe Black's empire. The operation was simple. The drivers picked up and delivered parcels all over the city. The firm's team simply did not record all their pick-ups and deliveries, and received cash payments that no-one recorded. But in the period leading up to Ron's death something had gone wrong.

The first sign of trouble had appeared when some of the deliveries assigned to Frank Jordan went astray. Jordan had protested his innocence. Ron had not believed him. Jordan's execution as a warning to the other drivers was now the subject of a police investigation.

A few weeks after Jordan's death, one of the deliveries of high grade product assigned to John Cameron had somehow trans-formed itself into low grade product by the time it reached its intended recipient. Ron's theory had been that someone was playing on their patch, and he had been determined to get Cameron to talk.

Ron's plan for getting Cameron to spill his guts hadn't turned out as he had explained it to Simon and Peter. What did happen had led to the police asking questions about the firebombing of Ron's house, and the disaster which the media was referring to as the Merlin Massacre.

Following Ron's death, Simon Flaherty and Peter Bolt were left to clean up the mess, which included stonewalling the police and wondering whether they would be next.

On the Friday morning following the Merlin Massacre, Simon Flaherty, who handled the firm's finances, was sitting at his desk staring at the screen of his computer, trying to fathom what had happened. There was less than a hundred dollars in the payroll account. In fact, there was next to no money in any of the firm's accounts.

'Pete,' he called across the office to Peter Bolt, who was reading the morning's paper. 'We have a problem. We can't make payroll. Someone's cleaned us out. We've got less than a thousand dollars in the bank.'

'Have you called the bank? Maybe it's a computer glitch.'

Simon telephoned the bank and spoke to their account manager. He couldn't believe what he was being told. 'Are you sure?' He listened to the response. 'Is there any way we can reverse that?' He listened again. 'Thanks. I'll get back to you.'

'What did they say?' said Peter, when Simon put down the phone.

'That Ron had used the funds to buy Bitcoin on Wednesday afternoon at three fifty, ten minutes before they closed off transactions for the day.'

'What the fuck was he up to?'

'You're assuming it was Ron. Think about it. He was here at three fifty on Wednesday, and I don't recall him being on his computer, do you?'

Peter Bolt stared into space.

'You're right. We were having afternoon coffee, and he was talking to Scaletta about making the meeting at the Merlin for nine.'

'Fuck, Pete! Do you know what that means?'

'Someone's got Ron's access code.' Peter walked across the room and looked at the city skyline in the distance. 'Is there any way we can retrieve those Bitcoins?'

'Not according to the guy at the bank. You need some special Bitcoin software key from the computer used to do the transaction.'

'Better check the Black accounts.'

Peter waited while Simon queried the Black accounts.

'Ron's account is empty but ours are intact,' said Simon.

'How much money are we talking about? How much have they taken?'

'Close to six million dollars. It's just as well Ron won't be needing his retirement funds.'

'Yeah, well let's hope the bastards can't get to ours. You'd better change the codes,' said Peter.

'You'll need to do yours,' said Simon.

The office was quiet while they reset their online banking access codes at B&A Bank, and in faraway Switzerland.

'We'll have to draw on the reserves. Get onto the bank and make sure Ron's access has been revoked before you transfer any funds into the payroll account. Make sure they understand we'll be holding them liable if they approve any more transactions authorised by his code,' said Peter, after he had updated his codes.

'You sure you want me to do that? Transferring funds from the Black accounts will leave an audit trail connecting them to us.'

'What else can we do?'

'We could get a few clients to pay early this month. An early payment discount should do the trick, and we can drip feed cash into the accounts. That shouldn't be a problem if we keep it below the cash deposit threshold.' Simon stroked his chin. 'If we have to, we can pay some of the guys in cash, we've got plenty of that.'

'Sounds like a plan. You work on that while I call the boys together for a war council. We could be in a lot more trouble than I thought.'

<hr />

The war council met over lunch in a back room at the Portside Hotel. In addition to Simon Flaherty and Peter Bolt, who were now in charge of operations, the war council consisted of Jim Rapier, Mike Steele and Barry Smart.

Jim Rapier ran the operation at the garage, including the production facility. Mike Steele was in charge of the nightclub security teams. Barry Smart managed the distributors, the people who actually sold the product to the public.

They called it a war council for a fairly straight forward reason. They were military men and they had decided they were at war.

'Six million! You're kidding me?' said Jim, when Simon briefed the council on their financial losses.

'I think the money is the least of our worries,' said Peter. 'After his little chat with the police on Wednesday, Ron told me we'd have to watch out for Jack Trimmer's boys. The police think they're distributing in some of the clubs we don't look after.'

'What? A good old fashion turf war?' said Barry.

'Ron thought these boys showing up at the same time as Cameron going off the rails might be more than coincidence. Cameron was close with Jack, before his accident,' said Peter.

'You thinking those snotty nosed kids have figured out that what happened to their old man was no accident?' said Barry.

'A lot of people went missing when Joe died. Who knows who knew what happened to Jack was no accident?' said Simon.

'How old would those kids be now?' said Jim.

'The older one would be about thirty, I reckon. What was his name?' said Barry.

'Glen,' said Peter. 'His cute little brother is Rory. He's a few years younger than Glen, if I remember correctly.'

'We should have kept an eye on them,' said Jim.

'Who knew they were going to get into the business. Come on, Jim, they were kids,' said Simon.

'Wasn't there a third one? A skinny little girl?' said Barry.

'Yeah, think you might be right. She couldn't have been any older than five when Jack went down,' said Simon. 'Maybe the mistake we made was not keeping an eye on Rosie.' Simon shrugged his shoulders. 'I never could figure out what Jack saw in her, she was such an airhead.'

'Jack wasn't interested in her head, you idiot,' said Barry.

Their laughter was interrupted by a knock at the door, before a waitress entered with a trolley to serve their lunch.

For a while, after the waitress left and closed the door, any intruder into the room would have thought he had stumbled across a group of business men having a quiet lunch in a private room.

'So what's the plan?' said Jim, as he finished his porterhouse and roast vegetables.

'We need to find those Trimmer boys before the police do,' said Peter. 'Barry, you have people on the ground. Get them to ask around. If they're trying to break into our patch somebody's sure to have heard something.'

'What about the boys at Black Trucks?' said Barry.

'Ron was sure Jordan was working for someone but Scaletta couldn't get him to talk, and Cameron isn't going to talk now, is he? Whoever is behind it has made sure there are no witnesses,' said Peter.

'What about the others?' said Jim.

'We'll know if any of them cross us,' said Barry. 'I've told my people not to pay until they have tested the contents of the package.'

'Can we trust them not to go to the police?' said Simon.

'Barry can remind them about what happened to Jordan with the next shipment,' said Peter, before turning to Mike Steele.

'Mike, get some of your people out visiting clubs we don't control. We have to find these bastards.'

CHAPTER 31

Bɪʟʟ Gɪʟᴇꜱ ᴏᴘᴇɴᴇᴅ the padlock in the iron bolt that locked the heavy wooden door of the ancient stone shed that housed the lawnmowers. There was nothing he could do about the building. Its fate was in the hands of the Church Insurance Office but the grounds were heritage listed. The gardens needed to be maintained, even if no-one was currently living in Gladesview House.

Bill had been the head gardener and maintenance manager at Gladesview House for thirty years. He was in love with the gardens. They meant more to him than the embittered woman he called his wife. He'd have divorced her years ago but for their Catholicism and 'death do us part' wedding vows. Coming to work every day was an escape from his private domestic corner of hell.

Hank and Wally, two of the men in the gardening team from St Franks that had arrived to cut the lawns and work on restoring the gardens, walked into the gloomy interior of the shed behind Bill and started preparing the lawnmowers.

'Tank's empty on this one,' said Hank.

'Grab the can from under the bench. I filled her up last week before we knocked off,' said Wally.

Hank walked to the bench up against the back wall of the shed and bent down to pick up the petrol can from its usual spot.

'You sure you put it here?'

'Where else would I put it, Hank?'

'How the fuck would I know? I'm telling you it's not here.'

'Oh, shit!' said Bill. 'Don't touch anything, boys. Think I had better call the police.'

'What are you going on about?' said Hank, who was not keen on being in the same space as anybody in a dark blue uniform.

'Didn't you boys watch the news last night?'

'Oh, fuck!' said Wally. 'The Golden Fleece can. I thought about that when I saw it on the news last night but decided it couldn't be ours, not with that bloody great lock on the door.'

Carl arrived at Gladesview House with Sergeant Dean Lang and his crime scene investigators within fifteen minutes of Bill's call. The gardening crew, smoking and hoping they wouldn't have to talk to anymore policemen, watched from under the large red gum in the back garden.

'Did you look inside this shed last week, Dean?' said Carl, as Bill Giles walked towards them.

'It was locked with a bloody great padlock in an iron bolt. No sign of forced entry, so we didn't bother looking inside.'

Bill Giles explained that, as far as he knew, the shed had not been opened since the last time the lawns had been mowed on the Wednesday before the fire.

'Who has a key to the shed?' said Carl.

'Me, and there's one, or rather there was one, on a hook in Fr Harris' office,' said Bill Giles.

Sergeant Lang examined the padlock and the iron bolt.

'I still reckon this has not been forced. If anyone entered this shed to get the can, they used a key.'

'Who was the last person to see the petrol can, Mr Giles?' said Carl.

'Wally.'

'Where is he?' said Carl. 'I'd like to speak to him.'

A man in his late fifties, with a gold earring in his left earlobe and greying hair pulled back into a ponytail, detached himself from the watching gardeners when called. As he approached, Carl recognised him as the same Wally he had arrested, and helped convict for dealing in stolen car parts, about five years ago.

'Hello, Wally,' said Carl, extending his hand.

Wally shook his hand and smiled. 'Nice to see you, Inspector.'

'Mr Giles tells me you were the last person to handle the missing petrol can.'

'Yeah. I filled it up the last time we were here while I was waiting for Hank to bring his mower in. Put it under the bench in its spot over there.' Wally pointed towards the wooden bench standing in the gloom against the back wall of the shed.

'Who locked the shed when you finished?'

'Me. Robert was here to pick us up, so I locked up after Hank put his mower in the shed.'

'Do you need a key for that?'

'Nah. You just push it together until you hear it click.'

'Did you check it?'

'Yeah, it was locked alright. Didn't want any of those local kids breaking in and pinching our stuff, Inspector.'

'I checked the padlock before I left,' said Bill Giles. 'The shed was locked.'

'Any idea how the can ended up inside the house after the fire?'

'Bill had to use his key to open the shed, Inspector. If that burnt can they showed on the news last night is our petrol can, I'd say someone with a key took it out. Have you seen the size of that bolt?'

'Yes. I was thinking the same thing, Wally.'

'Aren't you going to ask me where I was at the time of the fire, Inspector?'

'Do I need to ask you, Wally? I thought you were watching TV with Robert Sturm at St Frank's.'

'Oh, yeah. I forgot. The cute little girlie already asked.'

'Constable Priest.'

'Bit ironic, don't you think, Inspector? Someone knocks off poor old Fr Morrie and you guys send out a constable called Priest.'

'At least we know who killed Fr Skinner, Wally.'

Wally put his hands into the pockets of his jacket. 'You know, Inspector, I met John Cameron inside when I was doing time for something. Never struck me as someone who'd kill anyone. He was always meditating or praying but, you know, I never could understand why he didn't want to have anything to do with Fr Morrie.'

'I think we do now, Wally,' said Carl.

'All the same, Inspector, it's hard to believe Fr Morrie was one of those priests that abused little boys.'

Wally walked back to join the gardeners from St Frank's standing under the red gum in the centre of the back lawn.

Sergeant Lang directed his team to dust the shed and lock for fingerprints, and to look for fibres caught in the bench and the doorjamb.

'Where in the house was Fr Harris' office, Mr Giles?' said Carl.

'In the east wing, just inside the back door.'

'Do you think you could point out to us where that key would have been hanging?'

'I suppose.'

'Dean, let's see if we can locate the key in the rubble. Shouldn't be hard to find if it's still there.'

The three men walked over to the burnt-out building. The walls of the east wing were still standing even though most of the roof had fallen in. Burnt and twisted roofing iron and charred beams were piled in the courtyard next to the east wing, where the search and recovery team had dumped them.

They stood outside the hole in the wall that had been the window of Fr Harris' office and peered into the blackened interior.

'The spare key was on a hook behind the door, over there,' said Bill Giles, pointing through the hole.

Dean shone his torch into the gloom and illuminated what was left of the wall opposite the window. The key was still hanging on its hook.

'You're sure these are the only two keys?'

'I've never seen any others, Inspector, and I can assure you mine was at home on my key ring on the night of the fire.'

'That might explain why he left the can inside, Inspector,' said Dean, 'so he could put the key back before setting the place alight.'

'That means whoever lit the fire must have known it was there in the first place, doesn't it?' said Bill Giles.

'And he must have known where you stored the fuel for your mowers,' said Carl.

Dean went to get his camera and an evidence bag.

'Who knew about that key, apart from you and Fr Harris?' said Carl.

'Some of the gardeners. They'd have to get Fr Harris to open the shed if I wasn't here, and most of the residents, I guess. Some of them spent a lot of time with Fr Harris when he was here.'

'I suppose anyone that had lived here for years would know where the mowers were kept.'

'You think one of the residents burnt the place down, Inspector?'

'Wouldn't be the first time, Mr Giles, but let's not jump to conclusions.'

CHAPTER 32

HARRY WAS BRINGING his timesheet up to date when his smartphone started vibrating in his pocket.

'Hello, Detective,' said Jessika. 'Got five minutes?'

'Got forever for you, Miss Walsh.'

Lisa looked up from her computer at the sound of the smile in Harry's voice.

'Dad asked me to call. He wants to set up a meeting with your inspector. Can you arrange that?'

Harry looked across the office to where Carl was in conversation with Charlie Head in front of the wall map he'd filled with colored pins. 'When does he want to meet?'

'Can you arrange something today? Say this afternoon. Dad said he'd come to your office.'

'I suppose. What do you want me to tell Inspector West?'

'Can't discuss that on the phone, Harry. You never know who could be listening.'

'Give me a minute.'

Harry walked over to where Carl and Charlie were in deep conversation about the map on the wall covered with pins.

'Excuse me, Boss,' said Harry.

Harry waited for Carl to look at him.

'What's up?'

'Max Walsh wants to meet with you, this afternoon.'

'Did he say why?'

'They don't want to discuss it over the phone. Jessika said he'd come here.'

Carl looked at the calendar on his smartphone. 'Tell Max I can see him any time after two.'

Harry passed the message to Jessika and they agreed on two-thirty.

'That's all a bit mysterious, isn't it?' said Charlie. 'Do you boys always play secret squirrels with lawyers?'

Carl laughed and left Charlie scratching his head. He had an appointment with DCI Rankin.

The chief inspector looked up from the page he was reading. 'This could be tricky, Carl.'

'That's why I wanted your thoughts before taking the next step.'

'You're sure about this key?'

'As sure as I can be. Either we need to show that one of the gardeners is behind the fire or we're left with it being one of the priests. Either way it's not going to look good.'

'What about this Fr Harris?'

'He doesn't have an alibi for the night of the fire and neither does Sister Kite, the head cook, but what would be the motive for either of them?'

'I suppose it's possible that your hero, Sister Murray, could have started the fire as well.'

'Same problem.'

'Working that out, Carl, is why we're paying you the big bucks. Do some more background checks. There must be something we've missed or stuff they haven't recorded. Perhaps you should have a chat with that retired monsignor who worked for Bishop Knight.'

'I've got Charlie working on setting up an appointment with him.'

'Good.'

By the way, Chief, I've just had a call from Max Walsh. He's coming over at two-thirty. Wouldn't say what for but he wanted to talk today.'

'Keep me posted. He doesn't normally come calling unless he wants something.'

Walsh and Garcia was a member of the legal aid panel of law firms the state paid to defend people who couldn't afford a lawyer. Every officer on the force that had arrested anyone knew Max Walsh.

The renown defender of petty thieves and other minor criminals arrived at two-thirty.

Harry went down to escort Max up to Carl's office.

'You're looking well, Harry. Jess must be taking good care of you.'

'No complaints from me, Max.'

'Glad to hear it.'

Carl stood when Harry ushered Max into his office.

'Hello, Max.' The two men shook hands. 'Take a seat.' Carl waited for Max to settle. 'What's on your mind?'

'I have a proposition for you.'

'Go on.'

'As you know, Carl, we represent a lot of minor criminals. Most of them are idiots that do stupid things but every now and then we come across someone with half a brain, who realises he's in deep shit before you boys find out about what he's been up to. I've got a deep shit client that wants to talk to you.'

'Why would he want you to talk to me, Max?'

'He wants protection. He's scared shitless someone's going to kill him.'

'What's he done? I assume he's done something, otherwise you wouldn't be here.'

'Oh, he's done something. He worked with Frank Jordan and John Cameron.'

'Black Truck Couriers,' said Harry.

'They were part of a team delivering unregistered parcels for cash, without their employer's knowledge. Apparently, they'd get a text message alerting them to a pick up and the delivery address would be on the parcel. They got paid cash on delivery.'

'Apart from cheating their employer and the taxman, I can't see why that should be life threatening, Max,' said Carl.

'Those packages were full of meth tablets; ice,' said Max. 'Jordan and Cameron are both dead. My boy thinks he's next.'

'He want us to arrest him?'

'He wants protection in exchange for the information he can provide,' said Max.

'I'm happy to listen to his story but, as you no doubt realise, that's not my decision. We'll need to persuade the Public Prosecutor,' said Carl.

'I think we may be able to do that, Carl. My client claims his information will help you solve the Merlin Massacre.'

'We need to get Bob Reid in here. He's leading that investigation.'

'Are you interested in a deal?'

'Are you interested in a conference with Bob Reid and the Public Prosecutor's Office?'

'Can you set up a conference today?'

'Let me make a couple of calls.'

Harry and Max went to Lena's for a coffee while they waited for DI Reid and the Public Prosecutor to arrive.

'Jess tells me you're working on the Gladesview House arson case. Making any progress?' said Max, after they ordered.

'Still looking for a motive.'

'I wonder whether Michael Knight has a skeleton in his cupboard like Maurice Skinner,' said Max.

'It's well hidden if he does.'

'My father was close with the Church, too close for my liking, but then his brother was a bishop. He told me once that he'd advised his brother to be very careful about what he archived.'

'I'd say he took your father's advice.'

'Not much bloody help when you need to know what they were up to, is it?'

'No, and in the end it cost Fr Skinner his life,' said Harry.

'Yes, you wonder what would have happened to him if he'd been outed and sent to prison. Maybe that's why Uncle Pat sent him to prison as the chaplain. Mind you, it doesn't excuse him, but you do wonder how they saw things back then, don't you?'

'I have enough trouble working out how people see things today.'

'That's one of the joys of living with a member of the fairer sex, Harry. Let me give you some fatherly advice. She takes after her mother, so you'll save yourself a lot of trouble if you simply learn to see things her way. Works for me.'

'I read in a book somewhere that it was better to choose to be happy than insist on being right. Is that your philosophy, Max?'

'Damn right it is, especially in a man's own home. It's a different story in Court though. I'd rather be right there. That way I end up with a happy client.'

'We don't seem to get that option. Every time we're right our client is always unhappy.'

'Harry, I think you're forgetting that your client is the general public, not the criminal you've put away.'

Harry and Max bumped into the Public Prosecutor in the lobby of Police Headquarters when they were returning to Carl's office. They travelled up to the third floor together in the elevator.

Bob Reid was waiting for them with Carl. The conference convened in the meeting room down the corridor from Carl's office, simply because they needed more chairs.

The Public Prosecutor took control of the meeting. 'What's the deal, Max?'

'My client is prepared to name names in exchange for protection. He's prepared to confess to his part in distributing drugs but he'd rather not go to prison. I've explained to him that might not be an option but that you might consider a lesser charge if his information is correct, and if it helps you solve the Merlin Massacre.'

'What does your client claim to know, Max?' said the Public Prosecutor.

'Who was supplying the drugs and who Jordan and Cameron were working for.'

'Isn't that the same?' said Bob Reid.

'No, Inspector. The difference is what my client believes led to the Merlin Massacre,' said Max.

The Public Prosecutor asked the two inspectors to step out into the corridor.

'What are your recommendations, gentlemen?'

'If we can get the kingpin at the cost of a foot soldier, let's take the deal,' said Carl.

'I'm in,' said Bob Reid. 'We've already lost a couple of foot soldiers.'

They returned to the meeting room.

'Max, tell your client he has a deal,' said the Public Prosecutor. 'When can you bring him in?'

'He's waiting for my call.'

'Call him. Let's get him into witness protection. Once he's safe, DI Reid can take it from there. And Max, if he's bullshitting us, all bets are off.'

CHAPTER 33

JANICE GEORGE HAD BUILT a solid private investigation business uncovering other people's secrets. It had been a hard slog.
She'd spent five years learning the ropes from her father before
he'd succumbed to lung cancer, after a lifetime of standing
around smoking and watching other people do things they didn't
want either their boss or their spouse to know about.

The business operated from an office in Janice's seventh floor
apartment and advertised on a discreet webpage. She met with
clients in the coffee shop opposite her apartment building when
they required a face to face meeting. A lot of her assignments
came from referrals, and most of the work involved following
people and recording where they went and who they spent their
time with. It was tedious and often boring but people paid good
money for certain types of information, which could only be
gained by surveillance.

Janice called her mother every night. It was one of those
habits she'd fallen into as a teenager and carried over into adult
life. She might have broken the habit if she'd had a serious relationship but at thirty-five, despite numerous liaisons, Janice
hadn't found the man worth the investment a serious relationship
required. Most nights Janice spoke to her mother on the phone.

Some nights, when her target's movements didn't allow her the opportunity to call before nine o'clock, her mother had to be satisfied with a text message.

When Martha George hadn't heard from her daughter or been able to contact her for three days, she suspected something might be wrong and went to check on Janice, thinking she could have taken ill. When she arrived at the seventh floor apartment, Martha inserted the key Janice had given her and let herself in.

The smell hit her as soon as she opened the door. Thinking Janice must have left some meat out on the bench to thaw and then hadn't come home to cook it, Martha crossed the room and opened a window. Then she went to check the kitchen so she could do something with the rotten meat. But there was no meat on the bench. Puzzled, Martha opened the door to the bathroom and wished she hadn't. The smell of rotten meat nearly knocked her over.

She glanced into the bathroom. The floor was covered in a pool of dried blood, which had spread from the shower cubicle across the tiles to the vanity unit. Martha turned her head to look at the shower cubicle. The naked body of a woman lay crumpled into the bottom section of the cubicle, below white tiles splattered with blood and brains. Someone had turned off the shower. Martha realised it hadn't been Janice.

She rushed into the kitchen and threw up in the sink. When she'd recovered from her initial shock, Martha opened the tap and cleared the sink, before going downstairs to call the police.

There was no doubt about how Janice George had been killed. There was no gun in the bathroom, so it was obvious she hadn't shot herself. What Carl wanted to know was: Why had she been killed? And who'd pulled the trigger?

He wondered if she was the same Janice George that had stayed in the Surfers Apartments at Carrick, and if she'd been following John Cameron, seeing that her mother had told him she had been a private investigator, like her father.

The fact that there was no sign of forced entry and that the door had been locked, according to the victim's mother, suggested to Carl that whoever had killed her either had a key or had been let into the apartment by the victim.

'Bit strange that she was in the shower, if she'd let someone in, isn't it?' said Lisa.

'What do you mean?' said Carl.

'Well, if I'd been in the shower, I wouldn't have answered the door, and if I'd answered the door, I'd hardly have left someone sitting in here while I had a shower, unless it was a close friend.'

'What if it was her boyfriend and he'd arrived early, and she hadn't showered yet?'

'I guess that's possible. I suppose he could have slept overnight, too,' said Lisa.

Sgt Lang came into the living room from the bathroom with an evidence bag.

'What have you got there, Dean?' said Carl.

'A used condom, Inspector. Looks like it's been washed out but that's no guarantee it's clean.'

'Better take a good look at the sheets on that bed, Dean.'

While Sgt Lang and his crime scene investigators continued their forensic investigation of the apartment, Carl and Lisa went downstairs to interview the building manager in his office on the third floor.

'How do people get into this building?' said Carl.

'There's a concierge service from seven am to seven pm, Inspector. Outside those hours, residents use an access code on the keypad by the front door or the one by the door in the carpark. Any after hours visitors need to use the intercom at the front door to request access, which residents can grant from the intercom panel in their apartment,' said the manager.

'Any CCTV?'

'No.'

'Who provides the concierge service?' said Carl.

'Colin does the seven to one shift and I do the other shift.'

'Okay. I spoke to Colin on the way in,' said Carl, 'and he told me that, as far as he could recall, Miss George hadn't had any visitors during his shift since she returned to the building last Wednesday. What about during your shift, Mr Jones?'

Mr Jones checked his computer screen. 'I log all visitors, Inspector. I've got no-one since the week before last, when her friend Alison visited. She comes to see Miss George two or three times a month.'

'Do you have any details apart from her name?'

'Sorry.'

When Carl and Lisa returned to the apartment, Harry was sitting at the table in the room set up as an office, reading the contents of the victim's laptop.

'When did you get here, Harry?' said Carl.

'Just after you went downstairs.'

'Wasn't that thing locked?'

'Dean found the password taped to the underside of a drawer in the bedroom.'

'Found anything?'

'Extensive list of contacts in her address book.'

'Is there an Alison in there?'

Harry scrolled down the list. 'There's an Alison Ross.'

'Contact details?'

'Mobile, email and address,' said Harry.

'Give her a call and see if she's at home,' said Carl.

Alison Ross lived in a one bedroom apartment overlooking the ocean at Morton Sands. It took Carl and Lisa thirty-five minutes to drive across town to see her, once Harry had confirmed that she was at home.

'Miss Ross, tell me how you're connected to Janice George?' said Carl.

'I work for her, Inspector.'

'And, what exactly is it that you and Miss George do?'

'Janice is a private investigator. We do surveillance work. Mostly for insurance companies, but we do some private work. You know, things like seeing if a man is cheating on his wife. Stuff like that.'

'When was the last time you saw her?'

'Why are you asking?'

'I'm afraid Janice is dead, Miss Ross.'

Alison's eyes opened wide. 'Dead?'

'We're investigating her murder.'

'I can't believe it. Who'd want to kill Janice?'

'That's what I was hoping you might be able to tell me.'

Carl waited for Alison Ross to get her emotions sufficiently back under control so that she could answer his questions.

'I realise it's a bit of a shock, Miss Ross, but do you remember when was the last time you saw her?'

Alison took three deep breaths and placed her hands in her lap.

'Sunday before last. We met to discuss a case we were working on.'

'Which one?'

'I guess it's okay to tell you, seeing that Janice is dead. We were tracking one of the men killed at the Merlin: John Cameron.'

'Who for?'

'I never knew who we were working for, especially when it

was a private job. Janice looked after that side of the business. I helped her with the surveillance. You can't do twenty-four seven on your own.'

'Do you know if she had a boyfriend?'

'Not anyone serious.'

'Do you know if she was into casual sexual relationships?'

Alison shook her head.

'We found a used condom in her bathroom.'

'Was she raped?'

'I don't think so.'

Alison twirled a strand of her hair. 'She mentioned some guy called Rory a couple of times, but I've never met him.'

'Recently?'

'About a month ago.'

'When did you start the job watching John Cameron?'

'A couple of months ago.'

'So, you knew he'd visited St Frank's on the night Fr Skinner was murdered?'

'I was there. Janice said we couldn't say anything otherwise we wouldn't get paid.'

'Looks like Janice wasn't counting on getting paid this way. I guess you'll be out of pocket on this one.'

'Am I going to get into trouble for not reporting John Cameron, Inspector?'

'Too late to worry about that now, Miss Ross. Cameron's dead.' Carl looked her in the eye. 'Your boss might still be alive if you had.'

Alison dropped her head.

'Did you hear from Janice after you'd last seen her?'

'She called on Wednesday to tell me the job had been called off, and that she'd call me when she had something else for me.'

Carl looked around her small apartment. There was nothing

visible that betrayed her occupation. 'Do you have anywhere else to stay, Miss Ross?'

'I could go to my parents' place, I suppose.'

'I suspect Janice might have been killed by whoever employed you to watch John Cameron. Hopefully, they don't know about you, but it might pay for you to visit your parents for the next few days.'

'Do you think I'm in danger staying here?'

'To be honest, I don't know. It was just a suggestion.'

'Might be a good idea. Do you have a card if I need to call you, Inspector?'

Carl handed her his card and placed his hand on her shoulder. 'Don't blame yourself. It won't do you any good. Trust me, I know.'

By the time Carl and Lisa returned to Police Headquarters, Harry had compiled a list of the jobs Janice George had recorded on her computer.

'Anything we can use on that computer, Harry?' asked Carl.

'Most of the jobs are for insurance companies, and they're fully documented. I'd guess we could trace payments to her bank account for those, but there is also a list of jobs, including one for watching John Cameron, where there is no record of who was paying for it.'

'We might find cash deposits in her account for those cases,' said Lisa.

'What about all those contact details?' said Carl.

'I've got Charlie and Jane going through that list asking people about their connection to the victim.'

'Any news from Forensics?' asked Carl.

'They're running DNA tests on the condom and the pubic

hairs found in the bed. We'll have to wait for the results. You know what they're like and, I almost forgot, Dr Jonas wants you to call him.'

Carl went into his office and called Mike Jonas, who answered on the second ring.

'Carl, I've got the results back from Ballistics. The bullet that passed through Janice George's head was fired by one of the guns used at the Merlin.'

———

After hearing Dr Jonas' news, Carl met with DI Reid.

'Bob, it looks like Janice George was killed by someone using one of the guns used at the Merlin.'

'What else do we know about her, Carl?'

'She was a PI, and she and her offsider were watching Cameron, right up to the day he was killed. In fact, Janice came back from Carrick on the afternoon before the shooting at the Merlin.'

'Have you spoken to her offsider?'

'She doesn't know who wanted them to watch Cameron, and there's no record of that on her computer either. She did tell me though that Janice had been seeing someone called Rory,' said Carl.

'That's interesting. Word on the street is that a couple of young bloods going by the names of Glen and Rory Trimmer have been trying to break into the nightclub ice scene,' said Bob.

'Isn't that what you were chasing Zeitz for?'

'I'd pegged them as small fry. Maybe I've underestimated them.'

'Might be time to have a chat with your small fry, Bob, and when you do, get a buccal smear from each of them. We've got some biological material from Janice George's bedroom.'

CHAPTER 34

IT TOOK two days to arrange for Max Walsh's mystery client to be squirrelled away in a safe house under the control of the witness protection program. When DI Reid and DS Strong arrived at the nondescript suburban house to interview him, they were surprised to discover that the informant enjoying their protection was Brad Poland, one of the drivers they had already interviewed in relation to Frank Jordan's murder.

'Change of heart, Brad?' said DI Reid.

'Yeah.'

'Why should I believe anything you tell me, Brad? The last time we spoke you didn't know anything about anything.'

'Things change, Inspector.'

'Oh? In what way?'

'Before, they would have killed me for saying anything.'

DI Reid waited.

'Now, they'll kill me to make sure I don't say anything.'

'Who is they, Brad?'

'Zeitz.'

'Isn't he dead?'

'Ron's dead but he isn't Zeitz.'

'Ah, you mean the firm. Why would they want to kill you, Brad?'

'I work for them.'

DI Reid looked at DS Strong, and then back at Poland. 'I thought you worked for Black Trucks.'

'Yeah, them too, but that was only so I could do what Zeitz wanted.'

'Which was?'

'Deliver packages for Zeitz that Black Trucks didn't know about.'

'Why would that get you killed?'

'It's what was in the packages, Inspector. We've been delivering ice all over town.'

'Who's this we?'

'Me, Jordan and Cameron. We all worked for Zeitz.'

'So how did this little operation work, Brad?'

Brad looked at DS Strong. 'You got that recorder thing switched on?'

'It's recording, Brad.'

'I'd get a text message to pick up a package that didn't go through the office. When I picked it up it would have the address on it, and I'd drop it off between my other deliveries. The guy I delivered it to would pay me cash.'

'Where does the ice come from?'

'Zeitz have their own lab.'

'Here or offshore?'

'Here, Inspector. In their garage out at Northfield.'

'So, what went wrong? How come Jordan and Cameron are dead?'

'Glen Trimmer. Have you heard of him?'

'I know who you're talking about.' DI Reid waited.

'Somehow, he knew about the operation. He approached us a couple of months back and offered us a pile of cash to switch some of the packages. He'd get the stuff we were supposed to be delivering and we'd deliver his shit in its place. I told him I wasn't interested but Frank had gambling debts to pay. And you know what happened to him, don't you?'

'What about Cameron?'

'He told me he wasn't going to do it, but I think he must have.'

'Why do you say that?'

'He's dead, isn't he?'

'So's Ron Zeitz.'

'I reckon Ron's mate, Scaletta, shot Frank when they found out he had switched one of the packages.'

'Why's that?'

'Because the arsehole threatened to kill me if I ever did anything like that.'

'Well, he's not around to carry out his threat. Why are you talking to us?'

'It's a long story, Inspector. You see, me and Cameron go back a long way. We were in the army together. Ron Zeitz was our platoon sergeant. He gave us jobs when we left the army.'

'What sort of jobs?'

'We worked as bodyguards for a dude called Joe Black. I'm sure you've heard of him.'

DI Reid looked at DS Strong and raised an eyebrow.

'Yeah, I've heard of him. He's been dead for years.'

'But his operation didn't die with him, Inspector, it simply became part of Zeitz. The only ones who didn't make the switch were Jack Trimmer, on account of him being knocked off his bike and dying on the side of the road, and John Cameron, who ended up inside after a shootout with some of your lot.'

'Who got Cameron the job at Black Trucks?'

'Me.'

'Who do you think shot Zeitz and Cameron?'

'Trimmer.'

'Why do you think that?'

'Ron Zeitz killed his old man. Ran him off the road because he wanted to take over Joe's business.'

'And you think Glen Trimmer found out about it and wanted revenge.'

'That's what Cameron told me.'

'Why didn't you warn Zeitz?'

'What, so he'd know I'd been talking to Trimmer? I might be stupid, Inspector, but I'm not that stupid. Besides, I've got to get out of the game. I can't sleep nights knowing what that stuff does to kids. It's got to be stopped before we fuck up the country for good.'

'Conscience getting to you, Brad?'

'No, Inspector. Guilt. That was my cousin's kid that died of an overdose at the music festival last weekend.'

The Gladesview House arson investigation moved to the back-burner, while Carl and his people assisted DI Reid's team shut down the Zeitz operation and hunt for Glen and Rory Trimmer, who were now the prime suspects for the Merlin Massacre and the murder of Janice George.

'Excuse me, Inspector,' said PC Priest, when Carl walked past her desk.

'Yes, Jane?'

'I've done that research on Susie Morte that DI Reid wanted. She changed her name. She was born Susanne Rosemary Trimmer. She's Glen and Rory's sister.'

'Good work, Jane.'

Carl called Bob Reid.

'Bob, had any luck contacting Susie Morte?'

'No. We haven't been able to find her. Why the interest?'

'Jane's done that background check you wanted. Her birth name was Susanne Rosemary Trimmer. She's Glen and Rory's sister. Looks like Zeitz might have been fucked in more ways than one.'

'And you thought Harry was sleeping with the enemy.'

'Yeah, well I think we can live with Harry's sort of enemy. Think we need to treat Susie as an accomplice and not a grieving widow. I'll get an all points out on her.'

After releasing Susie's details to the media, Carl decided to see what Harry would make of the revelation that Susie Morte was actually Susanne Trimmer.

'Someone's planned this, Boss. It's starting to look like something you'd see in a movie.'

'Any idea where DI Reid got that photograph of the Trimmers?'

'It was on Jordan's phone.'

'How did we find out who they were?'

'Dean loaded the photo onto Facebook.'

'Facebook?'

'Yeah, apparently their face recognition software is better than the FBI's. If you have a photo attached to your profile it can recognise you in any photographs of you posted by anyone else, especially if you've been tagged.'

'Does that mean these guys have Facebook accounts?'

'They do. If we'd explored their mother's account earlier, we might have seen their connection to Susie Morte before now. Rosie's a professional photographer, mostly weddings. She has a Facebook Page for that but her personal account has a lot of family photos.'

'So, apart from the family connection, what do we know about them?'

'Glen's rumoured to be a small-time dealer but we have

nothing on him. In fact, his name didn't come up until DI Reid started on the Jordan case. The only thing we have on him really is the story Poland told DI Reid.'

'What about the other one?'

'He's got a computing science degree from City but doesn't appear to have a job. The interesting thing though is he owns several apartments, including one in the building that Janice George was shot in.'

'Might explain how he got into the building. If he owns an apartment he'd have the access code, wouldn't he? And, he'd know when the concierge wasn't on duty.'

'Yeah, I thought of that. By the way, Boss, Dr Jonas rang. He has the DNA profile of whoever was in bed with her before she was shot.'

'If it was Rory Trimmer, I wonder if that was how he was paying her for the surveillance.'

'I don't think she did anything for love, Boss. I had Lisa cross-check her bank account with her records. There are cash deposits that line up date wise for all of the jobs outside her insurance work.'

'I think he killed her simply because she knew about his connection to Cameron.'

'And, they killed Cameron so he wouldn't talk.'

'Makes sense, Harry, but it doesn't explain Susie's role. She doesn't appear to have shot anybody.'

'Maybe they were after his money as well. She was living with Zeitz. Who knows what she had access to?'

'Take a look at Zeitz's accounts while Charlie and I visit Monsignor Peterson, and be sure to let DI Reid know what you find out.'

DI Reid wasn't the only one looking for the Trimmer brothers. Ever since the war council at the Portside Hotel, Mike Steele had been on their trail. He was also looking for Susie Morte, but not for the same reasons DI Reid wanted to find her.

The first thing he discovered was that Rosie was now using her maiden name: Mortimer, and that she was still living in the house she had shared with Jack at Morton Sands. No-one answered his knock when he visited the house in Longbottom Street, so he talked to the neighbours. After he'd passed one of them a fifty, she told him that Rosie had driven off around ten o'clock on the morning of the previous Wednesday, the same day as the shootings at the Merlin, and hadn't come back. She also told Mike that the police had been around looking for Rosie.

A couple of days later, news reached Mike that Glen Trimmer had stopped supplying his dealers, who were now looking for alternative sources of supply. Under normal circumstances Mike would have seen a business opportunity to exploit but, after consulting with his partners, decided anything associated with the Trimmers would be high risk. The news also implied that the Trimmers had gone to ground, implicating them even further in Ron's death as far as Mike was concerned.

By the time Mike had located where the Trimmer boys were living, it was too late. He'd paid good money to hear a similar story to the one he'd been told at Rosie's. They hadn't been seen by their neighbours since the morning after the shootings at the Merlin. It looked like they'd run, which only confirmed Mike's suspicions that they were responsible for Ron's death, and the theft of the firm's money.

Then he learnt that Brad Poland had failed to show up for work. When he enquired further he discovered that, while Brad's van was still parked in his driveway, none of his neighbours had seen him for several days. One of Brad's neighbours, persuaded to divulge a little more information in exchange for cash, told Mike that Brad had left in a taxi in the middle of the night.

Mike called Barry Smart.

'Barry, are you aware Poland has disappeared?'

'I thought he was on the sick list.'

'Then why would he take a taxi ride in the middle of the night?'

'Fuck! You don't think he's done something stupid do you?'

'Barry, he knows way too much to be a loose end.'

'You'd better find him then. Too bad Scaletta's no longer around.'

'He's not the only one who knows how to take care of loose ends, Barry.'

CHAPTER 36

THE NIGHT after his interview with Brad Poland, DI Reid arranged for the police helicopter to conduct a thermal imaging reconnaissance flight over the building housing the Zeitz vehicle garage.

While the helicopter was thudding around the Northfield industrial park in the dark, DI Reid led a raid on the home of Glen and Rory Trimmer, in a quiet suburban street three blocks from their mother's house. There was nobody home but the house was not empty.

A team of crime scene investigators spent several hours examining the contents of the house and found a few items of interest, including an expensive laser printer, a card embossing machine, and several partially burnt blank plastic cards in a rubbish bin in the backyard. They also collected dirty underwear, hair and skin cells from the bathroom and beds.

Interviews with the neighbours revealed that no-one had seen the Trimmers since the morning after the Merlin Massacre. The woman living across the street told DI Reid that she'd seen one of them come home around eight that morning, before both of them left in a silver Ford around ten. DI Reid issued an all points bulletin for the brothers and their car.

Next morning, the images captured by the thermal camera in the police helicopter were on his desk when DI Reid arrived at work. They revealed a hotspot in the northwestern corner of the building housing the Zeitz vehicle garage.

Armed with the images and the information Brad Poland had given him, DI Reid met with DCI Rankin, who authorised the raids he requested. It took the better part of the day to organise the raiding parties.

By late afternoon, as Zeitz Security Services was gearing itself up for the coming evening of work across the city's night-clubs, DI Reid's raiding party was quietly surrounding the garage.

At four thirty, DI Reid got the signal he had been waiting for: everyone was in place and ready to go. He looked at DS Strong, who was sitting behind the driver's wheel waiting for his command, and smiled. He picked up the microphone attached to the car's radio. 'All units, go!'

Within seconds, all access to the garage was sealed off as fifteen heavily armed Special Weapons officers stormed into the building, ordering everyone to put their hands in the air.

Jim Rapier marched up to DI Reid as he entered the garage. 'What the fuck do you think you're doing?'

DI Reid took the search warrant out of his coat pocket and handed it to Rapier to read. 'I'm searching the premises and arresting everybody on site.'

'Are you out of your fucking mind?'

'Sergeant, read Mr Rapier his rights.'

While Jim Rapier was handcuffed and led away, DI Reid walked towards the north western corner of the building. 'That section there. Tear the wall down if you have to.'

'There's a door behind this partition, Inspector,' said one of the uniformed constables. 'It's locked.'

'Okay, let's see what's in there.'

Two officers stepped up to the locked door and swung their steel battering ram. On the second impact the lock gave way and the door swung open.

DI Reid stood in the doorway. He had expected to see a basic meth lab, not something that looked like a university research laboratory with half a dozen technicians, dressed in white coats and safety goggles, huddled together in the far corner.

'Bloody hell, Nina. This is some set up,' he said, as DS Strong joined him in the laboratory.

'The last time I saw a laboratory like this was when I was in hospital,' said DS Strong. 'Got to be the first meth lab I've seen with a clean floor.'

Once the people working in the laboratory had been hand-cuffed and taken outside to the waiting paddy wagons, Sgt Dean Lang and his crime scene investigators moved in to shut down the operation and catalogue the contents of the laboratory.

DI Reid called DCI Rankin and reported on the success of the raid. Then he started on the task of tracking down and arresting everybody who worked for Zeitz Security Services.

Carl sat with Harry in their silver Ford, waiting for DI Reid's signal. The twelve armed members of his raiding party had already reported that they were in place.

'How are things going with Jessika?'

'Pretty good, actually. At least I don't have to teach her how to cook. How's Nina doing with the cooking lessons?'

'She's making progress but I don't think I'm going to have a chef on my hands any time soon. You see much of Max?'

'Yeah. We ate at their place last night.'

'What do your parents think of Jessika?'

'My mother's over the moon. She keeps asking me when we're going to get married.'

Carl laughed. 'What about your Dad?'

'He thinks she's too good for me but he's become mates with Max. They've been playing golf together.'

'I didn't know your Dad was into golf.'

'He calls it his retirement planning. He started playing a couple of years ago. Says he has to have a plan to fill in his time when he retires, otherwise he'll go bonkers.'

'Your mother's not that bad, is she?'

'I don't think it's being with my mother. He can't stand not being busy.'

DI Reid's call came over the radio, effectively ending the conversation as they switched focus to the task at hand.

The six patrol cars moved out of their parking spots in the surrounding streets and blocked the front and rear entrances to the car park at the offices of Zeitz Security Services.

'What's going on?' asked the receptionist, when Carl and Harry walked into the building.

'Where can I find your boss?' said Carl.

'Here,' said Simon Flaherty, coming out of his office. 'What can I do for you?'

Simon stopped and stared as six uniformed officers walked into reception and stood behind Carl.

'What's going on?'

'Simon Flaherty, I'm arresting you on suspicion of drug trafficking,' said Carl.

'What?'

Carl took the search warrant out of his pocket and handed it to him. 'And, we're searching this building.'

By five o'clock, Simon Flaherty, Peter Bolt and Barry Smart, who had been finalising plans for that evening's security operations, and three other employees, had been arrested and trans-ferred to the patrol cars in the car park.

As the prisoners were being driven away, a crime scene inves-tigation team moved in to search the building and its contents, including every computer hard drive.

Carl called DCI Rankin to report that the raid had gone according to plan.

CHAPTER 37

'How WELL DO you know Monsignor Peterson, Charlie?'

'He was our parish priest in the years leading up to his retirement, Inspector.'

'What are you guys going to do when you run out of priests?'

'Ordain women, I suppose, or import more of them from India.'

'Guess I'd better get used to seeing Indian priests around town then. Anyway, what's the monsignor like?'

'He was a bit out of touch when he arrived in our parish. I don't think he'd had that much parish experience before Bishop Kerry decided he wanted his own man around, and sent the monsignor into the vineyard, as he was fond of telling me.'

'Who's Bishop Kerry's man?'

'That suave Monsignor Rivers that Lisa likes.' Charlie smiled. 'He's one smooth operator our Monsignor Rivers.'

'Yes, I've met him.'

'Well, Monsignor Peterson is nothing like that. He's definitely an old-style priest. You know, one of those priests that expect everyone to do their bidding. I can tell you, the first couple of years with him were a real nightmare, but he finally got with the program when he realised he didn't have any control over what happened in the parish. He was great after that. My kids love him.'

'Who's your parish priest now?'

'Fr Pradesh.'

Carl laughed. 'So, I guess we won't be seeing any of those women priests any time soon.'

'Guess not, Inspector. It's that house over there.'

The door was opened by a white haired woman in blue jeans and a faded FDNY sweatshirt.

'Hello, Carol,' said Charlie.

'Charlie, nice to see you again.' Carol hugged him. 'Richard is expecting you. Come in.'

She showed them into the sunroom, where a tall man with a welcoming smile greeted them.

'So, what brings you all this way, Charlie? And, who's your friend?'

'Monsignor, this is Inspector West. He's leading the investigation into the Gladesview House fire. He wants to ask you a few questions about the priests that were living there.'

'Can I get you a cup of tea, gentlemen?' said Carol.

'Yes, thank you,' said Carl. 'That's most kind of you.'

'Think nothing of it, Inspector. What about you Charlie? Still white no sugar?'

'Yes, thanks.'

While Carol busied herself in the kitchen, the men made themselves comfortable in the sunroom.

'I haven't been to Gladesview for a couple of months,' said Monsignor Peterson. 'I usually get up there for a visit three or four times a year. Guess I won't be visiting again any time soon after this dreadful fire.' Monsignor Peterson opened his hands. 'What is it you want to know, Inspector?'

'I'm trying to work out why anyone would want to burn down a retirement house while its residents were asleep. I understand you worked closely with Bishop Knight and knew most of the other residents, so I'd appreciate anything you can tell me about them.'

'I see. Where do you want to start?'

'How well did you know the three priests that died as a result of the fire?' said Carl.

'As you'd expect, I knew Michael Knight very well, Inspector. Apart from working with him for years, we were at the seminary together, so you could say we'd known each other for nearly sixty years.'

'So, you knew Maurice Skinner as a young man as well.'

'Until that fire, there were five of us left from our class. Michael, Maurice, Peter Wilson, Brendan North and me. Now there's only three of us.'

'Guess you're lucky you had somewhere else to live,' said Charlie.

'You're not wrong there, Charlie.'

Carol came back into the room with a tray holding a teapot, three tea cups and a plate of sliced cake, and served afternoon tea.

'I'll leave you boys to it,' said Carol.

'Did you have any idea about Maurice Skinner's past?'

Monsignor Peterson looked out at the waves breaking on the beach opposite the house.

'I knew there had to be something, Inspector, but I had no idea it was abusing altar boys.'

'What made you think that?'

'Not long after Michael became bishop, he offered Maurice a parish. Maurice wouldn't take it. Claimed his calling was to serve prisoners, to set them free from their sins. Quoted some scripture passage, from Luke I think. Anyway, he refused, and Michael let him have his way. But I often wondered why he'd turned down that parish. You see, when we were at the seminary all Maurice ever talked about was being a parish priest. It just didn't add up for me at the time. Unfortunately, it does now.'

'Did you ever think to look at Bishop Walsh's archive?'

'His archives are a mess, Inspector. It would be like looking for a needle in a haystack.'

'Afraid, I have to agree with you. I had some of my officers go through it with the help of Monsignor Rivers,' said Carl.

'Yes, I'm sure Bishop Kerry would have wanted his eyes there while you were digging around. Did you find anything?'

'Nothing of any use. What can you tell us about Fr Peter Wilson?'

'He only moved into Gladesview a couple of years ago. He was another one the bishop had to force into retirement. A real gentleman. He was a much better parish priest than I ever was, hey, Charlie?'

'You weren't that bad, Monsignor, once we'd retrained you.'

Monsignor Peterson laughed. 'I sure needed that retraining. I'd lost my touch after all those years in the bishop's office.'

'And, Fr Brendan North?' said Carl.

'He's been retired a bit longer. Had a few issues with depression after his heart attack. Another one with a great record as a parish priest. Spent most of his time in the south-east. Can't see anyone wanting to harm him, Inspector.'

Carl looked at his list of names. 'What about Fr James Porter?'

'Jim Porter. I worked with him when I was a young priest. We shared a parish in the mid-north that took in several small communities. Lovely guy. He'd been retired for at least ten years. Very poor eyesight. He was almost blind.'

'And, Fr Patrick Kelly?'

'Paddy Kelly. The last of the Irish priests. He'd lost the use of his legs. Been in a wheelchair for years. Could still tell a good joke though, and loved his whiskey. I used to take him a bottle every time I visited the place. What a character. I'm going to miss him. He was one of those loveable rogues, very popular with the nuns. I'm sure Charlie's sister could tell you a few stories about him.'

Carl looked at his notes. 'What about Fr Michael Brown? He seems a bit young to be living in a retirement home. According to my notes he's only fifty-five.'

'He's not a well boy, Inspector. He's one of the reasons the place has to be locked up at night. He's got early onset dementia. Very sad case, he was such a promising young priest.'

Carl waited while Monsignor Peterson took a sip of his tea.

'What about Fr Paul Flaherty?'

'He'd have to be the oldest resident. Paul was an army chaplain for most of his time. Did a few years as an assistant at the Cathedral before he retired. Can't say I know him very well. He likes to keep to himself, but I saw on the news the other night that you had arrested his nephew, Simon.'

'Simon Flaherty?'

'Paul was so proud of him. Company director of a successful security firm, and making use of his military skills to keep people safe at night. Guess he won't be so proud of him now.'

'Yes, I can see how that would be a bit of a let-down. What about Fr Kevin Martin?'

'He's another one with health issues. Have you met him?'

'Not yet.'

'We used to talk about seven capital sins. Some call them the seven deadly sins. I suppose we're all tempted by them to a greater or lesser degree. Unfortunately, Kevin couldn't fight off gluttony, despite two heart attacks and a triple bypass. Probably just as well he was in the west wing. Can't imagine how the firemen would have gotten him out of the east.'

The monsignor smiled and helped himself to a piece of cake.

'When you were working closely with the bishop, did you ever hear anything about any of them that would suggest someone would want to kill them?'

'No, Inspector.' Monsignor Peterson shook his head. 'Looks like the only priest we now know someone wanted to kill was murdered in his own house. Bit strange that it happened on the same night, don't you think?'

'Yes, but it appears John Cameron didn't go near Gladesview that night, so unless he had an accomplice, it looks like there is no connection.'

'How can you tell where he was?'

'He had his mobile phone with him. That's as good as wearing a tracking device.'

'Oh.'

'Do you think any of them could have set the place on fire?'

'I wouldn't think so, but who knows what someone suffering from depression might do. As I'm sure you know, Inspector, they often take their own lives and even priests are not immune from that.'

Carl waited as Charlie made a note of the monsignor's comment.

'Can you tell us anything about Fr Damien Harris?' said Carl.

'I would have thought Charlie here could have told you all you'd need to know about Damien.'

Carl winked at Charlie. 'I think Charlie might be biased, so I'd be interested in another opinion.'

'I'd say he was all set to replace me before he had his breakdown. Had a great record as a parish priest and had completed an

MBA. I was really disappointed for him. He was a different man after that episode.'

'Is that why he ended up as the administrator at Gladesview House?'

'Probably, but you'll have to ask Bishop Kerry about that. He got rid of me by giving me Damien's parish when he took sick and, of course, he kept me there until I retired.' Monsignor Peterson looked at Carl. 'If you don't mind me asking, Inspector, are you looking for a reason why someone would want to kill them or do you really think one of them set the place on fire?'

'Have you been following the case on the news?'

'Of course.'

'Did you see the story on the petrol can?'

'Yes.'

'Turns out that can belongs to Gladesview House. Whoever set the place on fire knew where to find the key to the shed the gardeners used to store their fuel, and was able to get into the building without breaking in. He even put the shed key back on its hook in Fr Harris' office.'

'So, you're thinking it could be an inside job?'

'Starting to look that way but I can't fathom why any of them or the people that work there would want to do it?'

'We're strange creatures, Inspector. Who would have believed that a priest would molest a child? No-one. But we know it happened. Investigating complaints of sexual abuse by priests was not a happy experience, I can tell you.'

'Were you aware that Fr Harris was an altar boy at North Summit when Maurice Skinner was there?'

'Can't say that I was. We never actually dealt with any complaints against Maurice in my time on the committee. What I can tell you though, from my experience of dealing with sexual abuse cases, is that it's rare for there to be only one boy involved. Have you spoken to Damien?'

'He denies anything happened.'

'That might be true, Inspector, but sometimes memories get so repressed that people genuinely don't remember the event, until something traumatic drags it all back up for them.'

As they were driving back to the city, Carl asked Charlie to set up interviews with the surviving priests and Fr Harris.

When he got back to the office, Carl reread the statements made by the people who had worked at Gladesview House and reviewed the records of the men on the gardening team. Nothing jumped off the page for him.

His smartphone rang.

'Are you coming home or am I eating alone tonight?'

'Be there in twenty minutes.'

CHAPTER 38

CARL ARRIVED home to a table set with flowers and wine glasses. Nina was in the kitchen stirring something in a pot that smelt good.

'I could get used to this,' Carl said, kissing her on the cheek. 'What's the special occasion?'

'Celebrate my news.'

'What news?'

'I got in to see Dr Merry today while you were off gallivanting around the countryside. She had a cancellation.'

'And?'

'She's given me the all clear. There is no reason why we can't get pregnant.'

Carl wrapped his arms around her and kissed her. 'That's great!'

After Carl released her from his embrace, Nina swept her hand over the table. 'Last drinks.'

'Aren't we supposed to wait until you're pregnant?'

'We are not taking any chances, Mr West. I don't want our child starting life behind the eight ball simply because we couldn't resist a glass of wine.'

'Does that mean no sex tonight?'

'There's no way we can get pregnant tonight, honey. Didn't you read that book Dr Merry gave us on the first visit? There are cycles we have to play by if we're going to get pregnant.'

'I'm happy to play any time.'

'Let's just say there are some times in my cycle when I'm more fertile than others, and you'll need to be around for them if we're actually going to get pregnant.'

'I'll do my best.'

'I'm sure you have every good intention, but you know what our schedules can be like.'

'Well, I've always got my equipment with me.'

Nina hit him in the shoulder. 'I'm not one of your streetwalkers, Inspector. I expect your full attention, not a quickie in some corner between appointments, now go and get out of that suit while I finish making dinner.'

Despite the romantic atmosphere, it wasn't long before they were talking about work.

'You making any progress on that arson case?'

'At least I've still got Charlie helping me. We went to Carrick today, to have a chat with a retired monsignor.'

'They sure have some funny titles.'

'I guess it's not much different with some of ours. It's just that their organisation is a few years older, and English isn't its language of choice.'

'Was it worth the trip?'

'I'm starting to think it was an inside job. The monsignor said a few things that have got me thinking.'

'Like what?'

'For starters, he'd worked on some of their sex abuse investigations, and he said it was rare for a priest to abuse one altar boy.'

'You think there must have been others, apart from Cameron?'

Carl put down his utensils. 'I'm thinking Fr Harris. Mrs Cameron told me he had been an altar boy with John.'

'Didn't you ask him about that?'

'He claimed Skinner hadn't done anything to him apart from giving him a hug, but the monsignor said something about people repressing their memories of terrible things. Apparently, some people repress things so far down they don't remember them.'

'I guess that's how people survive. Think of all those soldiers that have been to war or even some of the things that happen in our line of work.'

Carl looked at his wife but his mind had gone back to the day Peter James had been killed.

Nina waved a hand in front of Carl's face. 'Are you still here?'

Carl reached across the table and took her hands in his own. 'Sorry, I was thinking about Peter.'

Nina squeezed his hands. 'I saw Janice the other day.'

'How was she?'

Nina packed up the dinner plates and topped up Carl's wine glass. 'The boys are both at school now, and she's gone back to work. She said to say hello.'

Carl watched Nina as she packed the plates and brought the dessert to the table, and hoped no-one would ever have to tell her what he had had to tell Janice James.

'That's the worst thing that's ever happened to me. I know I needed help to deal with it but I'll never forget it. I think of Peter every time I have to knock on a door.'

Nina massaged his shoulders. 'I think of it every time you leave the office.'

'Let's go for a walk.'

'Not until you've eaten that apricot pie I worked so hard to defrost.'

CHAPTER 39

Simon Flaherty sat with his lawyer, opposite DI Reid and DS Strong, in an interview room that was long overdue for a fresh coat of paint. DS Strong turned on the video recorder and stepped them through the required introductions.

'Mr Flaherty, I take it you're aware that Ron Zeitz had cleared out your firm's accounts on the day he was killed?' said DI Reid.

'I'm aware the accounts were cleared out, Inspector, but I'm pretty sure it wasn't Ron.'

'Why's that?'

'I assume you've examined the accounts.'

DI Reid pulled several sheets of paper from his folder and placed them on the table in front of Simon Flaherty, who examined them closely until he found what he was looking for.

'See the time and date of that transaction, Inspector?' Simon pointed to the transaction he wanted DI Reid to read. 'We were having a coffee with Ron in his office at that time. There's no way he could have done that.'

'Who else has access to your online banking codes?'

'Peter Bolt, and he was having coffee with me and Ron.'

'So, who do you think authorised the withdrawals if it wasn't Ron?'

'Somebody who knows Bitcoin transactions are impossible to trace, Inspector.'

'Bitcoin?'

'The bank told us that's where the money went. It was used to buy Bitcoin. Apparently, they have an exchange that works a bit like a bank, but you need some sort of special software to play.'

'Any idea who it was?'

'No.'

'So, you think someone must have breached your firewall and got access to the codes?'

'You've got all our computers, Inspector, you work it out.'

'We have them all apart from Ron's laptop.'

'Ron still had it when those withdrawals were made. It was sitting on his desk. So even if whoever shot him took his laptop, they would have been too late.'

'If you were sure it wasn't Ron, why didn't you report the theft?' said DI Reid.

'What, and have you lot looking through our files?'

'Might have saved us all a lot of trouble, if you had.'

'Yeah, well I guess that's irrelevant now, Inspector. You've got the files.'

'Any idea why Ron was killed, Mr Flaherty?'

Simon Flaherty crossed his arms and smiled.

'You're not worried about being shot?'

'If I had been a target, Inspector, I doubt very much we'd be having this conversation. Besides, my safety is your responsibility now.'

DI Reid placed a photograph of Glen and Rory Trimmer on the table.

'Do you know either of these two, Mr Flaherty?'

'Can't say I recognise them.'

'Any idea why Mike Steele has been asking their neighbours about them?'

'You'll have to ask Mike about that, if you can find him.'

DI Reid placed a photograph of Susie Morte on the table.

'You do know who this is though, don't you?'

'Yeah, that's Susie, Ron's girlfriend.'

'I don't suppose you happen to know where she is by any chance?'

'No idea, Inspector. She's been ignoring my calls. In fact, Ron was complaining about not being able to contact her when we were having coffee with him the day he got shot. He was worried about her.'

'I interviewed Ron that day. He told me she hadn't come with him because she wasn't feeling well.'

Simon Flaherty shrugged his shoulders.

'These two are her brothers.' DI Reid poked the photograph of the Trimmer boys with his finger and watched Simon's eyes, which told him Simon knew more than he was saying. 'They're Jack Trimmer's kids, all three of them.'

'If that's true, it's no wonder I didn't recognise them. Those boys were little kids the last time I saw them. Jack's been dead for twenty years.'

'What do you know about Jack Trimmer's death?'

Simon Flaherty uncrossed his arms and looked at his finger-nails. 'Got knocked off his motor bike. Hit and run if I remember. You lot never caught the bastard.'

'I think we might know who it was now, Mr Flaherty.'

Simon Flaherty smiled. 'After twenty years. Forgive me if I'm not impressed.'

'Ron Zeitz, but you already knew that, didn't you?'

Simon Flaherty shook his head. 'Someone's been telling you shit.'

'Seems someone told those Trimmer boys that same shit, Mr

Flaherty, which is why Ron is stretched out on a slab in the freezer downstairs.'

Simon Flaherty looked straight at DI Reid.

'You're telling me those kids shot Ron?'

DI Reid smiled. 'I guess you'll be safe for the time being, Mr Flaherty. Can't see you going home anytime soon.'

'We'll be making an application for bail at the committal hearing,' said Simon's lawyer.

'And we'll be opposing your application,' said DI Reid.

Dr Jonas stood next to DI Reid in front of the group of officers crammed into the Incident Room.

'We got two DNA profiles from the biological material Forensics collected from the house where the Trimmer brothers were living. There's no doubt they're brothers. No surprises there.'

DI Reid surveyed the room of expectant faces. He knew they were waiting for something more than that.

'One of those profiles matches the profile we got from Janice George's apartment. When you marry that with the ballistics report on the bullet that killed her, I'd say there's a definite connection between her murder, the shooting at the Merlin and one of the Trimmer boys.'

'Thank you Dr Jonas.' DI Reid waited while the pathologist walked out of the room. 'That pretty well confirms Glen and Rory Trimmer as our primary suspects. We know where they've been and what they've done. We even have a possible motive. What I want to know is where the bloody hell are they?'

Everyone in the room shifted in their seat but no-one offered an answer.

'I want everyone on finding them, except you Wayne. Your

job is to find Mike Steele. Nigel, I want you to focus on car parks near the transport hubs. See if any of them have records of cars that have overstayed their bookings. They must have left their car somewhere. Sergeant, run another check with the airlines.'

'What about asking Border Protection?' said Nina. 'They scan your passport when you leave the country. If we can find out which airport they used it might be easier to find out where they went.'

'Get on to it.'

DI Reid was getting ready to interview Peter Bolt when Nina stepped into his office.

'Excuse me, sir. Border Protection has just got back to me. The Trimmers don't have passports. None of them.'

'So they must still be here somewhere then.'

'Not necessarily.'

DI Reid looked at her. 'What, you think they've done a reverse boat people number and slipped offshore on some leaky boat?'

'Maybe, but what if they got themselves passports in some other name?'

'Don't you have to produce ID to get a passport?'

'One of them is a computer whiz, and think about what we found in their house. He could have knocked up their ID.'

'How the hell would we find out if they'd done that?'

'The guy from Border Protection suggested we send them any photos we have of the Trimmers. They have a database of every photograph used on every passport, and a team of face recognition experts to double check the mismatches their system spits out when people arrive back from their holidays.'

'Well, you'd better send the photos.'

'Done. He said he'd get back to me in the morning.'

'Good work, Sergeant.'

CHAPTER 40

Jack Trimmer was one of those guys that looked great in a uniform, and twenty-year old Rosie Mortimer was hooked on men in uniforms. Their first encounter was in the front bar of the pub, frequented by off duty soldiers waiting to catch a bus back to camp after a weekend in town, where Rosie worked as a barmaid.

In a body hugging tee-shirt that gave full expression to her bodily assets, young Rosie was a bar-room ornament that attracted a high level of military attention. Joe Black, the pub's manager, paid her extra to remove her bra whenever the soldiers were in town. Rosie definitely had the boobs for it, and the soldiers had it for Rosie's boobs. Joe simply counted the profits from the extra beer sales and gave her a bonus.

Earlier in life, Rosie had discovered that it didn't matter how smart she was, it had been her looks and her willingness to drop her knickers that had gotten her places. On the night she'd dropped them for Jack Trimmer, in the tiny room upstairs from the bar she rented from Joe Black, her life took a new path. Rosie realised Jack wasn't like all the others, who only seemed interested in a quick fuck. Jack was into foreplay and pleasuring her, before he spent himself deep inside her. She had invited him back.

It wasn't long after that first night that they had become a couple, and six months after she'd met him, Rosie moved into the army married quarters as Jack's bride.

Rosie soon discovered that soldiers' wives spent a lot of time on their own, while their men were away playing war games or fighting in the real thing. To pass the time while Jack and his mates were away, Rosie indulged in her passion: photography. She enrolled in a class at the local community college, persuaded Jack to buy her a decent 35 mm SLR camera, and set up a small business operation taking photographs of family functions within the army community in which she lived.

When Jack was home, he indulged in his passions, and a little over nine months after their wedding, Rosie was pregnant with Glen. Life changed again for Rosie when she became a mother. At first she was apprehensive about being responsible for another little person but she soon realised she enjoyed motherhood. By the time of Jack's discharge, eight-year old Glen had a six year old brother, Rory, named after Rosie's father, and a baby sister, Susie, named after Jack's mother.

After leaving the army, Jack became part of the security detail surrounding Joe Black, who had moved out of pub management into the more lucrative cocaine business servicing the night-club scene. Rosie had no real understanding of the world Jack moved in. All she knew was that he was earning a lot more money than he had as a soldier, even if he worked odd hours. She had her kids, and with Jack earning more money, she was able to upgrade her camera and record every moment of their lives.

It had been the happiest time of her life, up until shortly after Glen's tenth birthday, when Jack was knocked off his motor bike in a hit and run accident. Jack died at the scene. The police never located the black car reported by witnesses.

At least Jack had listened to his father and signed up for some life insurance, so Rosie was able to pay off the mortgage and keep the house. Then, despite being written off by all of Jack's mates and associates as a blonde bimbo with three snotty nosed kids, Rosie set about establishing herself as a wedding photographer to pay the bills. In the early days, while the children were still young, Rosie's parents looked after them every weekend so that she could establish her business. By the time he was fifteen, Glen was looking after Rory and Susie while their mother worked to support them.

Although she still had her good looks and great figure, Rosie soon discovered that a woman with three young kids was not an attractive proposition to most men, and she was no longer prepared to drop her knickers to make her way in the world. She often thought that was probably a blessing in disguise, as it allowed her to focus on developing her business and looking after her children.

Glen and Rory had been sports mad as kids, and Jack's father had stepped in to foster their sporting interests. He attended every football and cricket game they'd played, until he succumbed to lung cancer in Glen's final year of high school. Susie, on the other hand, had shown no interest in sport. She became her mother's apprentice, and went on to study creative photography at City University.

The Trimmer boys drifted from the straight and narrow path following the death of their grandfather. Glen became part of the drug culture on campus as he tried to sort out his life. Much to his mother's disappointment, he dropped out of university after a few months of disillusioned study, and joined a network of distributors supplying all kinds of exotic tablets to kids with more money than sense.

Shortly before his twentieth birthday, Glen was admitted to hospital, and nearly died from an overdose. After that experience he stopped using, and concentrated on making money out of the weaknesses of others.

Rory learnt from his brother's mistake. He kept away from drugs and graduated with a computing science degree, and a serious addiction to hacking. At first, he'd played with breaking into websites across the globe for fun. Then he discovered that there were ways of making serious money trading data others were eager to own, and manufacturing documents to support the creation of false identities.

Life for the Trimmer boys might have taken a different path if they hadn't bumped into Marty Frost, one of Jack's associates from his Joe Black days, on the night of Rory's twenty-first birthday celebration.

Rosie spotted Marty in the lobby of the hotel as they were leaving the party and, for some reason, felt compelled to say hello. Marty engaged the boys in conversation, remarking that Jack would have been proud of them if he hadn't been murdered. That offhand remark caught Rosie's attention, and she'd asked him what he'd meant by saying Jack had been murdered.

The terminally ill Marty, who was on a mission to atone for his life of sin, told her what he knew about the hit and run accident. He also told Rosie about what had happened to John Cameron, who'd worked for Joe Black alongside Jack, and suggested she approach him for help when he was released from prison. Marty was certain John would help her square accounts with Ron Zeitz, once he knew who had set him up.

Rosie hadn't slept that night. Armed with Marty's information, she'd spent that and many more nights in the following years plotting for the moment she'd exact her revenge.

The opportunity presented itself ten years after the meeting with Marty, when Ron Zeitz purchased one of Susie's photographs, and pursued her for sex. Rosie was prepared, and her daughter was willing to drop her knickers for the cause.

Susie Trimmer, fascinated with romantic notions of death, adopted the persona of Susie Morte when she was at university. Her early works featured gravestones and funerals.

It was during this phase of her life that Susanne Rosemary Trimmer ceased to exist, thanks to the execution of a legal instrument on her twenty-first birthday, and Susie Morte became a legal entity.

When she moved on from her morbid interests and turned her camera onto old men, buildings and seascapes, the output of her creative genius attracted the serious attention of collectors. Susie Morte was very successful in the years immediately after university. By the time Ron Zeitz discovered her work, she was a darling of the local art scene with several international commissions under her belt.

Following her fortuitous encounter with Ron Zeitz, Susie's family ceased all overt contact with her. She moved into one of Rory's apartments on the southern edge of the city, where she lived until she had drawn Ron into their web, using that most enticing of baits only a sensuous young woman could employ on an older man.

While Susie worked on entrenching herself as Ron's woman, her brothers initiated the next phase of their mother's plan. Glen tracked down John Cameron and converted him to their cause. Rory developed a small software application for Susie's laptop; an application designed to listen quietly to Ron's laptop whenever it was on the same wireless network as Susie's. Ron inadvertently helped them by separating his private and business lives, which allowed Susie to continue her own career, and to communicate with her family without Ron's knowledge.

If the Trimmers had a defining character trait, it was patience.

Rosie had waited years to find out what had really happened to Jack. In no hurry, she was determined to inflict maximum damage to Ron and his operation. Rosie's plan allowed Susie the time required to gain Ron's trust and to enjoy the benefits of his willingness to spend his money on her.

Their agreed timeline factored in the time Glen needed to scale up his operation and mount a credible bid to capture a share of Ron Zeitz's market. While Glen expanded his business, Rory employed a small surveillance firm to keep an eye on John Cameron, after Glen had persuaded him to help them.

Once Susie's laptop had joined the wireless network in Ron's house, the Trimmers knew more about Ron's operations than most of his employees, and they possessed the access codes for his bank accounts.

When John Cameron agreed to join them, two years after Susie had opened her thighs for Ron, Rosie activated her end game. It all almost went amiss when John, for his own reasons, murdered the priest. Fortunately, Rory's surveillance team hadn't let him down, and they had been able to use John's decision to kill Fr Skinner to manipulate him into delivering the firebomb, and setting up the meeting with Zietz and Scaletta.

The one thing Rosie had learnt from the mistake Ron Zeitz made, when he killed her Jack, was that the best plan to execute was one that left no witnesses.

CHAPTER 41

CARL READ through the post-mortem report for Sharon Wilson.

Dr Jonas had listed an abnormally high level of salmonella in Sharon's gut, and he'd concluded that the only way that amount of salmonella could have gotten in there was if someone had put it there. He'd described the cause of death as drowning in her own vomit, induced by deliberate salmonella poisoning and aided by a duct tape gag over the victim's mouth.

That observation, coupled with the fact that she had been trussed up like a sacrificial lamb, clearly suggested to Carl that Sharon had been a victim of foul play.

Carl suspected that Scaletta was the likely killer, until he checked the estimated time of death. The report listed it as mid-morning of the same Wednesday that Scaletta had been shot and, according to the record of his phone's movement, Scaletta had not been anywhere near the warehouse they believed Sharon had been held captive in. He looked at the image of Sharon Wilson that Harry had found in Cameron's email, and wondered who had cast the second shadow captured in that image.

Carl went to talk to Harry.

'Harry, do you think your friend at Telstra would be able to tell us what mobile phones were in the vicinity of that warehouse we raided when we were looking for Sharon Wilson?'

'Wouldn't that be like looking for a needle in a haystack?'

'We know where the haystack is, Harry. We have the GPS for the warehouse. Someone had to administer whatever it was that made her vomit, and that someone had to be there sometime that morning. And, how did she get from the warehouse to Lang National Park? If she died in the warehouse, someone had to shift the body. I know it's a long shot but how else are we going to find him?'

'He'll want a court order to do that sort of search.'

'I'll get you one. Ask him if he can do it?'

In the end, it took longer to arrange the court order than to get the account details of any numbers that met their search criteria from Telstra's database.

Carl showed the list of names and addresses to DC Wayne Paterson, who knew more about Scaletta and his associates than anybody else.

Wayne ran his finger down the list of names and stopped it at Gino Rumore. 'That's one of Redmond's boys. He worked with Scaletta when they were Redmond's debt collectors. I thought he was still inside. Got done for bashing a punter a couple of years before we shut down Redmond's operation. Let's see what the system says about him.' Wayne keyed Gino Rumore's details into the database. 'He's been out for six months. Can you believe it? He got early release for good behaviour.'

'Guess we'd better pay him a visit,' said Carl.

'Why don't we see if we can track his phone for the days around that one, Inspector, before we visit him?' said Wayne.

'Good idea, Wayne.'

'While you're doing that, I'll confirm this address we have here. No point in turning up if this is fake.'

Fulfilling their request for the GPS data from Rumore's

phone took a little longer, but the results were a revelation when Harry plotted the locations onto his wall map of colored pins.

'Good call, Wayne,' said Harry, as he and Carl stood back and studied the trail of Rumore's phone. 'Looks like he was with Scaletta when they picked up Sharon, and he visited the warehouse a couple of times the next day, before visiting Lang National Park, right where Sharon was found.'

'Time for that visit,' said Carl.

'Think I'd better come with you, Inspector, and we'd better take some muscle with us. He's not going to be happy to see us, and the last time I arrested him we had to disarm him.'

It was early evening when Carl, Harry and Wayne arrived with their armed back up at the address Wayne had verified. The kids playing in the street all stopped and stared when three police vehicles turned into their street, and parked in front of number fifteen. They watched in excited silence as four armed officers in body armour walked up the driveway of number fifteen, with a large German Shepherd on a leash. Two of the officers and the dog went past the white van parked in the carport and around to the back of the house. The other two officers approached the front of the house and banged loudly on the door.

'Police! Open up!'

The front door of the house was opened by a tall man who had obviously spent a lot of time working out.

'Gino Rumore?' said the officer on the doorstep.

'Yeah. What do you want?'

'Step outside and put your hands on the wall.'

Gino did as he was told and allowed the officer to search him.

'He's clean.'

'Now what?' said Gino.

'Now we're going for a ride downtown, Gino,' said Carl, as he and Wayne joined the group at the front door. 'We have a few questions for you.'

'Fuck! I should have known it would be you.'

'Nice to see you too, Gino,' said Wayne.

'Who's your mate?'

'Detective Inspector West,' said Carl, showing him his badge.

'Why can't you ask your questions here?' said Gino. 'I got nothing to hide.'

'Formal interview, Gino. We have to record it. Remember?' said Wayne.

'Anybody else living here, Mr Rumore?' said Carl.

'My mother.'

'Is she home?'

'Nah, she's still at work.'

'Got your phone with you, Gino?' said Carl.

Gino pulled an iPhone out of his pocket.

'What about your house key?'

'On the kitchen table.'

Wayne went inside the house and returned with a bunch of keys. 'This them?'

'Yeah.'

'That your van under the carport?' said Carl.

'Yeah.'

'Which key?' said Wayne.

'The black one.'

'We have a search warrant, Mr Rumore,' said Carl, showing him the warrant.

'What are you trying to pin on me this time?'

Carl turned to the officer holding Gino. 'Take him in.'

As the armed officers led Gino away, Carl called Operations and asked them to get a crime scene crew out to search the house and examine the van.

'How long have you had your phone, Mr Rumore?' said Carl, as soon as Harry had completed the preliminaries in interview room three.

'About six months.'

'They're pretty handy, aren't they? Take it with you everywhere you go?'

'Yeah.'

Carl placed a print of the image of Sharon Wilson that Harry had found on Cameron's laptop on the table in front of Gino Rumore. 'Recognise this woman?'

Gino looked at the photograph and shook his head. 'Why would I know an ugly tart like that?'

'Paolo Scaletta had this woman's phone in his pocket the night he was shot, with this photo on it. Sure you don't know her?'

'I'm not responsible for Scaletta's poor taste in women. He'd fuck anything. I like my women to be pretty, not ugly tarts like that.'

Carl touched Harry's foot with his under the table and sat back to watch the suspect's face.

'Do anything with Scaletta since you got out, before he got himself shot?' said Harry.

'I'd seen him a few times. Just catching up for a drink and something to eat.'

'What were you doing the night Scaletta was shot?'

'You think I killed Scaletta? You've got to be joking. He was my mate, why would I want to shoot him?'

'Where were you that night?'

'Home, with Mum.'

'What time did you get home?'

'Around seven. She doesn't like me being late for dinner.'

Carl noticed the slight sneer.

'What were you doing before you got home?'

Carl watched as Gino's eyes looked up towards the ceiling and he placed his hand over his mouth.

'That was one of the days I caught up with Scaletta for lunch.'

'Where?'

'We went to that pizza place on the river, San Bernadino's.'

'What did you do the day before that, the Tuesday?'

'Spent that day home watching TV.'

'Sure you didn't visit a warehouse in Northfield?'

Gino stared at Harry without breaking eye contact.

'Why would I want to go there?'

'What about Black Truck Couriers office?'

'I don't even know where that is.'

Carl nudged Harry with his elbow and placed his smartphone on the table.

'Mr Rumore, do you know that these phones send out a signal to tell your mobile phone network where they are?'

'Do they?'

'They're a bit like a tracking device that can tell us where they've been taken.'

Carl watched as Gino's eyes widened, and he looked from him to Harry and back again. Then Carl touched the photograph on the table. 'This is Sharon Wilson. She was abducted from outside Black Truck Couriers and taken to a warehouse in Northfield the day before Scaletta was murdered. Scaletta sent this photo of her to her boyfriend, John Cameron, who was also shot at the Merlin. Funny thing, though Mr Rumore, is that her body was found in Lang National Park, which is a bit puzzling, since we believe Scaletta was using her as a hostage to get Cameron to meet with him and Zeitz.'

Gino Rumore crossed his arms on his chest. Carl pulled a

photograph of Harry's GPS map out of his folder and placed it on the table.

'This is a map showing where certain mobile phones were on the day Scaletta was shot, and for the days before and after that day. Those green dots show us where Scaletta's phone was. The blue dots are Sharon's phone, and the pink dots, Mr Rumore, are your phone.'

Carl traced the line made by the pink dots and lingered over its intersection points with the green and blue dots. 'This trail here takes your phone from the warehouse in Northfield to Lang National Park. Want to tell me about that?'

'I want a lawyer.'

CHAPTER 42

DC Wayne Paterson parked their dirty silver Ford behind a red Mazda, five houses down the street from Mike Steele's house. DC Nigel Beard, sitting in the shotgun seat, moved the switch for the interior light into the off position, and adjusted his night-vision binoculars to get a clear view of the driveway. The officers in the red Mazda pulled out and drove off down the street.

Mike Steele had been smart enough to turn off his smart-phone so they couldn't locate him using its GPS signal, but he hadn't counted on them hacking into his young wife's email account. Mike Steele might have known how to hide, but it seemed he couldn't bear to be apart from his wife for longer than a week.

They knew Mike's wife was in the house. They knew she was going to him. They just didn't know where he was or when she was going. For the second night in a row, they waited.

Three hours later, at one in the morning, Wayne abruptly stopped snoring, when Nigel poked him in the ribs and brought him back into the present. 'She's leaving.'

Wayne rubbed his eyes and farted. He pulled himself up into the seat and waited. They watched as Mike's wife backed her black BMW into the street and accelerated away from the house.

Wayne started the engine and followed her at a distance. He waited until she had turned out of the street onto Cross Road before turning on the Ford's headlights.

Nigel opened the window to refresh the car's interior air supply, and alerted Operations. Ten minutes later he was speaking to the observer in the police helicopter idling quietly overhead.

'Black Beamer travelling east on Cross Road, just gone through the intersection with Fullarton.'

'Give me an illumination.'

Nigel switched on the car's GPS positioning beacon.

'She's about a hundred metres in front of us.'

'Got her.'

'You can back off, Wayne. They're locked onto her.'

Wayne allowed the BMW to draw away from them. 'Will you put that bloody window up? You're freezing my balls off.'

Nigel hit the button to close the window. 'What the fuck have you been eating?'

'Target vehicle is turning onto the freeway,' said the voice on the radio.

'Back up units are mobile,' said the voice from Operations.

They continued up the freeway, keeping their distance from the car they were following, and waited for the next update.

'Target is turning left on Piccadilly.'

When they reached Piccadilly Road, Wayne turned left. There was no sign of her tail lights.

'Slowing. Target is taking a right at Wiley.'

Wayne slowed as they approached Wiley Street.

'Stopping. Target is entering driveway, first on the left after the bend. On station.'

Wayne switched off the Ford's headlights and turned onto Wiley. He parked twenty metres back from the driveway.

'Driver has entered house. Thermal is showing two spots. I repeat, two spots only.'

Nigel checked out the area with his night-vision binoculars. 'There's the Beamer.'

'Be there in five,' said a voice on the radio, that sent Nigel into heaven.

'Keep your mind on the job, lover boy,' said Wayne. 'This guy's probably armed and I don't want Lily shooting you by mistake.'

Two police vehicles without headlights pulled up behind their Ford. PC Lily Chan, wearing a helmet and body armour, and carrying enough weapons to make her lethal, tapped on Nigel's window.

'Which house?'

Nigel slid out of the car and pointed. 'That one.'

PC Chan and one of her colleagues disappeared around the back of the house, while two others approached the front door and knocked. The police helicopter hovered in stealth mode high above the backyard of the house.

'Open up. Police!'

They waited three seconds, then kicked the door in and rushed into the house with weapons drawn.

The spotlight from the helicopter illuminated the rear of the house.

'Drop the gun! Put your hands in the air!'

Nigel had never heard Lily shout before. A shot rang out. Nigel nearly shit himself.

'I said put the gun down!'

'You shot me, bitch!'

'I'll blow your fucking head off if you don't drop that gun!' said a very loud male voice.

A couple of minutes later, PC Lily Chan came through the front door of the house. 'I need an ambulance,' she said into the radio attached to her vest. 'We have a male with a gunshot wound to the shoulder. He's lost a lot of blood.' She stopped and listened to the crackled voice from Operations. 'There's nowhere for them to put down. You'll need to send an ambulance.'

Lily walked towards Nigel and Wayne. 'Dickhead pointed a gun at me.'

Nigel had never felt more relieved in his life.

Lily took off her helmet and smiled. 'You should have seen his face when he came out the back door and the spotlight came on. He sure wasn't expecting to see me and Rick.'

Wayne went inside to complete the formalities of the arrest.

Nigel stayed with Lily to wait for the ambulance to arrive, and to assure the neighbours that everything was under control.

The police helicopter thudded off into the night on its way back to the city.

CHAPTER 43

Nina's contact at Border Protection called her shortly after DI Reid had dismissed the team from their morning briefing in the Incident Room. As she was speaking to Border Protection, Nina received an email with four attachments.

When she opened the attachments, she smiled, thinking to herself that the Trimmers weren't quite as smart as they thought they were. She thanked her Border Protection contact and then called DI Reid.

'I have copies of their passports. All four of them.'

'How did they do it?'

'Changed their last name to Shearwater and had them sent to a Post Office for collection.'

'So, the whiz kid managed to fool them with fake IDs. Must be pretty good.'

'Yeah, but he didn't know we'd get hold of his photograph or that Nigel was adding shots of his sister to his portfolio,' said Nina.

'Did you find out if they've left the country?'

'Flew out the day after the shootings at the Merlin. Took the ten-twenty pm flight to Dubai and then on to London.'

'Start the paperwork to brief the Public Prosecutor so he can send their details to Scotland Yard and Interpol. He'll need to start on the extradition orders, and the Feds will want in on the passport fraud. Better give them a heads-up. Let's hope they're still in the UK.'

Nina called the Australian Federal Police liaison officer and then spent the morning putting the paperwork together for DI Reid to take to the Public Prosecutor's office.

By the time Nina arrived for work the next morning, Scotland Yard and Interpol had been briefed.

Rory Trimmer put down the copy of The Guardian that had been delivered with their breakfast. 'Not much coverage of news from Australia.'

'Let's hope it stays that way,' said Glen, closing his suitcase.

Rory looked out at the grey clouds gathering in the sky. 'They call this summer. Haven't they heard that summer's supposed to have sunshine?'

'What would be the point of travelling if it was all like home?'

'Where's Mum?' said Rory.

'They went for a walk. Susie wanted to take some photos of the hotel before we leave for France.'

'What time do we have to leave to catch the train?'

'Around ten,' said Glen, looking at his watch. 'You got your bag ready?'

Rory pointed at his suitcase by the door. 'Who ever thought we'd be going through the Chunnel?'

'Who ever thought we'd be all expenses paid tourists?'

'And all thanks to dear old Uncle Ron,' said Rory.

They laughed.

'Ah, the life of the idle rich. At least we're in the right country for it. Too bad we can't just stay here.'

'I agree with Mum. I think it's best we keep moving for now. Besides, there's a lot of world out there to see.'

The door to their hotel room opened and Susie and Rosie walked in, dragging their cases behind them.

'You boys ready? We need to get going,' said Rosie.

They made their way downstairs, paid their account, and left the Great Northern Hotel. Then they crossed the road and entered St Pancras International Station, without pausing to appreciate the beauty of the red brick facade of the building. At the check-in point for the international platforms, they inserted their tickets, waited while their passports were scanned by the young woman in the Eurostar uniform, and then made their way to the French passport control point.

Glen handed their passports to the bored looking official and waited while he keyed their numbers into his computer. After he'd keyed the first number, the official looked up and closely compared Glen's face with his passport photograph, before keying in the remaining passport numbers. Glen watched as the official scanned through several screens on his computer.

'I am sorry, sir, but your party cannot board this train.'

'Why's that?' said Glen. 'We've got tickets.'

'Your passports are not valid.'

'What? The bloody things are brand new.'

The young man shrugged his shoulders.

'What's wrong with them?'

'All of these passports have been cancelled by your government. You need to contact your embassy. I am sorry, but I cannot let you through.'

'Can we have our passports back to take to the embassy?' said Glen.

The official stood and looked over Glen's shoulder, but did not make any attempt to hand over their passports. 'It would appear that the British wish to speak to you, sir.'

The Trimmers turned and watched as four Border Force officers make their way up the queue of passengers waiting to pass
through the passport control point.

Glen looked at Rory, who simply shrugged his shoulders.

'What's going on, Glen?' said Rosie.

'He says there is something wrong with our passports.'

The French official handed their passports to the senior
Border Force officer.

'Mr Shearwater?' said the senior Border Force officer.

'Yes,' said Glen.

'You and your party need to come with us.'

'What's going on?' said Glen. 'Why won't he let us on the
train?'

'There's a problem with your passports, sir.'

'I don't understand. They were only issued a couple of
months before we left Australia.'

'That's what we need to sort out, Mr Shearwater. Now, this
way please.'

They grabbed the handles of their suitcases and walked back
down the line of bemused passengers, with their Border Force
escort, to the Eurostar check-in point, where the attendant
opened the exit gate.

'This way, please.'

The Border Force officers shepherded them through a
doorway and into a small room off the main concourse.

'Wait here.'

They sat on the plastic chairs surrounding their suitcases,
acting as if nothing was wrong and it was all a big misunderstanding.

After fifteen minutes, a man dressed in a navy blue suit,
white shirt and light blue tie came into the room.

'I'm Inspector Dawson, from the Metropolitan Police. I've
been asked to detain you by the Australian Federal Police.'

'Why?' said Rosie. 'We haven't done anything.'

'According to my information, madam, you're travelling on fraudulent passports.'

'There must be some misunderstanding,' said Rosie. 'There's nothing wrong with our passports.'

'In that case, madam, it shouldn't take too long to sort it out.' He turned to the male members of the group.

'I have been asked to detain you two for extradition on the suspicion of murder.'

Rory stared at the inspector. 'Murder? You're joking, aren't you?'

'I don't joke about murder, Mr Trimmer.'

'Trimmer? My name is Shearwater. You've mistaken us for somebody else.'

'I'm afraid the game's over, Mr Trimmer. They're on to you back in Australia. This way, please.' Inspector Dawson opened the door and indicated for them to go out into the corridor. 'You can leave your bags here. My people will take care of them.'

They were handcuffed and led out into the street, where they were bundled into waiting police cars and taken to Islington Police Station. From there they were remanded in custody to await their extradition to Australia.

CHAPTER 44

FR MAURICE SKINNER's reformation didn't come until he was well and truly entrenched in the ministry of chaplain to prisoners, which he lived as his vocation for thirty-five years. In a way, Maurice Skinner served a life sentence for his crimes. Bishop Walsh may have been understanding of his weaknesses as a man at the time of his failing but, motivated by his desire to protect the good name of the Church, he had done all he could to keep Maurice away from small boys. Bishop Walsh had not, however, been forgiving. Maurice had entered his ministry in the prisons as an ostracised servant of God. He had not been invited to fraternal gatherings of his fellow priests, and had been assigned to living quarters in a decommissioned parish, away from public view.

It had taken Maurice a long time to redeem himself in his own eyes, let alone in those of his superior. Fortunately for Maurice, by the time he'd made peace with God and realised that he had found his calling, Bishop Walsh had been killed in a car accident and his friend Michael Knight was the bishop. Michael had agreed to allow him to serve out his time as prison chaplain, where Maurice felt he belonged.

Unfortunately, John Cameron wasn't the only altar boy that

had felt the cold hands of Fr Skinner on his innocent body. In his wake, the young Fr Skinner had left a small tribe of troubled young boys, who were now men in their fifties.

As they'd matured, most of the boys had managed to brush off their encounter with Fr Skinner as nothing more than an unpleasant or confusing experience. They were the lucky ones. They were the ones who had only experienced a fleeting skirmish with the unholy young priest.

There was one other, however, like John Cameron, who had been one of the young priest's sexual playthings, and who had struggled to come to terms with his demons for the rest of his life. Unlike John, he hadn't told anyone, and he hadn't turned to substance and people abuse. He had followed in his tormentor's footsteps and taken the same vow of celibacy that the young Maurice Skinner had failed to keep, in the hope that a life of service to God would atone for his sins, and somehow make him clean.

However, Damien Harris finally came to understand that his lifetime of service had not healed his pain or removed his feelings of shame. It didn't matter how many prayers he said, Masses he offered, or people he helped; he still felt defiled and unworthy. It had almost cost him his sanity. It had certainly cost him any hope of realising his dream of becoming bishop, as nobody wanted a spiritual leader with the mental health issues he endured.

In a way, Damien had been lucky that the role of administrator of Gladesview House had become vacant when it did. It had coincided with his recovery from the debilitating depression that hit him following the death of his parents, when their house burnt down. The role had given him somewhere to hide and, when he realised Maurice Skinner was planning to move into Gladesview House on his retirement, it had presented him with a solution to his problem.

Once he'd decided to punish his tormentor in a premeditated

act of revenge, the voices in his head, which had tormented him for years for being such a coward, fell silent. He'd tried forgiveness and known no peace. He'd turned the other cheek for fortyfive years. It was only when he'd decided it was time to strike that he'd finally found the peace he had spent his life searching for.

Armed with the knowledge of Maurice Skinner's close friendship with Bishop Knight, he'd chosen a different course of action than John Cameron for delivering his intended punishment. In Damien's mind, killing Fr Skinner would not have hurt him anywhere near enough. His aim had been to deny him the only pleasure he had to look forward to in retirement. He'd wanted the bastard to suffer a sense of loss like he had. But, thanks to John Cameron, things had not worked out as he had planned.

Now he was filled with remorse. He'd killed three people and burnt down Gladesview House, for nothing and, to make matters worse, it looked like it would only be a matter of time before the police had worked out he'd done it.

Fr Harris sat in his car looking at the five metre length of 60 mm plastic tubing and the screw operated steel clamp on the back seat. He'd told the assistant in the hardware store that he needed to clean out his rainwater tank. He smiled. He didn't even have a rainwater tank.

He'd driven to his favourite boyhood spot, a secluded glade of trees in the valley below what had been his parents' orchard. He'd often returned to this spot to think and sort things out, and thought it wouldn't be such a bad place to die. So many happy memories from his boyhood were connected with the trees growing alongside the creek that he had played in, before his parents had sent him to boarding school.

He got out of the car and walked over to the edge of the creek and listened to the water that gurgled through the trees. He sat on the large rock by the creek and watched the water slowly making its way over the stones before disappearing into the shadows. He sat there for a long time, contemplating the water and thinking about the disaster that was his life, and how easy it would be to disappear into the shadows.

But those shadows troubled him. He'd read Dante's *Inferno*. He studied theology. He'd preached hell and damnation.

He knew the pain of his suffering would cease with the ending of his life but he was worried about the pain of suffering for eternity in the fires of hell, or within the frozen lake as Dante had described it. He knew he could ask for forgiveness for what he had done, after all, he hadn't intended to kill anyone apart from Bishop Knight, but he was not so sure God would forgive him for taking his own life, especially since he had not confessed his sins.

He knew there was no point in asking God for help. Damien thought he already knew what God would say, and it wouldn't involve using the plastic tubing in the car. The feel of a wet splash on his leg, followed by several more, roused him from his thoughts.

He made it back to the car just as a thunder clap roared across the hills and the heavens opened to release a deluge upon the valley. Maybe God had answered him after all. He knew if he stayed where he was it wouldn't be long before he wouldn't be able to drive out of his secluded hiding place.

Damien started the engine and drove to St Clare's Retreat House, where he had told the bishop he was going to spend a few days to get over the shock of the deaths in the fire, and hoped he'd made the right decision.

CHAPTER 45

WHEN FR HARRIS didn't turn up for the monthly meeting of the St Vincent de Paul Society, Charlie Head was worried. The last time that Charlie could remember that Fr Harris had unexpectedly not turned up for an event or left a message with someone about not coming, had heralded the onset of a bout of severe depression, which had led to him being transferred from parish duties. Charlie decided to call in on Fr Harris on his way home.

Charlie hoped it was something else, even though he'd half expected Fr Harris to lose it after the fire at Gladesview House. He'd seen his friend suffer up close when the black dog had last visited, and it had not been pleasant feeling totally powerless to help him. At least he knew Fr Harris had access to a good psychiatrist.

The doorbell made its ding-dong sound inside the priest's house but there was no other sound, and no-one came to open the door. Charlie called Fr Harris' number again, and found himself listening to the priest's voice mail message for the second time that night. He left a message and went home, resolving to follow up with Monica Carey, Fr Harris' housekeeper, if he didn't hear from him.

Charlie was getting ready for work the following morning when Monica Carey rang.

'Charlie, Fr Harris didn't turn up for Mass this morning.'

'It's not like him to sleep in.'

'His bed's not been slept in, Charlie. I can't find him. He's not answering his phone either, and his car's gone.'

'Ring the bishop's office, Monica. They might know where he is. Give me a call back if they don't.'

When he arrived at work, Charlie noticed there was a text message from Monica Carey on his smartphone, asking him to call. He rang her number, hoping she'd have good news.

'Charlie, the bishop's office says he's gone on retreat at St Clare's. They're not sure when he'll be back,' said Monica.

'Perhaps the shock of the fire has finally caught up with him, Monica.'

'That may be so, Charlie, but I'm still worried. It's not like him to go off and not tell me. You know what happened last time.'

'Well, let's hope he's made the right choice.' Charlie ended the call and wondered why Fr Harris hadn't let him know he was taking time out, especially since they still hadn't closed the case.

Charlie went to find Inspector West and tell him they probably wouldn't be able to speak to Fr Harris for a week or more.

'A retreat, Charlie. Surely he would have told someone?'

'Sounds like he told the bishop's office, but to be honest, Inspector, I'm surprised he didn't tell anybody else. I thought he'd at least tell me. He didn't even tell his housekeeper.'

Carl wondered whether Fr Harris was doing a runner. 'Do you think he could have done it, Charlie, you know, torched the place?'

Charlie scratched his head. 'I've been wondering the same thing, Inspector.'

'What's got you thinking that, Charlie?'

'He had a key to the back door and the key to the shed was kept in his office. No doubt he would have known where the gardeners kept their equipment, and he doesn't have an alibi. I just can't believe he'd do such a thing. I mean, he's such a nice guy. Why would he do something like that?'

'I'm having some trouble there too, Charlie, but as you said, things are stacking up to make him look like the logical suspect. I can understand why someone like Cameron would kill Fr Skinner, but why would Fr Harris set fire to Gladesview House? It's not like he'd have anything to gain from the insurance money.'

'Maybe he's got more mental health issues than depression, Inspector. All I know is he was different after the breakdown he had when his parents died, and it took him months to recover.'

'See if you can confirm that he's actually at that retreat house. If he's not there, we'd better get an all points out on him. I think we need to speak to him before he does anything silly.'

'You might want to take DS Fuller or one of the others, Inspector. I'm not sure I'm the right person if we're going to arrest him.'

Carl noticed the slump in Charlie's shoulders. 'You okay, Charlie?'

'Damien's been my friend for years, Inspector.' Charlie pressed his fingers into the corners of his eyes.

'Come on, Charlie, let's go for a coffee.'

DC Templar called St Clare's Retreat House to confirm whether Fr Harris was in residence or not, and spoke with a woman who introduced herself as Sister Anne.

'Hello, Sister. Detective Constable Templar from City Police. I'm wondering if you can confirm for me whether Fr Harris from Gladesview House has arrived at St Clare's?'

'I'm sorry, but we don't usually give out that sort of information.'

'I appreciate that, Sister, but I need your help. I'm part of the team investigating the fire at Gladesview House and I need to locate Fr Harris. The bishop's office has advised us that he's taken leave and gone to St Clare's. I just need to confirm that he has arrived, so that we know where he is if we need to contact him again. It's important, Sister, otherwise I wouldn't be asking.'

There was a brief pause. DC Templar could hear Sister Anne talking to someone her end, explaining her request and asking if would be alright to tell the police that Fr Harris had arrived.

'Fr Harris arrived yesterday afternoon, Constable,' said Sister Anne. 'I can take a message if you like.'

'No need to disturb him, Sister, but I would appreciate if you'd ask him to call me before he leaves.'

'He's booked in for a seven-day retreat, so I wouldn't expect a call from him until the end of the week.'

'Thank you for your help, Sister.'

DC Templar reported to DI West that Fr Harris was at the retreat house, and that he was booked in for seven days.

'Thanks Lisa. Where's Jane?'

'She's with DS Fuller, they're still working with DI Reid.'

DC Templar waited while DI West rang DS Fuller and asked him to send Jane to his office.

PC Priest walked into DI West's office five minutes after he'd spoken to DS Fuller.

'You wanted to see me, Inspector?'

'Yes, Jane. I'd like you to come with us for a drive. We need to arrest a priest.'

HOLY DEATH

Carl let DCI Rankin have the pleasure of informing Bishop Kerry that they had arrested Fr Harris on suspicion of being the Gladesview House arsonist. The bishop had promptly arranged for Robert Klein, from Ratten and Brown, to represent Fr Harris. The lawyer, dressed in a dark suit with matching tie, sat beside Fr Harris in interview room three, opposite Carl and Lisa.

Lisa switched on the recording equipment and stepped them through the required introductions to start the interview.

'Father, do you want to tell me about the tubing we found in your car?' said Carl.

Fr Harris looked up from the spot on the floor that had been holding his attention. 'Tubing? What tubing?'

Carl extracted a photograph of the plastic tubing on the back seat of Fr Harris' car from his folder, and placed it on the table in front of the priest.

'This was taken inside your car, Father, and according to Forensics that tubing is brand new. It's never been used. What were you planning to do with it?'

Fr Harris looked at Carl and then at his lawyer.

'You don't have to answer any of their questions, Father.'

Carl thought the priest was going to cry but he waited for him to say something, anything.

'I was going to kill myself. You know, gas myself in the car.'

The lawyer sent by the bishop put his hand over his eyes and took a deep breath.

Carl waited but the priest said nothing else.

'Why would you want to do that, Father?'

'You don't have to answer that, Father,' said the lawyer.

Father Harris faced his lawyer. 'That's where you're wrong. I have to answer for all of it, whether I tell these people or not.

283

There's no escaping accountability with God. All I can hope for is that he will be merciful.'

The lawyer crossed his arms.

Fr Harris turned back to Carl. 'It's a long story, Inspector.'

'We've got all day, Father. Why don't you start at the beginning?'

The priest leant back into his chair. 'Remember when you asked me about John Cameron and Fr Skinner?'

'Yes. You told me nothing had happened.'

'I didn't exactly tell you the truth.'

'Oh, and what is the truth, Father?'

'It happened. He abused us. Me and John.' Fr Harris shrugged his shoulders. 'At the time, I thought it was all a big game. I enjoyed all the attention he gave me.' He looked at Carl. 'Do you have any idea what it's like to be ignored by your parents? They were too bloody busy with their precious orchard to pay any attention to me and my sister.'

Carl noted the red flush in Fr Harris' cheeks.

It took the priest a few moments to refocus.

'And, there was Fr Skinner. We were the centre of his attention. We'd do things with him and he'd give us treats, you know, lollies and things that our parents never bought us. Then John went and spoilt it all by blabbing to his mother.' He shook his head as if he couldn't believe someone would do that. 'I was really angry with John when he told me, and Fr Skinner left the parish and didn't come back. When my father asked me about what Fr Skinner had been doing to us, I told him nothing had happened. I told him John had made it all up. Can you believe that? The bastard was having us do blow jobs on him and playing with us in the bath, and I told my Dad nothing had happened.'

'How old were you?' said Carl.

'Seven or eight when it started.'

'I suppose you weren't old enough to really understand what you were doing was wrong.'

'You may be right, Inspector, because it wasn't until years later, when I was in high school, that I realised what we'd been doing with him wasn't right. By then, I was too ashamed to do anything about it, and I was too scared to admit it to my Dad, so I tried to forget about it.' He paused and fingered the cross sewn into the collar of his shirt. 'I thought that if I gave my life to God I could atone for my sins.'

'Is that why you became a priest?' said Carl

'Basically. I couldn't see any other way to do it.'

'From what Charlie Head tells me, you were a pretty good priest. What happened?'

'I suppose he's also told you I had a breakdown about ten years ago?'

'He did mention it.'

'That was when my parents were killed. Their house burnt down in the middle of the night. By the time the fire truck arrived it was too late. I didn't like my father much, Inspector. He was a hard man. I don't know how my mother put up with him, but she stayed with him. Not like these days, when people want to get divorced at the first sign of a disagreement. Anyway, no-one deserves to die like that, barbecued in their own bed. It was horrible.'

Carl couldn't help but notice the irony in that statement.

'My sister sold the farm after that. I couldn't bear to go back there after the funeral, and she didn't want it. That was one of the hardest things I ever did, presiding over the burial of my parents. I thought God was punishing me for what I had done.' Fr Harris stopped talking and looked down at his hands, crossed in his lap. 'I don't remember much about what happened after that. I remember being in a hospital. They said I was clinically depressed, but I got over it.'

'You didn't mention your abuse to the doctor treating you?'

'There are some things that are nobody else's business.'

Carl wished he'd seen it otherwise, but it was too late now.

'How did you end up as the administrator of Gladesview House?'

'The bishop sent me to Gladesview to recover when I came out of the hospital. I liked it there. It was really peaceful. The administrator died while I was there, so I asked the bishop if I could have the job. He said I could have it as long as I took on the role of chaplain for St Vinnies, but he wouldn't let me live there. Said it would turn me into an old man before my time. That's when I got that busybody housekeeper, Mrs Carey. The bishop insisted that I let her look after me.'

'I guess he was worried about you.'

'More likely he wanted her to keep an eye on me.'

Carl paused to let the priest's anger subside.

'Tell me about the fire at Gladesview.'

Fr Harris' lawyer took out his notebook and pen.

'We'll give you a copy of the tape, Mr Klein,' said Carl.

'Just need to write down a few thoughts, Inspector,' said the lawyer.

'The fire, Father?' said Carl, after the priest hadn't said anything.

'The voices came back.'

'What voices?'

'They kept telling me the only way to really find peace was to get even with Fr Skinner.' Fr Harris looked up. 'I really tried to resist them. I just couldn't get them to shut up. They kept at me night after night. I could hardly get any sleep some nights. Then one night the solution just popped into my head. That was the night I saw the testimonial to Fr Skinner on the TV. They were portraying him as a saint, as a man who had devoted his life to serving prisoners and helping them get back on their feet. I wanted to throw up. The man's whole life was a lie. That was when I realised I really hated the man.'

'So why didn't you just expose him?'

'I didn't want people's sympathy. I didn't want to shame him. I wanted to hurt him like he had hurt me. He'd taken my innocence and destroyed any chance I'd had of a peaceful life. I decided the best way to get my revenge was to take away the joy of his retirement. He was so looking forward to spending his last days at Gladesview with his friend, Bishop Knight.'

'Is that why you set Gladesview House on fire, to kill Bishop Knight?'

'I wanted to destroy everything he was looking forward to enjoying. The house, the companionship of his friend, the tranquil setting of the gardens. That way he'd suffer the pain of loss, like I had.'

'Want to tell us how you set the fire?'

'That bit was easy. I knew Bishop Knight would be out to it once he'd taken his sleeping pills. All I needed was a can of petrol. I didn't even have to buy one. There was one in the shed used by the gardeners, and I had the key to the shed in my office. I simply let myself into the house by the back door and poured the petrol over the floor by the bishop's room and dropped a match into it. The mistake I made was leaving the can inside the house. I thought any evidence would be destroyed by the fire. I'd seen what a house fire could do.'

'The mistake, Father, was locking the shed and putting the key back. That's what told me it had to be an inside job. Anybody else would have had to break into the shed or bring his own petrol with him. Guess you were unlucky the can was an antique.'

'We're all wiser in hindsight, Inspector. I thought I'd covered my tracks at the time.'

'So why did you want to kill yourself?'

'It didn't go the way I wanted it to, did it? I ended up killing three people, and for what? Bloody John Cameron spoilt it for me all over again. Can you believe it? The bastard killed Fr Skinner the very night I set fire to Gladesview.' Fr Harris dropped his gaze to the photograph on the table. 'If I'd waited another night none of this would have happened.'

'So what stopped you, Father? Why didn't you kill yourself?'

Fr Harris looked up and smiled. 'I don't know whether you believe in God or not, Inspector, but I realised God would forgive me if I confessed and took my punishment. He probably wouldn't if I simply killed myself. I guess I'm a coward, Inspector. I don't want to spend eternity burning in hell.'

'I hope you've made the right choice, Father.' Carl looked at the clock on the wall above Fr Harris' head. 'Interview terminated at three sixteen pm.'

Carl waited for Lisa to shut down the recording equipment.

'Father, we'll have a transcript of your confession typed up for you to sign.'

'Thank you, Inspector.'

Carl turned to the lawyer. 'I'll let you know when we have a time for the committal hearing, Mr Klein.'

CHAPTER 46

SOLVING the riddle of the Merlin Massacre and destroying the Zeitz drug operation turned DI Reid into a front page media sensation, at the expense of his superiors. The arrest of the Trimmers in London and their subsequent extradition to Australia was news fodder for weeks.

During her trial, Susie Morte briefly enjoyed heroine status for having seduced Ron Zeitz to get access to his bank accounts. When the media finally grasped the meaning of what she and her brothers were doing at the instigation of their mother, she was vilified as a scheming slut.

When the details of the Zeitz operation came out at the trial of Simon Flaherty and his associates, especially the bit about how the operation had gone undetected for more than twenty years, there was wild speculation in the media about who must have been on the take. Even the Commissioner got mentioned as being asleep at the wheel or corrupt, or both. There were calls for a commission of inquiry into police incompetence and corruption.

The Leader of the Opposition in State Parliament was repeatedly featured calling for the resignation of the Police Minister and the sacking of the Police Commissioner. No-one in Government took him or any of the others calling for something to be done seriously, and it all died down as the trials dragged on for months.

Although the media was all over the Gladesview House arson trial, their interest was in the tortured life of Fr Harris and the embarrassment of the Catholic Church over its failure to properly address Fr Skinner's transgressions. There were several calls for Bishop Kerry to be charged, despite the failure being on the part of his predecessor, but there was no interest in the policing that had cracked the case.

Six months after his arrest, Fr Harris faced the Court for sentencing. Although he'd pleaded guilty and his lawyer had argued for diminished responsibility in light of his mental state due to his abuse, the judge applied the full force of the law. He was sentenced to twenty-five years, with a non-parole period of eighteen years. His lawyer launched an immediate appeal on the severity of the sentence, and everyone else lost interest.

Carl was happy to escape the media spotlight, and SC Head was more than happy to return to community policing. PC Priest finally gave in to the pressure and enrolled in the detective course, with a recommendation from DI West.

With the closing of the case, Carl decided it was time for a celebration. But instead of the usual pub gathering, Carl thought they needed a night at Massimo's.

Massimo's, located on the opulent ground floor of the International Hotel in the centre of the city, was Carl and Nina's favourite restaurant. The restaurant belonged to one of Carl's boyhood friends, Massimo Ranieri, known to everyone as Max.

The last time Carl had organised a group gathering at Massimo's it had been to celebrate his marriage to Nina.

When Carl and Nina entered the restaurant, Harry and

Jessika were seated at the table talking to Lisa and her husband, and Charlie and his wife were chatting with Jane.

Max rushed over to greet Carl and Nina, and the others watched in amusement as Carl's boyhood friend kissed Nina on both cheeks and made a big fuss of pulling out her chair for her. Usually, after making a fuss over Nina, Max would then pour her a glass of champagne, but tonight he poured her a glass of sparkling mineral water. Then he poured one for Carl, before pouring everyone else a champagne.

'You on the wagon, Boss?' said Harry.

'We have an announcement,' said Carl.

That got everyone's attention. Carl turned to Nina.

'We're pregnant,' said Nina.

The party erupted into a round of congratulations and baby related questions.

Carl sat back and wondered whether he really was ready for the responsibility of parenthood, and wished he'd never agreed to support Nina by not drinking alcohol during her pregnancy.

It was going to be a long nine months.

If you enjoyed ***Holy Death,*** you can help other readers share your enjoyment by telling them about the book and writing a review.

Drop by at **www.petermulraney.com** and join my **Crime Readers Group** to download a free copy of ***Deadly Sands*** and be one of the first to know when my next book will be released.

ACKNOWLEDGMENTS

None of us really do this alone, despite all rumours to the contrary. I'm grateful for my friends in The Novelist Circle and at Crime Writers SA, whose support and encouragement make my writing life easier and my writing better.

Thank you to Cettina O'Neill for her assistance in preparing the manuscript for publication.

Finally, I'd like to acknowledge the ongoing support of my wife, Toni, who, despite hearing every possible twist of the tale, several times, by the time I finish a story, still wants to read the book when it's finished.

A whistleblower exposes other people's secrets.

Death exposes the secrets of all, including a whistleblower's.

Inspector West investigates the death of a public service whistleblower, and discovers the whistleblower has a few secrets of his own.

If you like murder mixed with mystery, and a story full of twists and surprises, you'll enjoy Whistleblower, the fourth book in his Inspector West series.

CHAPTER ONE

On the Tuesday before Christmas, the board members of the Walker Group gathered for their final meeting of the year. As chairman, Peter Walker sat at the head of the table in the boardroom on the top floor of the group's head office on East Terrace.

Seventy-year old Peter Walker, with thirty percent of the group's shares, was the majority shareholder. He'd started the company in his early twenties, building sheds and warehouses, and had grown it into one of the most successful property developers in the country.

The board usually followed his advice on which projects to pursue, given his track record, and the fact that his connections still held enough shares to represent the majority in any vote, especially when his ex-wives followed their usual practice and voted with him.

To Peter's right sat Mario Imbroglio. Mario had a twenty percent holding in the group, acquired as part of the finance package he had brought to the table when the group was facing insolvency at the height of the global financial crisis, when the banks had stopped lending.

Next to Mario sat Warren Hunter, who owned a fifteen percent interest. Warren had been with the company from the start as its accountant. He'd found ways to finance Peter's dreams and had been rewarded with a significant stake in the company.

Opposite Mario, with his back to the window that opened on to a vista of the hills that stood on the eastern rim of the city, sat Dustin Walker, Peter's grandson. Twenty-five year old Dustin had inherited a ten percent interest in the group following his father's death in a skiing accident the previous year. Dustin did what his grandfather told him to do when they met for lunch before each board meeting started.

Next to Dustin sat Monica Webb and Rachel Foley, Peter's first two wives, who held twenty-five percent of the group's shares between them, thanks to their divorce settlements.

Peter shuffled the papers in front of him and took off his glasses, before placing them on the table. He looked across the table at his ex-wives. 'I've decided to retire.'

'As chairman?' said Monica.

'No, Monica. I mean retire as in stop work. I've been doing this for almost fifty years. I want to enjoy myself for a bit before it's too late.'

'You're not thinking of asking Dustin to take over the business, are you? He's only a boy,' said Rachel.

'Dustin and I have had a long chat. He's not ready to take on that sort of responsibility.' Peter looked down at his hands. 'Things would be different if James was still alive. I'd planned on handing things over to him when I was ready to retire but, well, you know why that won't be happening. So, I've had to make other arrangements.'

'What other arrangements?' said Rachel.

'I'm selling to Mario.'

Peter watched the color drain from the faces of Monica and Rachel as they realised the impact of what he had said. He enjoyed witnessing their consternation bubble to the surface and repaint their faces with the red of anger. He hoped Mario would screw them like the bastard had screwed him. 'We wouldn't be here if it wasn't for Mario's intervention when the banks wouldn't help us. I've given him first option, and he's made an offer I'm prepared to accept.'

'That would give Mario fifty percent,' said Monica.

'Sixty, actually,' said Dustin.

His grandmother and her successor turned to face him.

'You don't have to sell just because your grandfather tells you to,' said Monica. 'I don't think your father would be pleased with that decision.'

'My father's not here, Grandma, and there are other things I can do with the money.'

'When is this happening?' said Monica.

'As we speak. The papers were signed yesterday. I'd like to congratulate Mario on becoming the chairman of the Walker Group.' Peter stood and offered his seat to Mario.

'No need to be that formal, Peter, but thank you anyway.' Mario faced Monica and Rachel. 'I'd be happy to make you the same offer I made Peter and Dustin.'

'What about you, Warren?' said Monica.

'I've accepted Mario's offer,' said Warren, without looking up.

'And, what is your offer, Mario?' said Rachel.

Mario opened the folder on the table in front of him and slid a sheet of paper across the table to her, and then slid one to Monica. 'I think it would be best if you signed before you leave. That offer will not be on the table after today.'

Mario Imbroglio moved into what had been Peter Walker's office during the first week of January. He'd been a board member of the Walker Group for six years, ever since the opportunity to insert himself into the business had presented itself during the global financial crisis, when he'd introduced himself to James Walker after receiving a tip-off that the group was in financial trouble.

The big banks had withdrawn from the financial facility backing one of Walker's multi-million dollar projects when the group's cash flow had suffered a sharp downturn. Mario had also been aware that James' father, who controlled the group, had been living beyond his means for several years. The man's ego was insufferable but Mario had been trained to manipulate the egos of powerful men.

After constructing a financial package with his backers, who were keen to find legitimate businesses for their money laundering purposes, Mario had persuaded James Walker to introduce him to his father as the group's saviour, as the one who could pull them back from the brink of bankruptcy. His price had been a twenty percent stake in the business.

The old man had called him every name under the sun. He'd even threatened to disinherit James for bringing someone like Mario into the boardroom. But, in the end, he'd signed. His ego couldn't face the prospect of bankruptcy and the exposure of his personal failings as a businessman.

Mario had joined the board and studied the way Peter Walker did things. He didn't like the old man but he admired his way of doing business. Walker seemed to be able to create money out of thin air, provided he had the backing of someone's money to finance his dreams. Mario was particularly amused when he learnt that one strategy the Walker Group used was to build office towers for gold-plated government tenants, sign contracts with the tenants to clean their offices, and then sell the buildings to superannuation funds, who liked the regular income government tenants provided. The group would then build another office tower in another city and repeat the process.

Over the years, Mario had developed a successful working relationship with James Walker, who had been slated to take over the business when Peter retired. But the Walker world had changed when James met with an accident during a skiing trip to Austria. The old man hadn't been the same after his son's death. He'd lost interest and within a year had offered the business to Mario and his backers.

He'd told Mario he didn't have the time or patience to school Dustin, so that he could take over the business, and confided that it was probably just as well, since it was always the third generation, the grandchildren, that squandered a family's fortune. Mario had reflected on that comment in light of what he knew, and concluded that Peter Walker was blind to his own failings and the cost of his extravagant lifestyle.

Mario's backers were delighted. They liked the diversity of the group's interests, which included ownership of two shopping malls, that would provide them with numerous opportunities for laundering their black market money.

By the time Mario had taken control of the group, several of his lieutenants, including Trevor Hunter, were already holding positions of influence within the group. He knew he'd have to keep the core group of executives in the property development division in place, the people who knew how to turn Peter Walker's dreams into reality, but there was plenty of scope for expanding into operations that Peter Walker would never have considered, not even in his wildest dreams.

Peter Walker's last useful role, prior to his retirement, had been to introduce Mario to his friend Richard Nelson, the Minister for Recreation and Sport. Nelson was another man with a big ego, which Mario planned to massage during negotiations to build and operate the city's second casino.

Mario looked at the final plans for Long Street on the desk in front of him, and decided it was time to start working on the Minister.

CHAPTER TWO

On the last Friday in April, John Drake sat at his desk in The Office of State Supply reading the agency's whistleblowing guidelines, for what must have been the fifteenth time, waiting for four o'clock. John was convinced he was doing the right thing but he was also aware of what often happened to whistleblowers, despite all the words in the Act.

He also knew it was too late to regret looking at things he hadn't been asked to investigate, even though he wished he hadn't let his curiosity get the better of him during the slow period around Easter, when he'd started opening folders on the share drive and reading the contracts behind the payments he administered.

Initially, he'd thought it would be interesting to know the specific terms and conditions in the individual contracts. Then he'd decided it would be useful to understand the agency's procurement policies and guidelines, since the agency was charged with getting the best value for the government's dollars when buying products and services.

When he'd noticed that some of the more expensive cleaning contracts hadn't been awarded to the companies that had submitted the most competitive tenders during the last round of contract reviews, he'd looked into the companies those contracts had gone to, and found a pattern of common ownership.

Aware that contract reviews were conducted by a three person committee of senior officers, that included Sonya Curtis, the head of the agency, he knew there was no way he would be confronting any of them directly. He was intimidated by every one of them, especially Sonya Curtis, who was known among officers at John's level as 'The Bitch'.

John knew he had to tell someone or he wouldn't be living up to his obligations as a public servant. After a week of anxious deliberation, he'd decided to escalate his concerns to the Auditor General, which was one of the options available to him in the whistleblowing guidelines. But, because he would be reporting senior officers, he'd decided it would be prudent to discuss his concerns with Pam Watson, his immediate supervisor, just to be sure he hadn't misunderstood something.

At four o'clock, he put two copies of the document he'd compiled into his bag, picked up the third copy he'd printed for Pam, and walked over to her office.

Pam smiled as he sat down with the document in his lap. 'So, what's on your mind, John?'

'I'm not sure how to say this, but it looks like we might not have done the right thing when awarding some of the big dollar cleaning contracts.'

'Oh? What makes you think that?'

John shifted in his seat. 'Well, I thought I'd read some of the contracts I administer, so I had a look on the share drive. I ended up reading some of the tender documents, you know, to see how the whole process works.' John could feel beads of perspiration forming on his brow. 'Anyway, I reviewed the documents associated with the cleaning contracts I administer, and it looks like several of those contracts went to companies belonging to the Walker Group, even when they weren't the most competitive tender.' John looked up. 'We're supposed to accept the most competitive tender, aren't we?'

Pam leant back into her chair. 'Do you realise what you're suggesting?'

'Yeah, that's the scary bit. If I'm right, it looks like we have a problem at the top. You know who's on the contracts committee, don't you?'

'That's a pretty serious allegation to make, John. And, it's not like you're experienced in these matters, is it? You've only been here a few months.'

Those words hit John like a backhander across the face. He stared at Pam. She didn't intimidate him like the others.

'I've been working in contracts administration for at least ten years, Pam. It's what I was doing at Transport before I came here. I think I know what the rules are and I've studied the guidelines we're supposed to be following, so I think I know what I'm talking about.' John paused to regain his composure. He didn't want to start an argument. 'Sometimes a fresh set of eyes sees things that others have missed, but,' he held his hands up in front of him, 'I could be wrong. That's why I thought I'd better discuss it with you before taking my concerns any further.'

'Wise decision, John. So, what have you got there?'

'It's all in here.' John passed her his document and watched the color drain from her face as she scanned its contents.

'I don't have time to study this now but I'll read it and get back to you as soon as I can. In the meantime, I want you to keep this to yourself. If you've read the whistleblower guidelines, which I hope you have, you'll know they offer you no protection if you leak anything to the media, even if you're right.'

'I intend to stick with the guidelines. Wouldn't look too good if I didn't, would it?'

'If I agree with your findings, this will have to be escalated to the Auditor General. On the other hand, though, John,' Pam flashed him a smile, 'if I don't agree with your interpretation of the data, I'll be advising you to drop this. I'd hate to see you make a career ending mistake simply because you misinterpreted something outside your area of responsibility.'

John felt the wind being sucked from his sails. The tone in her words, along with her body language, told him he wouldn't be getting any support from her.

'Look, you've done the right thing bringing this to my attention.' She looked at her watch. 'I'll catch up with you on Monday, after I've had a chance to study this.'

John returned to his desk and decided that talking to Pam hadn't been the mistake he'd thought it might be. She obviously didn't want him to take his concerns any further, despite her words of support, but the look on her face when she'd scanned the report had told him what he'd wanted to know.

While he packed up his workstation, he decided to post a copy of his report to the Auditor General on the way home, and live with the consequences.

———

Pam slipped John's document into her briefcase and watched him pack up his workstation and leave for the weekend. She admired him for wanting to know about the contracts he was administering. That was more than any of his predecessors had done. But, she wished he hadn't been so inquisitive. Now they had a problem they would have to deal with before he did anything. She hoped to God he'd do as she'd asked him and wait for her to get back to him.

As John walked past her office on his way to the elevator lobby, Pam picked up her personal smartphone.

'Sonya, we have a problem.'

ALSO BY PETER MULRANEY

Inspector West series

After

The Holiday

Whistleblower

Twisted Justice

The East Park Syndicate

Living Alone series

After She's Gone

Cooking 4 One

Sanity Savers

Living Alone (Collection)

Stella Bruno Investigates

The Identity Thief

A Gun of Many Parts

Bones in the Forest

A Deadly Game of Hangman

Taken

Fallout

The Identity Thief Collection

The Fallout Collection

Novella

The New Girlfriend

Everyday Business Skills series

Everyday Project Management

Everyday Productivity

Everyday Money Management

Writings of the Mystic

Sharing the Journey: Reflections of a Reluctant Mystic

A Question of Perspective

My Life is My Responsibility: Insights for Conscious Living

I Am Affirmations: The Power of Words

Beyond the Words: Reflections on I Am Affirmations

Mystical Journey: A Handbook for Modern Mystics

Sharing the Journey Coloring Books

Mandalas

Mandalas by 3

Sharing the Journey Coloring Journals

Sharing the Journey Coloring Journal

Discovery

Reflection